arla

Funny money

George Reeves, top-flight 'creative' accountant and beloved 'Georgie-boy' to Muriel, his mid-fifties, portly wife, had flown the coop. Scarpered with a bit of fluff? Cleared the office safe and done a bunk? Both seemed likely to 'Mitch' Mitchell, late of Radio Brum, who had recently set up as a private eye.

For the past four years, George had worked for Arno Czinner, a financier who'd make a corkscrew look like a railway line. So when, in the cold light of a winter's dawn, a cadaver crushed under a roller was found in the grounds of Czinner's spacious residence, suspicions of foul play were fully aroused.

Why did Czinner's girl friend, the luscious Daisy Sharpe, Drusilla in the TV 'soap', *Motel*, keep bugging equipment in her clothes cupboard? Who'd employ a Financial Director who was a flagrant transvestite? And what was behind Muriel Reeves's abrupt disappearance?

In her second 'Mitch' Mitchell crime novel, Valerie Kershaw has surpassed herself in inventive characterization and plotting. *Funny money* is a page-turning joy, and as clever as paint.

Also by Valerie Kershaw

The snow man (1979)
Rosa (1980)
The bank manager's wife (1981)
Published by Duckworth

Rockabye (1990)
Published by Bantam

Murder is too expensive (1993)
Published by Constable

FUNNY MONEY

Valerie Kershaw

Constable · London

First published in Great Britain 1994
by Constable & Company Ltd
3 The Lanchesters, 162 Fulham Palace Road
London W6 9ER
Copyright © 1994 by Valerie Kershaw
The right of Valerie Kershaw to be
identified as the author of this work
has been asserted by her in accordance
with the Copyright, Designs and Patents Act 1988
ISBN 0 09 473050 4
Set in Linotron Palatino 10pt by
The Electronic Book Factory Ltd, Fife.
Printed in Great Britain by
St Edmundsbury Press Limited
Bury St Edmunds, Suffolk

A CIP catalogue record for this book
is available from the British Library

1

There had been a heavy fall of snow during the night but for most of the day the sun had been out, low in the sky. Now it was lower, a dull red against white-capped chimney pots. Almost all the householders had cleared their drives and the pavement in front of their houses. The cul-de-sac was a chequerboard of black and white. A snowman stood in one of the gardens, a baseball cap on his head and a blue and white Birmingham City scarf tied round his neck.

Mitch skidded a little as she braked. The TVR nosed into the fringes of cleared snow which was heaped over the kerbside. She looked across at 41 Selbourne Close. It was a semi-detached house with bay windows on two storeys and a recessed porch. She opened the driver's door and thrust one reluctant boot out into the cold. Swinging her bag over the shoulder of her red coat she hauled herself out of the rakish racing driver's seat. It was too low but she told herself that if she could pull her bones out of bed in the morning she could damn well get them out of the TVR. She might not be as young as she liked to think she passed for, but she was sure as hell too young to drive a motorised shopping trolley.

The door bell played the line of a tune. 'There's no place like home,' it chimed. A large woman opened the door. Through the porch glass Mitch could see expanses of turquoise track suit. The woman fingered a white plastic bead on her necklace before opening the porch door. 'Yes?' Warm air and a strong smell of linseed oil wafted out.

'Mrs Muriel Reeves? I'm Mitch Mitchell.'

'I'll get you some slippers. You can leave those in the porch.'

Mitch looked down at her boots, turned, sat on the top step and hauled them off. Mrs Reeves returned with a pair of fluffy pink mules. 'That's a ladder,' she said.

Mitch examined the toe in her tights.

'Boots are a devil for that,' said Mrs Reeves.

Shit, said Mitch, silently, dumped her boots in the corner of the porch, and followed the woman into the house. In the hall a coat stand was hung about with a blazing array of colours; the least alarming was the violet hue of a voluminous three-quarter length jacket. The floor was a skating rink of highly polished parquet. Getting across it in mules which were two sizes too big for her proved possible only if she didn't lift her feet. She shuffled.

'I keep myself occupied. Oh yes,' Mrs Reeves said, showing her into the lounge. 'Fill a minute, fill a day. Just excuse me while I wash my hands. I've been oiling my teak.'

'Teak?' Mitch was bewildered until she turned round and saw a roomful of 1960s furniture, all oilily gleaming. Over the tiled fireplace there was a mirror with a wrought-iron surround. Mitch went up to it, fiddled with her hair for a moment and then settled herself in an uncut moquette easy chair by the gas fire.

When Mrs Reeves returned she carried a large tray heaped with teacups and home-made cakes and scones. 'At times like this, Miss Mitchell, the proper thing to do is make sure the engine's well stoked. What's the good of being ill? Who does that help, may I ask?' She put the tray down on the coffee table and then silently handed Mitch a bar of soap. Mitch stared at it uncomprehendingly.

'To stop the ladder. Might as well make the best of a bad job.' Mrs Reeves nodded in approval as Mitch hitched up her tight skirt and lifted her foot. 'Actually, I like comfortable clothes myself. At our age.'

'How do you think the Mitchell and Orient Bureau can help you?' Mitch asked, soaping away and wondering whether even an apostle would be Christian enough to come to this woman's rescue.

'Do have a scone.'

Crumby, a little bit of butter on the edge of her coat,

Mitch found herself saying a minute later, 'Delicious. Really wonderful,' somewhat astonished, meaning every word.

'Try one of these Stanhope Firelighters, dear. Too many people look down on an oat. My mother was a good cook. She's the one that got me going. The only thing you learn from a book is how to tartify. Real cooking is goodness through and through. Like your mother's milk.' She laughed and shook her head. 'Men.'

Mitch found herself studying her more closely, trying not to calculate how many scones and butter and Stanhope Firelighters went into the manufacture of those rolling thighs. Mrs Reeves was in her mid-fifties, hair tightly controlled in little permed curls. She was by no means all fat. There was plenty of muscular strength in those shoulders and legs, though Mitch guessed she had never been near a health club. Splitting clumps of Michaelmas daisies, tossing mattresses, heaving carpets over lines, that all seemed more likely.

Mrs Reeves suddenly put down a half-eaten *langue de chat*, brushing off crumbs from her track-suit top. 'No point in going all round the houses. My Georgie boy's gone.'

Mitch said nothing. She was remembering childhood nit nurses, headmistresses and a certain bus conductress. None, in her recollection, was more impressive than Mrs Reeves.

'Might as well come out and say it. Get it out in the open.'

'Flown the coop?' Mitch suddenly found herself thinking of missing budgies. Or perhaps a marmalade cat?

'He left the house on Thursday as normal to go to work. He has a very responsible job, Miss Mitchell. In his own quiet way. Not, of course, that he's ever been given the credit. Well, they don't, do they? Credit costs. He left about a quarter past eight. We have a nice little green Golf. Snow was forecast but he has to drive to work, Miss Mitchell. It's way out of town. Near Burton-on-Trent. By rights he should have a company car. Not that he's not been promised. But there you are.'

'Your husband left to go to work on Thursday and you haven't seen him since.'

'I went to see the coppers. Fat lot of good that did.'

'When was that?'

'Friday. Oh, I could see what that desk sergeant thought. I

could have boxed his ears for him. And before you get any such notion, Miss Mitchell, let me tell you that Georgie boy and I go back a long way. I know what that sergeant was thinking. He's had it away with some young tarty piece. I may not be a vamped-up dolly in one of those body things but Georgie isn't exactly the latest thing either. Look, we've got no children, him and me. We've always had to be all in all to each other. I'm not saying he's not run off with a bit of fluff. The Lord knows men are daft enough for anything. Give any living creature a didgeridoo and what have you got? Lack of mother wit, that's what. But we make do, Miss Mitchell, don't we? Not got much option, after all.'

Mitch put down her teacup, opened her handbag and took out a notebook.

'That's moving a bit quick,' Mrs Reeves said. 'How much do you cost?'

'One hundred a day. Reasonable expenses. If I take the case.'

'You place a high value on yourself, don't you? We're not rich, you know. I got reorganised out of a job last November and missing husbands don't pay wages.'

'The Bureau would require two hundred pounds in advance. In our line of work, Mrs Reeves, we rarely come up with good news. Most people don't like forking out for bad. No one wants to hear the truth, let alone pay for it. Two hundred pounds buys you two days' work, at the end of which you get a report. You decide then if we carry on – if that's necessary, of course.'

'Sixty a day is about as much as I can go to. And that's breaking the bank.'

'It's not negotiable, Mrs Reeves. You can take it. Or leave it.'

'You can find him in two days?'

'I don't know. It's quite likely though.'

'Have another of these Frenchie *langue* things. Five ounces of cream in them. The French are beggars, aren't they?'

Mitch, to avoid the pressure of Mrs Reeves' gaze, took one. The clock, set in a miniature brass ship's wheel, began to dominate the room.

'I expect I'm a chump. I expect I'll land up kicking myself. But my Georgie boy is all the world to me. We've always been all in

8

all to each other. All in all. I nursed him, you know. That's how we first met. He had a bad fall.' She sighed. 'He's not been easy work. Terrible trouble with his nerves. Though I will say he got over all that. Never had a good chest. But he's such a nice fellow. I've knocked about in my time and, believe me, nice people are as rare as a butcher with a windowful of greens. Well. Chop, chop. At the moment you're all notebook and no pen. Not take the case indeed. When I hire people they're damn well hired and no nonsense. And if you don't give satisfaction, Miss Mitchell, you'll know about it. *Tout de suite.*'

Mitch scrabbled about in her bag and came up with a biro.

'My George's full name is Wenlock George Reeves. He's fifty-six years old next May and we've lived in this cul-de-sac for twenty – I tell a lie there – nineteen years. Georgie trained as an accountant but because of his nerves he never took his final exams. Later, when he was better, his mother was all for me getting behind him. Making him retake them. But that was for George to decide, wasn't it? Not her. Not me. Or the Queen of England come to that. And I was earning a good wage. I'd given up nursing because of the hours and taken this shorthand-typing course. Of course, they've all got these word processors nowadays. In those days there was skill to it. Spell checks, indeed.'

Pausing, she tapped her head.

'That's all the spell check I'll ever need. But all most bosses are interested in is the shape of their secretaries' bums. What they want in their female staff is a fair degree of idiocy. Puts them in a good light, does that. And a thirty-eight bra size and the job lot not more than twenty-five.' She leaned forward. 'What they mean by a willing girl, Miss Mitchell, is not what we mean. When I tell you–'

'George,' interrupted Mitch, who could see Mrs Reeves was getting well into her stride, 'where did he work? I mean, does he work? I presume you've checked there?'

'For the past four years he's been with Arno Czinner Enterprises at Aston Clinton.'

'The financier?'

Mrs Reeves nodded. 'He did work in the accounts department of Jane and Jarrod's for twenty-three years before that.'

'Chocolates.'

'Very nice people to work with. One of the old school was Mr Jane. Always a personal card at Christmas. But the business was taken over by Arno Czinner. And, to be honest, George thought he would be at the front of the queue when it came to redundancy. But he had a stroke of luck. Harry Vine, a chap he'd been to school with, turned out to be a very big cheese at Czinner's. Harry's an accountant, you know. At Czinner's he was called Development Manager and he wanted George to be one of his little team. They came under the Finance Department.'

'What did they do?'

'Arno Czinner buys and sells companies. Just like a grocer buys sugar to sell it at a profit. The Development Manager and his team looked out for opportunities. Ran the rule over what might be a good prospect. That sort of thing. That's how George put it. He loved it. He was a changed man when he first went to Czinner's, Miss Mitchell. Harry knew his Georgie, see. Knew him from the old days. Georgie's a wizard with figures. Harry always said no one could read balance sheets like George. I expect he found it dull all those years at Jane and Jarrod's but he rarely complained. Just got on with things. That's George all over.

'When he went to this new job he brought all Czinner's old company balance sheets home. One by one. Read them just like they were bestsellers.

'It all seemed to fit in so well. Just before Mr Czinner bought Jane and Jarrod's he moved his head office out of London to Aston Clinton. We shouldn't have liked to move to London. Not at our age. Apart from anything else it's such a mucky place. No pride down south. That's the trouble. It's a wicked shame.'

'So he's very happy at work?'

'Well, it didn't last, dear, did it? Two years ago they got this new Finance Director. Mr Toby Trubberman. You know the type. All posh accent and broad braces. Hardly into his thirties. And, of course, the recession didn't help.

10

'We heard, just this last Christmas holiday, that Harry Vine was leaving. He'd been ill, granted, but it wasn't that. Harry and this new Finance Director had never got on. Not since day one.'

'How did George feel about that?'

'Well, it's the end, isn't it? My husband was Harry's appointment. George is just there caretaking until Czinner appoints someone to take Harry's place. Then he'll get the push, too.'

'Let's go back to last week. The days before George went missing. Was there anything unusual in George's behaviour? Did anything strike you as odd?'

She shook her head. 'I've had all the time in the world to think about it. Georgie was just the same as usual. I've been through all his things. Nothing is missing. Not as far as I can see.'

'Has any money gone from any bank accounts?'

'Everything's in joint names, Miss Mitchell. Bank and building society. I checked again before I got in touch with your office. He's not drawn on any of it.'

'Could he have an account you don't know of?'

'I suppose it's possible.' She spoke slowly, pushing away the plate of cakes. 'I don't believe it. Where would the money come from to put into it?'

'You've been in touch with his office?'

'I was down there this morning. I saw Miss Havelock.'

'Who's that?'

'She was Harry Vine's secretary. They – that is Harry and my George – thought she'd been put there by this Mr Trubberman.'

'The Finance Director? Why would he do that?'

'To keep an eye on them, they reckoned.'

Mitch raised her eyebrows.

'Well, to tell you the truth, Miss Mitchell, office politics these days seem more like one of those old Cold War spy stories than anything else. If you ask me, they all watch too much telly. The way of it is, I suppose, that most of the time business is boring and people like a bit of excitement, don't they? If they don't get it, they manufacture it.'

'This Finance Director . . .'

'Everyone reckoned that Harry Vine should have got that job.

11

George told me the only thing Trubberman has is connections. Reckons the chap is pretty US.'

'Trubberman was out gunning for Harry and at Christmas managed to oust him?'

'That's about the size of it.'

'When you saw this secretary – Miss Havelock . . .'

'She told me George was at the office all day Thursday. Left at the normal time. She said he seemed just the same as usual.'

'And what do they make of your husband's disappearance?'

'Everyone there thought he was ill because that's what I told 'em at first. I mean, what would you do? They rang on Friday to ask why he hadn't come in and I said he had flu. At that time I kept thinking he'd walk through the front door and shout, "Home, Mu!" like he always did. But last night I came to my senses. Something had got to be done and it was obvious the police weren't doing it.' Her arms moved towards Mitch, palms up, empty-handed. 'I mean, it's Monday now. He's been gone over three days.'

'So you saw Miss Havelock and explained the situation . . .'

'Mr Trubberman was on his way back from Switzerland and Mr Czinner, well, he's still in Liechtenstein. There was no one else there to tell. The Accounts Department is different. That's even in another part of the building. Only Harry and my George worked in Development. And the secretary, of course. The team was run down, you see. Because of the recession.'

'You've heard from nobody at Czinner's since you visited Aston Clinton this morning?'

'No.'

'Do you have an address for Harry Vine?'

'He has a cottage near the Aston Clinton estate. To be handy. I should have thought of him. He could know something. Just shows you. I hardly seem to know how to think straight any more. Or what to think. I've been up to Harry's place once or twice. There's a set of traffic lights before a single-lane bridge near a village called Yoxall. Immediately after there's a track off. Cross-in-the-Hand Lane. It's up there. Pond Cottage. Right after you come out of an S-bend. I wonder . . .'

'Don't worry. I'll see Mr Vine. Did George have any other

friends or interests? A pub where he liked to drink, for instance?'

'He sometimes dropped into the Spread Eagle on the way back from work. That's off the A38 just past the crematorium. Not half a mile from here.'

'Did he belong to any clubs, societies? What are his interests?'

'George likes his home. He's a home body, Miss Mitchell. Sometimes we go to a musical. I like a nice musical. But where's this getting us?' She leaned forward. 'Put this down. He was wearing his nice pale grey suit with the thin chalk-stripe. Blue striped shirt with the detachable collar. He had a white collar on. Sheepskin jacket. Tweed trilby. Grey slip-on shoes. M and S. They do a very nice line in slip-ons, do M and S. Fair Isle gloves my sister knitted him for Christmas. Using up odd bits and pieces. She's a right knitter that one. She's always something on the go. White vest and pants. We don't go for coloureds.'

'Well, I'll need the registration number of his car. And a recent picture of him, of course.'

'You don't get yourself photographed all over the place when you're our age, Miss Mitchell. You're more thinking where you're going to put another lot of blessed snaps. Nothing like them for cluttering up drawers . . .' but she heaved herself out of the chair. 'Won't be a mo.'

Mitch got up as Mrs Reeves left the room and wandered over to the window. She lifted the edge of the net curtain. There was a swirl of falling net in the bedroom of the house across the way. Everyone in the street will know, she realised. They probably knew almost as soon as Mrs Reeves that her Georgie boy had flown the coop.

'Here we are then,' Mrs Reeves said.

Mitch turned and saw her holding an eight-by-ten photograph away from her so she could focus more accurately. 'I suppose it'll do. It was taken just before Christmas. They had a do up at Aston Clinton. I will say that for Mr Czinner. He knows how to put on a good spread.' She gave her the photograph and an envelope. 'That's your money. I shall want a receipt, mind.'

'Let's take a look at the photograph first, shall we?'

'Georgie boy's next to Mr Czinner. Mr Czinner's the little chap in the centre, see? Pink shirt and all.'

Mitch looked at the photograph. She recognised Arno Czinner at once. She'd often seen his pictures in the paper.

'Georgie's on the left of Mr Czinner. That's Mr Czinner. Harry Vine's on the right. Both tall chaps, aren't they? My George and Harry. The one who is fancying himself – the one with the blond curls – that's Toby Trubberman, the Finance Director. Always in the gym seeing to his body. That's what I've heard.'

Mitch studied the photograph more closely. 'I've seen Mr Czinner's picture in the newspapers. Isn't he the one who goes out with the actress who plays Drusilla in that soap?'

'*Motel*. That's her. Quite the lady of the manor is our Miss Daisy Sharpe.'

Mitch studied George Reeves more closely. His birdlike head was a little too small for his frame, but nevertheless he was an attractive-looking man. Not at all the sort of husband she'd imagine Mrs Reeves would have. In fact, he's more the sort of fellow I could picture myself with, she thought, shocked. What on earth had he seen in this caricature of a stout middle-aged housewife? 'Right,' she said crisply. 'I'll give you that receipt.' She slipped the photograph in her handbag. 'Oh. The registration number of the car.'

Muriel Reeves wrote it on the envelope for her. 'If George hasn't had it mended there'll be no glass in the offside mirror. Kids, Miss Mitchell. Couldn't you strangle them?'

'And George was always home in the evenings? Never went off – say – to night school? Anything like that?'

'Bar Tuesday evenings. But that was work, Miss Mitchell. There was a strategy meeting every Tuesday evening at Aston Clinton. And I daresay they had a pint or two afterwards. Georgie was always home though by about nineish. Oh, he was never a stop out. Not my Georgie.'

Five minutes later Mitch was on the doorstep pulling on her boots.

'Can't imagine what they're doing without a zip,' Mrs Reeves said, watching her. 'And not even a fur lining in them to keep

14

your tootsies cosy. Fashion! Still, it keeps the tills ringing, I suppose.'

Mitch was glad to escape down the path to her parked car. Turning on the engine, she sat there for a moment. There were lights appearing in the houses now. The front door of the semi across the way opened. A woman appeared with a cat in her arms and stood staring across at Mitch. She put the cat down. As she walked back into the house, the animal followed her.

The neighbours know all right, Mitch thought, as she turned on the lights and put the TVR into gear. She looked over her shoulder. Mrs Reeves had drawn the net curtain from the side of the bay. She, too, was watching.

2

There was a sniping wind rattling the panes. Powdery snow, caught up in the sash bars of the Victorian window, whirred against the glass and slid down; the bowl of the Gas Street Basin was liquidised into oranges and reds spitting through blacks and greys. Mitch, elbows out, hands clasping her head as if trying to hold each detail of her new surroundings in her mind, was gazing out.

She turned and looked at her first-floor office. Good grey wool carpet, fitted on Friday, balls of fluff still rising out of the pile, grey filing cabinets, blond wood desk, two black Italian chairs. The computer sat on its steel table against the wall, empty shelving above. When she'd first come in this morning she'd felt – and she'd had to analyse the sensation it was so unfamiliar, so breath-taking – happiness.

Happiness? Are you sure?

She was trying to recapture that feeling now and, when she couldn't, anxiously questioned herself.

Was I kidding myself this morning? God. If you can't be honest with yourself, what's left?

She'd no difficulty in recapturing that unbelievable moment

three months ago when Freya Adcock, the manager of Radio Brum, had told her: 'I'm so sorry to have to let you go, Mitch. Believe me. We're really going to miss you. The budget has been sliced back to more than the bone. We're in there, bang in the tissue. Right where it hurts like hell.'

Even when she'd left Freya's office, walking along the blue-carpeted corridor to the Production Office, she'd been unable to believe it. She passed a framed photograph of herself, one of a clutch of local radio 'stars', and told herself there was going to be a gap on the wall. But it can't be true, she'd thought. I feel just fine. This is like any other day. Everything is going on in the same way really.

It wasn't until two hours later that her knees had given way. She'd gone and shut herself in the lavatory so none of the other broadcasters could see how violently she was shivering. She'd been all right after half an hour and she'd presented her show, *City Talk*, as usual that evening.

What she thought of now as the awful messiness had come later. It was all so physical. When her stomach had vaporised and every organ in her body was caught in the turbulence. That was better than tears, though. When you cried too much there was a point when you no longer cried because life was unbearable but because crying made muscles and ligaments hurt too much.

It was only when anger hit her, almost a week later, that everything had firmed up again. Why hadn't Freya fired that bastard Quentin Plunkett? The stuff he did was total crap. Or that frightful new little girl they'd got doing the breakfast show? Not to mention Digger Rooney. He'd been actively looking for a different job even then, before this new programme organiser had been appointed.

Christ. Why me? I'm better than the lot of them. Is thirty years' experience in the trade worth nothing?

If it hadn't been for Tommy Hung she might have made that classic Pilgrim's Progress into the Slough of Despond. Though she would probably have drowned in gin instead of muck. But there was Tommy, buzzing on the phone, buzzing in and out of her house in Bristol Road, buzzing with this crazy idea he'd had since last summer about them setting up a detective agency together. Earlier that summer, much against her better judgement, she'd agreed to use her talents as an investigative journalist to look into the suicide of a wealthy young researcher. She'd met Tommy in the course of her enquiries and in no time she'd found him helping her.

The case had been solved successfully and she had pocketed ten thousand pounds. But that didn't mean the pair of them would be able to get a detective agency off the ground. It was surprising, though, how the thought of going down to the DHSS offices concentrated the mind. Mitch had never drawn dole in her life. Logically she knew that there was no stigma attached to it, that this was what everybody did these days. But somewhere deep down in her lay the prejudices she'd learned in childhood from her parents. Shame felt so dirty she'd wanted to shower. She'd realised then that if the only job open to her was cleaning lavatories she'd jump at it. As it was, there was Tommy's offer. This crazy idea of his that they should set up a detective agency.

Tommy came into her office now, carrying plain white china on a black melamine resin tray. He had a face which had dropped off the back end of Hong Kong, a seventy-year-old Oriental with eyes which said he was going on two.

She'd taken her boots off when she'd come in and now arched her foot and wriggled her toes in the wool pile. 'I never thought an office of my own would feel good,' she said. 'I'm beginning to understand why suits fight over territory. But, Tommy, if we go down the tubes you're going to lose a packet.'

'When one is as old as I am, my dear, there's only one tube one worries about. The rest is by the jolly old way. Anyway, the Mitchell and Orient Bureau already has its first client.' The kind of English he spoke was that of stiff upper-class Forces types up against it in the black and white films of her childhood. After a while she'd found herself falling in with this illusion of a double-barrelled true blue Anglo-Saxon. She'd more than once had to remind herself that Tommy probably thought in Mandarin or Cantonese or even in something truly exotic like Fukienese.

'Two hundred in advance.' Mitch opened her large patent

leather handbag. 'Here we are. In tens. You don't often get paid in cash these days. It made me wonder if Muriel Reeves had short-changed us. But it's all there. We're in business.'

'I never had any doubts,' Tommy said, leaving the envelope on the desk. Mitch was silent as he concentrated on his English tea ritual. To do small things perfectly seemed to give him not so much pleasure as a sense of security as he practised his control over the physical world. Mitch had to admit that watching him could bring her impatient soul to screaming pitch.

Handed her tea at last, she told him about her interview. Years of being a stand-in bulletin editor in radio and television newsrooms made her account brief but succinct.

Tommy, feet touching at heels and toes, sat with his spine well away from the back of one of the expensive Italian chairs she'd chosen and he'd paid for without losing his sense of humour.

'What bugs me is that woman's dry eyes. Not to mention the haggling over price.' She paused, thinking it over more carefully. 'And yet in spite of that the impression I have is that she's very fond of her Georgie boy.'

'Could she be in shock?'

'It's possible,' said Mitch, remembering her inability at first to believe she'd been fired. 'Though he's been missing four days. And that's quite a long time.' She found her hand touching the very expensive leather of the Italian chair. And I bought two of them! How could I spend so much? I don't know that Tommy is rich. He might have blued his life savings on this little set-up. She was saying: 'If we're going in for a bit of skull-lifting what about our old friend guilt? She's split his head open with a lump of frozen lamb, buried him under the Michaelmas daisies, and now wants me to find her out. At cut rate if possible.'

Tommy laughed. 'Can I see his picture?'

'It's the one on the left of Arno Czinner. See?' said Mitch, giving the photograph to him. 'A good-looking chap if you go for the studious type. And though Muriel's origins are certainly working class I'd say he's a son of the middle classes.' Mitch shook her head. 'Her door bell actually plays "There's no place like home". What's a guy like that doing married to our Muriel?'

18

'One never realised you were a snob, Mitch.'

'Muriel would make anyone prejudiced.'

'The woman irritated you?'

'And how. Telling me there was a ladder in my stocking–'

'Which there is.'

'Making me take my boots off in her porch.'

Tommy laughed. 'One can see you'd have difficulty living with her. But this chap was apparently happy to marry Nurse. You did say that was her job when they met?'

'But you'd have thought he'd have grown out of her by now.'

'One is often surprised by the partners others have.'

Mitch was thinking. 'She's practically a caricature of your working-class lady with the support stocking. And yet I occasionally got a glimpse of a very sharp mind. Or did I?' And then she nodded her head. 'Yes. I did. And can she bake. She's master class.'

'But the likelihood is that her husband has run off with another woman?'

'I think it must be, although she says he's not raided their savings. That's got to be unusual in such a set-up. And she did mention that he has "nerves" or, at least, used to be a bit wonky in that direction. This chap's boss has been fired, he's about to lose his own job . . . God forbid, but he could be at the bottom of a lake.'

'Why choose water?' Tommy was curious.

'I don't know. He'd have been found if he'd thrown himself under a train, wouldn't he? Or jumped off a building?'

'Why hasn't his car been found, then? He's been missing almost four days. And apparently his behaviour seemed to be perfectly normal on the day he went missing. He goes to the office as usual, leaves at the usual time . . . no one notices anything amiss . . .'

'So Muriel said.'

'He worked at Czinner's headquarters? At that place out at Aston Clinton?'

'One of the Development team apparently. Do you know anything about Arno Czinner Enterprises?'

'Only what I've read in the financial pages. It is – or was – a fast-growing conglomerate. The recession must have slowed it down a bit. Czinner bought mainly construction businesses in the first place – getting in on the ground floor after the 1970s recession. But property is very cyclical so they began to branch out in other directions. They bought Jane and Jarrod's, the chocolate people, among others.'

'What do you mean by cyclical?'

'When the bad times come some industries get hit far worse than others. Cars, for instance. People tend not to buy cars in a recession. Too busy paying the electricity bill. That has a knock-on effect. Steel, glass, paints and components have a bad time as well. Raw materials and manufacturing of all kinds bat on a very sticky wicket. Construction, too. People don't move house if they fear they're going to be put out of work. But they do buy food. That's practically recession-proof. And drink to drown their undoubted sorrows.'

'So if Arno Czinner is mainly in construction he could have had a bad time of it? Georgie boy's firm could be in trouble?'

'Not that one's heard, my dear. Everyone seems to believe Arno Czinner is a very shrewd blighter.' He shook his head. 'One has to go for the simple explanation. At least in the first place. Our chap George has left his wife for pastures new.'

'I'll try and dig out his ex-boss Harry Vine first thing in the morning,' Mitch decided. 'By all accounts there was more to their relationship than boss and employee. Then I'll take a look at Aston Clinton. If he has got a bit on the side I'm sure the secretary will know.'

'You mentioned a pub?'

'The Spread Eagle.'

'I'll toddle along there. What about the neighbours? From what you say, nothing much would escape them?'

'We don't want to antagonise our client,' warned Mitch.

'I could be from the insurance company. His car has been reported missing.'

'Leave it for now. I don't want a run-in with Muriel.

She's quite capable of giving me a bloody good hiding. So undignified.'

'Mitch!' Tommy laughed.

'If nothing turns up we might take a closer look at Czinner's,' she said. 'Do you know, I'm fifty years old and I simply can't ever recall having met a millionaire.'

'Billionaire.'

'Really? I wonder how many posh frocks and swimming pools that is?' She thought about it and then gave up. 'I certainly hope I'm as calculating as the next female. But – and this is really awful, Tommy – I don't even know how many noughts there are in a billion.'

'In this country it's one million million. In America the sum is different, I believe. One thousand million.'

'One man has all that?'

'Not actually. He's usually borrowed it from the banks. It's our money, my dear.'

'When you're good for a billion of other people's money you've got to be worth knowing. Good for a billion.' It made Mitch's head reel. 'Jesus. How can you be that good this side of the angels?'

'You show a lamentable lack of knowledge about finance. You of all people. I've always thought of you as a woman of the world.'

'One really doesn't want to spend one's day thinking about money matters. Not when finances are in the state mine always are. Sort of like looking at a dead rat. One tries not to. But if there *are* up to a billion in freebies going, perhaps I ought?'

'High finance isn't a matter of freebies. The banks want their money back! With interest.'

'That's their problem. I'd have quite enough spending it. The trouble is that as I get older I don't want sort of – things – in the way I did. To be honest, Tommy – and shut your ears if you don't want to hear – a decent chap, a good fuck and the sun's belting out in my world. Of course, I don't mind the odd bottle of champers thrown in. Or a trip to somewhere exotic. But that's about my limit.'

Tommy never seemed to have learned how to be inscrutable.

21

He had a very pained expression, a drawing together of eyebrows, a pulling together of nose and lips. Mitch thought he looked as if he'd sat on a patch of frog spawn.

She found she'd tried to emulate his look. One foot was off the carpet, sole up towards her and toes pulled over the ball of bone and agonisingly scrunched. She laughed. 'Still, I wouldn't mind meeting Mr Mega Moneybags. One never knows . . . But, in the mean time, it's back to George. I hope he's not one of these dopy men who always fall for the same type. One Muriel is quite enough in my book.'

'I must be off, my dear.' Tommy had not entirely lost his pained expression. 'I'm taking a friend to a Simon Rattle concert at the new Symphony Hall. A small whisky at her place first. One does so like one's music to prickle in the skull. Mr Rattle succeeds more often than any other conductor I know.'

'I won't be in first thing. I'm going straight over to Vine's place.'

'You'll phone him first?'

She shook her head. 'I'm not going to give the guy an excuse to slide out of seeing me. Eight o'clock will see me on his doorstep.'

'Then you'll go over to Aston Clinton?'

'Probably.'

Tommy picked up Muriel's cash.

'Hardly in the Arno Czinner league,' said Mitch.

'It's a beginning. Oh, by the way, Freya Adcock rang. She wants you to get in touch. It sounded urgent.'

Her ex-boss's name sandpapered flesh, sparking anger. She can go and get stuffed. But she didn't say that. Not out loud. She didn't want to conjure up again that pained expression Tommy always wore when she came out with a bit of coarse language. He makes me feel so vulgar, she thought. As though I were a Balsall Heath tart. Well, in her soul she was, wasn't she? Legs wide open to all her opportunities.

Which is why I managed to land up with a Miss Prune of a Chinaman as a partner, she thought when he had gone. Shouldn't fate be a big word? All Hollywood symphonies, wailing violins? Not plain ridiculous. But she calmed down as she quartered her office again, realigning the phone, fondling the top of the computer's monitor.

How could she have lived for fifty years and not realise how wonderful it would be to have her own office? Territory. Yes. It had its attractions, all right. And thinking of territory, her mind turned to plants. Not just piddling little things, she further thought. A palm that will knock your eyes out. No, no, no, she told herself. You only like to imagine that Tommy has pots of money. Aren't the Chinese supposed to go in for this thing called face? He's not going to tell you if setting up this little venture has practically wiped him out. She sighed. Two hundred pounds – the only thing Muriel's money did was make their Uniform Business Rate look fractionally less like Mount Everest.

No palm, she told herself.

She thought again about the bizarrely random events which had brought her and Tommy together. But now she decided she was ungenerous to rail against her fate. Here she was, principal partner in the Mitchell and Orient Investigation Bureau, in an operation entirely financed by him. He had found their premises in the centre of Birmingham. He'd rented a small white-painted terraced house on the canal bank in the Gas Street Basin, sandwiched between an antique dealer's and an architect's office. He'd given her the best room, on the first floor with a good view of the basin, and allowed her to furnish it as she wished on the condition that he had a free hand with the rest. And he hadn't stinted on the money. Surely he must have pots of the stuff?

Tommy had created a series of miniature Victorian smoking rooms with lots of buttoned leather, brass lamps of Arabic design and Persian rugs. 'One wants to achieve a feeling of rock-solid respectability. Of being a long-established institution. We're combating a very sleazy image, my dear. One doesn't think of your private investigator as a solid citizen. There's too much of the mean streets and dirty raincoat . . . We are after people's trust. We must make them feel they're visiting the solicitor the family have used for generations – the chap they know will help them out of a little bit of local bother.'

23

'Most people don't have a family solicitor like that,' Mitch pointed out.

'Of course not,' said Tommy. 'But they'd jolly well love to have one and that's where we come in.'

Mitch had been looking at a brass hanging lamp she'd thought would be more suitable for a harem. She asked: 'Isn't it a touch over the top?'

'People like stuffed leather. It's full of sterling worth,' Tommy told her.

Mitch privately thought that their clients would think they'd seen too many Sherlock Holmes films or taken a course in the very latest trends in pub interior design, but she didn't want to hurt his feelings.

He had no such qualms. 'Your office could be in a car sales showroom,' he'd told her and his expression said that she'd let the side down badly.

God knows how it will all turn out. She looked round her room again. An office in a car showroom. Oh, he knew how to administer a rabbit punch. The little rat.

Did it really look like that?

Time to knock off and have a drink. If I really let myself think about what I'm up to I'll lose my nerve completely.

Outside the front door a humped-back footbridge crossed a spur of canal. It led to a narrow causeway which separated two stretches of water. Narrow boats were moored off wooden jetties on either side. At the other side of the basin was a neo-Edwardian pub complete with atrium.

Mitch, surveying the scene, turned her collar up. On the walkways paths had been worn through new falls of snow to the old snow underneath, brittle with the gleam of ice. The water was black and pooled with refracting neon light. Beyond the pub on the other side of the basin the city glowed orange and rumbled as the rush hour gave it belly-ache. Among the rooftops she could make out the Holiday Inn and the outline of one of the city's two television centres.

Still letting her new surroundings feed into her bones – am I really going to feel at home this end of town, am I going to like it? – she cautiously made her way across to the pub.

24

Shaking out the cold, she let a fumy warmth of central heating, alcohol and tobacco draw her through the atrium towards the bar. She saw Digger Rooney, a half-drunk pint at the elbow of his sheepskin jacket, sitting on a bar stool. He'd had his hair cut so it stood on end, or should have stood on end. In Digger's case there was a rebellious little droop. It was damned if it was going to bristle. 'This is a bit off the beaten track for Radio Brum, isn't it?' she asked him as he raised a plumpish hand. 'In my day everyone went to the Scales.'

'I heard there was a researcher's job going in telly. So one visited one's hairdresser, had one's left ear pierced, chose a discreet ear-ring, and chanced one's luck. One simply can't stay at Radio Brum. Too, too gruesome.'

'What's the telly show?'

'*Up For Grabs*. A new prize quiz thing. And before you forget to ask, blossom, I'll have another pint.'

'Any luck?' she asked and ordered.

'Double gin? And I thought you made the right decision when Freya fired you. The only thing to do is leave that place.'

'You could do that. Any day of the week.'

'But the money. How could one's bank manager do without one's money? He's practically a stretcher case already.'

'I liked working at Radio Brum.'

'You are weird. Anyway, it looks as if I'm stuck there.'

'Your foray into television came to nought? Ah, that's the ear-ring. Turn your head a bit more.'

'Gavin – he's my chap at the hairdresser's – says it makes me look younger. More artistic. What do you think?'

'You're too round for it, Digger. Too full of sponge pud and booze.'

'It made me feel quite sexy for a while. One had a bit of a preen in front of the mirror . . . you know how you do when you're in something new . . . and I felt this very odd stir. Hormones at it. There's been very little going on in that department lately, I can tell you. That being so, one will certainly keep one's ear-ring. In fact, I was thinking of investing in a bloody great big one.'

25

But Mitch was thinking of other things. 'Actually, Digger, I'm very glad I ran into you–'

'No. No, no and no.'

'The actress Daisy Sharpe–'

'Implants. I'll stake my life on it. You can't be that thin and have a pair of warheads that size.'

'So you do know her? I thought you did.'

'In a previous incarnation I did some seasons in rep with her. I would say she's a worse actor than me. And that's not good news. But the gods are fickle. Here the little lady is, opening supermarkets by the barrelful and giving the general populace her views on what to eat, what to wear and how to approach one's Kierkegaard. Oh, if only I could be the naughty knickers in a pricky little soap.'

'Do put your malice away for a minute, Digger. Give me a break. All I want to know is if she still goes out with a financier called Arno Czinner.'

'Isn't it truly horrific? The luck some people have! My last bit of comfort and joy scarpered with my video. And here's Daisy wallowing in millions. Anyway, what's your interest in her? If it's not bad news I don't want to know.'

'I don't know I have one yet, though it could be that I might want to meet her–'

'Oh, I'll certainly fix that. We're old friends. Absolutely bosom buds. Perhaps I'll have a whisky. You wouldn't believe the day I've had.'

'Mine's a gin,' she said. 'Come on. Pay up, pay up and play the game. I haven't asked you for a favour yet.'

'By the way, Freya dropped by my desk this morning. Our boss lady couldn't raise you at home and wanted your new office number.'

'And you gave it her.'

'Never occurred to me until later. I suppose when you left you pinched that Uher there's been such a song and dance about.'

'What would I want with a tape recorder? I'm not a broadcaster any more.'

'It was a naughty thing to do. I wouldn't want Freya Adcock

after me. Many words come to mind when one thinks of Radio Brum's station manager. Animal, vegetable or mineral aren't among them.'

3

Each blade of grass stood out from its fellows, suited in a fur of ice, millions springing into the beam of light as Mitch opened her front door. Surveying downspouts growing out of roots of ice, fantastical flowers of lace blossoming on shrubs, a driveway full of giant pearls, she said: 'Oh shit.' She tried hard to reverse this first opinion, to tune into the beauties of this winter wonderland, but all she could think about was how she was going to get her car down the icy steepness of her driveway and on to the dual carriageway beyond the stone-topped gateposts.

'Oh shit, shit, shit,' she said and went indoors to get a drum of table salt. She again promised herself she would find out if it was any good salting after ice had formed. She should know these things, she told herself. Excuses had run out about two decades ago.

Today she wore a navy blue duffle coat over a short jacket, thick tights under her red wool pants, and her Royal Stewart tartan scarf climbed right into her nostrils. On her feet were an old pair of fur-lined boots her daughter had described as 'seriously unsmart' five years ago. There had been a time, perhaps not too long ago, when she would have ventured out into the snow in high heels, a skirt high above her knees, and some little velvet blouson number standing in for a coat. But she'd found, particularly in this cold snap, she'd been listening to the marrow of her bones as she'd never done before. If she listened any harder even Muriel Reeves was going to be proud of her.

She threw down salt, waited thirty seconds for a miracle to happen and when it didn't took the salt back into the kitchen, picked up her patent leather handbag, switched off the hall light and stepped into the night which was morning. Her breath rose up before her. She steamed like a coal-powered cargo boat as she tracked cautiously across the ice. She spent the next five minutes scraping the ice off the windows of her TVR. She didn't let herself know that all this would have been unnecessary if she'd put the car into the garage the evening before. She had a feeling this was going to be a difficult enough day without beating herself over the head at the start of it.

Should she start the engine or let the car roll down the drive? What were the rules when driving on ice? Though she'd had a licence for thirty years that, too, foxed her. Her trouble was that she was an optimist; bad weather never turned up and when it did she was optimistic enough to believe she'd enough true grit to see her through.

Well, here we go. Letting off the handbrake, she coasted down through the gates and – this was the tricky bit when performed on ice – swung round on the pavement so she could squeeze into the northbound traffic. Engine on, through first into second, choosing to slide on to the road in front of a Jaguar. It was an article of faith with her that chaps in expensive cars would, for the love of their toy, make way for her. Amen.

She edged down the Bristol Road, swinging through the tunnels and over the loops of Spaghetti Junction, seeing the frosted Tudor domes of Aston Hall glowering in the neon light. She dropped down on to the Tyburn Road and then forked north towards Derby.

The car heater was now working full blast and as she warmed her spirits rose. She planned to arrive on Harry Vine's doorstep at eight o'clock and stay there until he let her in.

She came off the A38 at Barton-under-Needwood. It was still dark as she pushed through the elongated village street into open country. As she forked left, away from the village of Yoxall, there was a hardening of shapes. Day was coming. She found the turning Mrs Reeves had told her about, just before the traffic lights at the bridge.

She passed scattered farmholdings and then began to climb. As she swung out of an S-bend she saw a woman in a skin-tight balaclava and matching mauve anorak, with sap-green track-suit bottoms. Slamming a gate shut with a red boot, laced with yellow, the slender figure bounded into a black Mercedes and cautiously drew away from snowy hedgerows.

Mitch overshot the gate, stopped and carefully reversed. A sign which said 'Pond Cottage' was nailed to the bumpy trunk of an old apple tree. She couldn't see a house. Volleys of gunfire sounded in the distance as she got out of the car. It wasn't until she opened the gate that she saw the tiled roof fifty feet below her, down winding brick steps. The reason for the gunfire was immediately apparent. Not six yards away a pheasant's tail was disappearing under a rhododendron bush.

Taking hold of an iced handrail, Mitch negotiated the steps.

The snow was melting over the eaves of what Mitch guessed must have once been a thatched cottage. Thank God, she thought, that means the central heating's on. When it came to her creature comforts, Mitch's abilities as a detective rose into the Sherlock Holmes class.

An uncleaned ship's bell hung in the porch. The peal hadn't quite begun when the plank door opened and a man stooped to thrust his head under the lintel. Startled, he withdrew a little. His hair was wet and he was pulling the collar of his shirt out of the neck of his sweater. 'Do I know you? You somehow look familiar.'

'Mr Vine? No, we've not met. I'm here on behalf of Mrs Muriel Reeves. I believe you worked with her husband George?'

'Mu? Good God.' His brow hiked above widening eyes.

'You are Mr Vine?'

'Mu? Who the devil—'

'I am speaking to Mr Vine? You did work with George Reeves?'

'Certainly I know George. What's this all about? You'd better come in.' As he led the way in he shouted: 'Watch your head. Nothing's more brutal than an oak beam. Indeed not. Not even iron.'

The porch door led directly into a low-beamed lounge. A green couch with paw feet was pulled up before a fireless inglenook. The air was impregnated with the smell of wood ash. Looking at the grate it seemed to Mitch that papers as well as logs had been burning there a few hours before. Curls as large and delicate as dead leaves were heaped in a corner against the fireback.

He took her through to a kitchen dining-room, full of cheerful pine furniture and willow pattern. A collection of treen covered a sideboard. French windows led out on to a terrace and not far beyond this, at the edge of a short lawn, she could see a fringe of frozen reed. 'So you do have a pond,' she said. 'I was beginning to wonder. The hillside's so steep.'

'The cottage is built in a sort of hollow half-way down to the valley. It gets pretty steep again at the bottom of the garden. The previous owner had mallard ducks. But I've never had the kind of lifestyle that would allow ducks. Or any other kind of livestock. Still, a computer isn't such bad company.'

'What happened to the ducks?'

Harry Vine laughed. 'I expect they found their way down some good citizens' gullets. Actually, I was making fresh coffee. Would you like some?'

'Thanks.' He appeared younger than he had on the photograph, more mid-forties than fifties. And yet if he'd been to school with George he must be in his fifties. He was one of those men whose hide only just seems to have enough elastic in it to stretch over all the knuckles and knobs. It was as if he'd been jointed by a series of jumbo granny knots. Still, he was not unattractive with lots of boyish hair which was beginning to curl a little as it dried. Three curved furrows, one on top of the other on each side of his brow, gave him a look of being permanently surprised.

He put two cups of coffee on the butcher's block which did duty as a table. 'Take a pew,' he said, indicating a rush-seated dining-chair. 'Now what's this all about? Just who are you? That'll do for starters.'

'I'm Mitch Mitchell, a partner in the Mitchell and Orient Bureau. Muriel Reeves called me in yesterday. Her husband disappeared four days ago and she wants me to find him. She's extremely worried.'

'George? Old George?'

30

'He went missing after work last Thursday.'

'George?' He couldn't seem to stop looking at her. Looking for what, she found herself asking herself. 'I . . . well, I hope you don't mind my saying this, my dear, but I don't know you from Adam. It could be a lot of shim-sham. George?' and he shook his head. 'He's a steady fellow is George. Conscientious almost to a fault. Good heavens. Jumped the traces . . . Look, before we have a natter I'm going to ring Muriel. Sorry and all that . . . but you turn up on my doorstep out of the blue . . . She's not let on to me. Gone? Just like that?'

'You find that hard to believe?'

'You don't know George. Believe me, you could set your watch by that chap. People like George don't do a bunk. No wonder the wifey's worried. I'll just give Mu a tinkle if you don't mind.'

'No. No. Go ahead. Ring her.'

'Won't be more than a jiffy.'

When he'd gone Mitch got up, and, cup in hand, padded round the room. The geranium on the window-sill was a corpse and she would have been able to draw in the dust on some of the shelves. Perhaps Harry Vine had also been fired by his cleaning lady? Near the draining board was a small brown bottle of pills, still a quarter full. Propped between it and the wall was a folded prescription. She picked up the bottle. Amiodarone. The name of the drug seemed to ring a distant bell. Amiodarone? The prescription was for repeat medication. She replaced them and went to view the collection of dusty treen.

'No reply,' Harry Vine said as he came back in. Though he didn't skip there was that kind of springiness in his legs. Mitch couldn't work him out. When she'd first mentioned Muriel Reeves to him he'd been plainly startled, when she'd told him about George he was unbelieving . . . and now? Why the man almost seemed exhilarated. 'I expect I'll just have to believe you, won't I? More coffee?'

'Thanks. No. Is there another woman? What do you think?'

Another hike of the eyebrows. 'If there is he's never mentioned it. There's never been a hint.'

'And it would surprise you?'

'He's a diffident chap with the females, is George.'

31

'He married Muriel.'

'Mu married him.' He thought about it. 'All the world knows how terrifically fond she is of her Georgie boy. She tells everyone often enough. My God she does.'

'But what about George? Is he fond of her?'

'I agree. At the moment that's more to the point.' He shrugged. 'Look, I've never been married. I don't know what goes on. And all this speculation doesn't really get us anywhere, does it?'

'I'm trying to find out what George is like in the hope of getting some inkling as to where to look for him.'

'Aren't you kidding yourself? Far be it from me . . . but it sounds pretty much needle in the haystack stuff.'

'Still, if you'll bear with me a bit longer . . . Weren't you at school together? What was he like then?'

'Painfully shy. Thin-skinned.' He thought about it. 'A bit of a prat. But he was clever all right.'

'The sort of boy other lads pick on?'

'Was he bullied, do you mean? I only got to know him in the Sixth. I expect he was when he was in the Lower School. After we left we didn't see each other again for a few years. But I did hear he'd had some kind of nervous breakdown and landed up in hospital. I met his mother round about that time and she said he was on the look-out for a job. Did I know of anything? The old bitch told me he'd just come back from Australia! He was always far cleverer than the rest of us. But the poor devil has always been too screwed up to use his grey matter to his advantage.'

'An ineffectual man?'

'You're hard, Miss Mitchell—'

'I'm simply listening to what you are telling me.'

'I suppose you're right really. Hasn't made much of himself, has he? He'd have been on the dole when Czinner took over Jane and Jarrod if I hadn't taken him on. Mind you, it very much suited my book at the time. To be blunt, Miss Mitchell – and why not, I no longer work there – I thought I could use his brains and take the credit. At that time I was gunning for the Finance Director's job. But when old Pierrepoint finally retired we had Toby Trubberman foisted on us. Had to be pull. The chap's not really up to it. Unlike Czinner, that. He usually goes for the best regardless.'

'And George? His wife seems to think that your going will be a prelude to his sacking. He'll get the push after your successor gets his feet firmly under the desk.'

'Right. That's the way it operates at Aston Clinton. You have your team. One out all out.'

'Seems wasteful.'

'It's the way Arno likes it. Thinks everyone will pull out the stops if they know it's sink or swim together. Thinks it promotes loyalty to the team leader and through him to the firm. It's a lot of crap, if you ask me. George and I did well as a team because I used his brain to the full. He liked that. He'd been sitting in the driving seat of a Rolls Royce all his life and never got out of first gear. Never motored. I showed him how to.'

'You did well as a team?'

'I'd say so.'

'Yet you were fired.'

'If you want to keep rabbits eagles won't do.'

'So George *did* know he was for the chop. He has a history of mental instability. Could that have pushed him over the edge?'

'Suicide?'

'I'm afraid it can't be ruled out. Did you see him after you left Czinner's?'

'A few times. Muriel had me over for a meal once. I went for a drink with him at lunchtime now and then. As a matter of fact I saw him last Monday.'

'Three days before he disappeared.'

'He met me for lunch at a pub near here. He seemed quite his usual self. Cheerful, good appetite.'

'If one were to choose between possibilities, that would make it seem more likely that another woman was behind this—'

'That's not much of a possibility either, if you ask me.'

'What does that leave? I suppose George could have cleared out the safe – if you can do that sort of thing in a plastic money age – and scarpered.'

'You don't know our George. He has principles, Miss Mitchell.

Everything by the rule book. He never looked beyond that. Didn't see – wouldn't be capable of seeing – that the rules were made up by bastards out to get and keep the lion's share.'

'We're getting through the possibilities pretty quickly. What about murder?'

That startled Harry Vine so much that his cup clattered into the saucer. 'Look, George is a nice fellow. A decent chap. Why should anyone want to bump him off? Ask anyone. They'll tell you he's a nice guy.'

'His wife said that. She said people as nice as him are as rare as a butcher with a windowful of greens.'

'Did she really? It must be very worrying for her. Upsetting. If only I could be of more help. But they always do say *cherchez la femme*, don't they?' And he nodded as if trying to convince himself. 'Even blokes you could set your watch by fall for the ladies now and then. Good Lord. That's it.'

'What?'

'You're a dead ringer for her. The woman who used to present that investigative consumer programme on the telly. What the hell was it? *Square Deal*. That's why I thought I knew you. That's why you looked so familiar.'

'*Fair Play*. That's ten years ago now.'

'Funny. The name didn't ring a bell.'

'People do sometimes recognise me. But scarcely anyone remembers my name.'

'It's a long way from presenting a television show to being a private investigator.'

'I worked in radio after that. Finished up in local radio.'

'And now you're chasing after George. It's a funny old world.'

'I like it. My job, I mean.' Do I? she wondered. Well, she certainly liked having an office. That was something. That was a start.

Harry Vine had been thinking. '*Cherchez la femme*. Got to be, hasn't it? The old bugger. I'd never have guessed. He's certainly kept her under wraps.'

'How should I go about finding her?'

'Try Tina. Tina Havelock. Our secretary.'

'Are you implying–'

'Good heavens, no. It's just that all incoming phone calls go through her usually. Also, she's a nosy bitch. If she *does* have an office boyfriend I'd say it's Toby Trubberman.'

4

Mitch rang the office from a village post office and general store. She was sitting, legs splayed apart, on two cartons of baked beans. Her bag was open between her feet and the contents strewn about. She'd not been able to remember her office number. 'Good morning,' said the voice at the other end of the line. 'This is the Mitchell and Orient Bureau.' She got an unexpected thrill from that. My name, she thought in wonder. My firm.

She became very brisk. 'I think I ought to have a car phone.'

'Really? Aren't they for spivs?'

'Tommy, there aren't any spivs any more. Spivs are entrepreneurs. Or they're the Governor of the Bank of England or Lloyd's insurance brokers.'

'Still, a car phone. So *déclassé*.' The way he lingered over day-class-aye would, Mitch thought, have scythed every spike off a porcupine.

Mitch was made of stern stuff. 'I'm a flashy lady,' she told him. 'And I don't like phoning you from on top of cartons of baked beans. They aren't even Heinz. Anything your end? Has our ad produced lots more cases?'

'I'm in the middle of opening around forty to fifty letters.'

'You're joking.'

'Unfortunately they all relate to the ad I put in for a secretary.'

'I didn't know you had. Can we afford a secretary?' she asked him and then answered the question herself: 'Of course we can't. All we've roped in so far is Mrs Reeves' two hundred quid.'

35

'I'll be the judge of that.'

'We haven't the time to interview all those people!'

'I'll make a short-list. For a start one does expect one's secretary to be able to spell. That consigns above sixty per cent of the letters to the bin. How are you getting on, my dear?'

'I've seen Harry Vine.'

'And . . .'

'Hmm. Not sure. I'll mull it over with you later. Meanwhile, do you think you could find out all you can about Arno Czinner's business activities? I'm on my way over to Aston Clinton now.'

'Will do.'

'Listen, are you really sure we need a secretary, Tommy? They cost a lot of money and in my experience spend most of their time phoning their boyfriends and having period pains.'

'How can one convey the impression that one is a flourishing concern when one hasn't even got a secretary? My dear! If one isn't flourishing one isn't considered to be any good. In the real world, as you should know, appearances are all.'

'I don't see why one just can't plunge in and get on with it,' grumbled Mitch.

'There won't be anything to get on with if we don't attract clients.'

'But Tommy! Looking good can't be better than being good!'

'As far as making money goes it is. Certainly it is. But the Mitchell and Orient Bureau will both look good and be good. One finds anything less than excellence tacky. I am seventy years old. One hasn't time for tackiness.'

'Believe me, a car phone will look very, very good to a Brummie,' Mitch said as she felt the cardboard split beneath her bum. She banged the receiver down.

She pushed through the grubby lemon and white strips of plastic which formed a screen between the hallway and the shop and asked directions to Aston Clinton as she gave the woman at the till a pound coin.

'Going to snow again, ducks,' the woman replied. 'That's the weather for you. You wouldn't catch me driving in this. But would 'e listen? Our Wayne's brains got washed away in that

36

poncy jacuzzi of 'is. Letting a jet of water excite you! Christ, you've got to laugh. Kids today.'

Mitch asked for directions again. And learned them while also hearing how much phlegm it is possible to cough up while in the grip of pneumonia and acquiring some facts she didn't like about Bright's disease. 'If you ask me it's better altogether if you don't know where your kidneys are,' the woman told her. 'It's when you think about things that trouble starts.'

Mitch emerged into a deserted village street. Though it was not yet eleven o'clock in the morning lights were on in some of the semi-detached houses across the way. The pub sign whined as it swung in a stiffening wind. Flutters of snow fell as she turned the car on to the Sudbury Road. First she switched on her sidelights and then her headlights as the snow became heavier.

Missing the turning to Aston Clinton, she had to go back and look for it. The fork was to the left of a water pumping station isolated in sheets of white fields. Hedgerows gave way to stands of trees. As she entered a hairpin bend a Jaguar closed up behind her, beginning to push, to ride her bumper. 'Bastard,' she said aloud and she dropped her speed, forty, thirty, twenty. The Jaguar's horn let out a yell of rage. 'Cry, baby, cry,' Mitch sang. 'While I shove shit in your eye!' and she swung towards the hedgerow and let him have it. A volley of snow rose up from her wheels.

The hairpin straightened and a shallow half-moon driveway appeared to her left. Brass shell shaded lights illuminated the plaque on the eight-foot-high park wall. ASTON CLINTON. She pulled in, stopping at lodge gates. The Jaguar, still hooting, swung through a matching gateway marked OUT.

The porch of the lodge had been adapted to form a glass booth. Mitch got out of the car and went across to the window. 'Who is that cretin?' she asked the security man.

'Black Jaguar? One of the A team. Mr Trubberman. Ha! And what can I do for you, girlie?'

'I'm looking for a Miss Havelock. I'm told she's Financial Development.'

'Main door for you then. Ask at the reception there.'

'What did you mean? The A team?'

'The hit squad. They all drive black Jags. When Mr Czinner buys a business they go in and pull the place apart and then put it back together again the Czinner way.'

'What way's that?'

'Not enough left on the bones for a worm's supper. Still, all's fair in love and war. Eh, ducks?'

Mitch climbed back in her car and nosed through a long winding drive to the car-park. As she entered it she saw a blond, curly-headed man bending to lock the black Jaguar. Oh, yes. Very nice if you can get it, she found herself thinking as she viewed his body with a discerning eye. I bet he's got a pair of those Tory blue eyes; call me Tarzan. Pity no Tory in his right mind would think me Jane. Shielding his curls with a pink wodge of the *Financial Times*, he raced down a path cut through shrubbery to the entrance of Aston Clinton. 'Trubberman,' she said out loud, and then placed him. Czinner's Finance Director.

Duffle coat hood up, head down, gloved hands balled in pockets, she followed him at a more sedate pace. Before she reached the entrance her cheeks were tingling.

Aston Clinton was a Tudor-turreted Nonsuch Palace constructed in Victorian times with a large, recently built neo-Georgian wing. Portland stone entrance steps led to a rectangular vestibule with a black and white chequered marble floor. Beyond heavy oak doors more steps led to inner doors. Two suits of crusader armour, visors down, articulated finger plates resting on hefty broadswords, were on guard.

Mitch entered a huge two-storey hall decorated with the flags and banners of ancient regiments. Copies of Napoleon's campaign chairs lined one linenfold panelled wall. A fan of rapiers containing a smaller fan of flintlocks was arranged on the wall above a roaring log fire. The reception area was at the bottom of the hall, across yards of highly polished black and white marble. Above a carved reception desk spotlights played on a twenty-foot oil canvas showing a lot of cannon, gun smoke, rifles and mutilated bodies. The bleeding flesh was rendered so beautifully that Mitch wondered whether Goya was the painter.

'Go down the corridor to the left of you. Go as far as the staircase and then turn right. The door is straight ahead of you,' said the doe-eyed eastern beauty who luxuriated in her suit like a Persian cat in its fur. Mitch took her duffle coat off and swung it from her shoulders.

The corridor was eighteen feet wide and covered with Persian rugs. Rows of cannons interspersed with pyramids of cannon-balls were lined up under leaded windows. Opposite, pikes, arranged as Roman numerals, marched along the wall. She came to a huge carved staircase lit with Pre-Raphaelite glass showing scenes from the legend of King Arthur. Beyond, in gold lettering, a door pronounced itself to be the entrance to the Development team's office.

She knocked and entered and found herself alone in dazzling Pre-Raphaelite light. The team had inherited the family chapel. The stained glass, showing the conversion of St Paul on the road to Damascus, gleamed in lancet windows. Kelim-covered sofas faced each other across the body of the chapel and there was a marble-topped table with some magazines on it. The two steps up to the altar remained but the altar itself was now a large smoked glass and steel reception desk. Two smaller doors were set into fluted stone doorways behind it.

Mitch, turning slowly so she could better observe the carved stonework and glass, felt the roots of hair at the nape of her neck stiffen. She was an atheist who firmly believed in the wrath of God; indeed she was now looking upwards. But no thunderous face appeared through the painted panels showing Jesus, cross over his shoulder, toiling upwards.

Miss Havelock, a file in her hand, came in from one of the doors at the back of the altar. She gleamed like a golden boy; thick, blonde hair, parted in the middle, shaved off below mid-ear, tumbled over urchin eyes. The masculine cut of her silk shirt, the baggy slacks, seemed to emphasise the subtle femininity of her slight figure.

Mitch, finding herself in the candid gaze of this candidly not very impressed kid, found herself drawing her body up. On parade, not a slack muscle to be seen.

'Yes?'

'It is Miss Havelock? I'm Mitch Mitchell. I've been employed by Muriel Reeves, the wife of George Reeves.'

A low sound emanated from Miss Havelock's fluorescent pink lips. It was with a sense of shock Mitch realised it was a whistle. 'She was here yesterday. I never imagined . . . no . . . Are you a private detective? Shit a brick. You are!'

'I'm a partner in the Mitchell and Orient Bureau. Mrs Reeves has hired us to try and find her husband. I wondered – well, to be blunt, Miss Havelock, one tends to look for the other woman in a case like this.'

'George is older than my dad!'

'Yes. I expect he is. But older people do . . .' Mitch found herself desperately looking round for the right words.

'Do it?' Miss Havelock began to giggle. 'Tina. Call me Tina. I know they do. But George – well, he's a nice man, Miss Mitchell, really he is. A sweetie. And sort of not . . . well, nice. And more than a bit behind the door. If you know what I mean. Shy.'

'He couldn't have been nice all the time!'

'Well, he's a bit of a stickler. A place for everything and everything in its place. But I drew the line at dusting the files. I mean . . . well. And if he wanted the phones sprayed he had to do it himself. But if you were in trouble over anything he'd always stick up for you. I know he's finicky and drives you mad but still . . . he's a serious sweetie. Honest. If he's really got up his nerve and left that old cow – well, all I can say is I'm pleased for him,' and she shook her head in wonderment.

'Are you absolutely sure he wasn't fond of anybody? At the office, for instance?'

'Not that I know of.'

'No gossip about him at all?'

'Not that sort of gossip. But it was rumoured he was going to be sacked. He was Harry Vine's appointment, you see, and Toby – that's to say Mr Trubberman – had to get shut of that man Vine. And I don't think poor George will suit Mr Skeog. That's the man who is taking over from Mr Vine. Toby – Mr Trubberman – thinks we need lots of young fresh blood. We're moving into the twenty-first century now. The twentieth century is old hat. Kaput.'

'Do you know how George felt about the prospect of being sacked?'

'Oh, that wouldn't be George. He wouldn't say a word. Toby says they cracked the mould when they made George's stiff upper lip! Actually, he seemed to work even harder than usual. Often in earlier and he worked late more than once. He wanted everything to be left just right for the next man. Of course, it's been about eighteen months since any real work was done in this office. If it had been up to Toby that Vine man would have gone a lot sooner. Toby was so worried about his loyalties he didn't even let him know what the latest strategies were. It's been very difficult for Toby. Really it has.'

'All calls to this department come to you?'

'Yes.'

'So if a woman were to ring George you would know?'

'Well, I should think so. I'm sure I'd have twigged if someone were ringing him at work.'

'And she wouldn't ring him at home,' Mitch said, more to herself than Tina Havelock. 'Did George have any personal calls of any sort?'

'Nothing that I specially remember. His wife sometimes–'

'He could have called out without the call going through you? On a direct line?'

'Certainly.'

'But the calls that went through you . . . nothing springs to mind.'

'There were one or two calls which worried me a bit if you really want to know.'

'From whom?'

'Some clinic. I wondered if he had something wrong with him. I mean, I liked him. I just hoped it wasn't serious.'

'Which clinic? Can you remember the name?'

'Something Hope. Something Hope Foundation.'

'The Glick Hope Foundation?'

'That's it.'

'The calls came over a period of time?'

She frowned. 'Three or four maybe. Spread over the last

twelve months. I thought it would be his ticker. I mean, he's no spring chicken, is he?'

Mitch, lips pursed, didn't answer her. Then she said: 'The last day he came in to work. Thursday. Did he act differently in any way?'

She sucked the end of her forefinger as she thought it over. 'No. I wouldn't say so.'

'Cheerful?'

'Oh yes. He was quite a cheerful sort of chap on the whole.'

'His behaviour all that week? He didn't do anything different, did he?'

'Tuesday.'

'What did he do then?'

'It was what he didn't do, Miss Mitchell. He always stayed late at Aston Clinton on Tuesdays. Had his tea here. But actually I saw him in the car-park. He left the same time I did.'

'Why did he usually stay late on Tuesdays?'

'I believe he always went to a meeting of some kind or other. He hadn't time to go home first. He had his tea here and then went off to some – well, club, I always thought – in Birmingham.'

'Not to a meeting here of any sort? Strategy, something like that?'

'Oh no. Never.'

'Did he have any particular friends among the staff here?'

'Not really. Not after that Vine man left.'

'You told me that George rarely showed his feelings. Stiff upper lip and all that. But I want you to think carefully about that Thursday. He seemed in no way worried? Depressed? Anxious?'

'If anything he was . . . well . . . "full of vim" – that was the expression he used. I can see him standing where you are now, rubbing his hands together, and I said something about he was getting out of the right side of bed these days. He laughed. "Full of vim, eh? Life in the old dog yet." Something like that.'

'And yet he thought he was going to be fired?'

'I said to Sammy – she's in Accounts proper in the new wing – I said I thought all the rumours were wrong. That he'd be staying. But she said if she knew she were going to be paid off in a few weeks' time she'd be doing a jig.' Tina suddenly descended down the two altar steps, pushing hair out of her eyes with her free hand and leaning forward: 'Her dad has got a pair of cuff links made from human molars.' She nodded her head. 'It's true. She showed them to me. Ace.' She began to laugh. 'George really has gone off, has he? If he had something tasty tucked up his sleeve he would be full of vim, wouldn't he? Wait till I tell Toby – Mr Trubberman . . .'

'You've not told your boss yet?'

'Lily – on reception – has only just phoned me to say he's back. He was in Switzerland. But he's gone straight up to see AC. That's Mr Czinner and he's just back from Liechtenstein. He stopped in London overnight and arrived about fifteen minutes ago. We've got a helipad here, you know.

'So no one knows yet that George has gone?'

'I'll tell Mr Trubberman as soon as he's free. Look, I'm sorry, Miss Mitchell – but I don't really think I should be talking to you. I know I haven't said anything but . . . well, they can be a bit funny here. They may not like it.'

'Don't worry. I'm not going to let anyone know.'

'I don't expect it matters at all . . .'

'Of course not.' Mitch turned round once more. 'It's a bit of a rum place to have an office,' she said, inspecting a neo-Norman column. 'Still, the Unitarian chapel I went to as a kid is now a hat factory.'

'At least the ceiling's high,' said Tina.

Mitch stared at her.

'We can do our skipping at lunchtime without the rope catching. Me and my friend Sammy do fifteen minutes a day.'

'Good for you. Well, thanks, Tina.'

'Take care the bugs don't bite,' Tina shouted after her.

Mitch put her duffle coat back on in the great hall, tucking her curls in the hood as she clattered down the entrance steps. Bending into the wind, she plodded back to the car-park deep in thought.

She banged her hands together before turning on the engine of the TVR. Switching on the front and back wipers, she

43

reversed. The car juddered as the wheels gripped. She juddered too as the bumper hit something.

'Balls . . .' she moaned to herself and got out to inspect the damage.

At first the shape, much of it half buried in snow, was a mystery to her. She made out two horizontal drums, one mounted on top of the other. Driving wind was blowing snow off the drums and on the top one she could make out lettering which said WATER. There was an irregular hump behind this and then a long handle which ended in a circle of snowy tubing. Two sticks with a knob on each sprouted from within the circle. She examined the bottom drum of this ton weight of machinery more closely and slowly realised she was looking at a petrol-driven roller. The bumper had knocked off a wedge of snow as it had crunched into a flat steel bar mounted above the roller. There was a scrape in the fibreglass body of her vehicle but the TVR had made no impression on the bar.

No real harm. Relieved, she climbed back into the car.

By the time she'd reached the gates of Aston Clinton the road had disappeared under a layer of white.

5

'Arno Czinner isn't an industrialist. He doesn't make anything. He's a trader. A buyer and seller of companies. He buys cheaply, sends in his team to sort things out, and then sells dear. Like all traders, he makes his money on the turn,' said Tommy Hung. Lifting the white china teapot, he paused for a moment to view the Washingtonia palm Mitch had bought on her way back to the office. 'They most certainly always have one of those in car showrooms.' His nose grew to his trouser bottoms as he looked further and further down it.

'But they have plastic ones. This is real. Tending plants is good for the soul.' This is what Mitch had told herself when she'd charged the plant to the Mitchell and Orient Bureau. Tommy, she'd decided, must have pots and *pots* of money if he intended to hire a secretary.

'Perhaps one could have chosen something . . . something less . . . perhaps flowers?'

'Flowers are bad value,' Mitch said. 'They're always dying. Though, apart from that, I've nothing against them.'

Tommy began to pour the tea. 'He came from a family of Hungarian Jews who emigrated to Egypt. His father set himself up in some sort of export-import business. He died before Arno was twenty-one. Arno dropped the exporting side altogether and it is said – though it has never been proved – that, among other things, he imported bits and pieces of military hardware the West didn't want Middle Eastern leaders to get their hands on. He had enough sense to get out of that as soon as he could and came to England in the mid-seventies. He went bottom fishing in the property sector after the secondary banking crash in 1975.'

'So his credentials don't really bear examining?'

'My dear, if you're not Prince Charles, the only credential you need is cash. Czinner bought his first public quoted company for five million in 1982. Today he's capitalised at just under three billion. In the eighties the value of his shares multiplied by almost fifty. Dividend growth was three times the UK average. Earnings per share grew at a rate of something like forty-two per cent.'

'Stop fogging my mind. What the hell does all that mean?'

He gave her a cup of tea. 'It means he's in the super-star league. Of course, the roaring eighties have given way to the wheelchair nineties but even here he seems to have managed to circumnavigate the fate of many of his erstwhile pals,' and Tommy turned his thumb down to demonstrate what had happened to them. 'In fact, he's earned the reputation of being able to walk on water.'

'Perhaps he made the right decision after all then.'

'What do you mean, my dear?'

'This guy's Financial Development Department is housed in a retread family chapel!'

'He's certainly been in need of divine aid. When the music

stopped in 1990 he was left holding a huge half-completed office development down by the river in London. He'd also paid way over the top for two companies – the chocolate people Jane and Jarrod and an aero-engine business in Preston. For a long time his shares did nothing but go south.'

'South?'

'Down. But they've gradually been creeping up for twelve months now. He's coming out of the woods.'

'So he's sound? Who gave you all this gen?'

'Willie French, a partner in Shakespeare, Salmon and Spivey.'

'Stockbrokers? Out on Colmore Circus?'

'That's them.'

'Would your Willie French buy Czinner's shares?'

'He's not a believer.'

'Why not?'

'He says he doesn't even believe Jesus Christ could walk on water. But he tells me his is not the general view. Most analysts think the shares are in for a re-rating as the after-effects of the recession finally die away.'

'What do you think, Tommy?'

'Czinner's shares always carried a risk. Not for widows and orphans. Apart from the public quoted companies he's got, there's a network of private companies. Some of those must have haemorrhaged badly during the recession. My fear would be that too much money has been siphoned out of the main businesses to prop those up. But they do say that Czinner has never yet failed to repay a bank loan. He's somehow managed to squeeze enough money out of his assets to keep his empire afloat.'

'How far does all this get us with the disappearance of George Reeves?' Mitch wondered. She got up from behind her desk and, hands on hips, turned to look out of her first-floor office window. Snow was floating on to ice which was spreading from the banks of the waterway towards the centre. Beyond the still black heart of the basin, lights were already winking in the pub, though it was not much past three o'clock in the afternoon.

'By the way, your ex-boss has been ringing again. Twice. I do wish you'd get in touch with her. She made one feel one

46

had let the side down badly by not producing you before now.'

'I'm not in to that woman. Not ever.' Oh, my God. There go my boobs. Heaving with indignation. It's uncomfortable to discover how much of a cliché one's responses are.

There was some tremor, too, as she recalled her erstwhile programme assistant Sean saying, in an effort to cheer her up: 'We'll have the biggest leaving party ever. We'll make the roof dance. Honest.'

'I don't think I'm quite that glad to see her go,' Quentin Plunkett had told him as he spliced tape. 'And to be quite frank, dear boy, if I'd been given the boot I'd like to exit on the QT.'

'Quentin's quite right. Anything else is too, too grotesque as Digger would say.' Mitch had spoken brightly though it was not long before she'd beaten a retreat to the lavatories. Lick your finger and put this on the plus side, she told herself now. You never cried in front of any of those bastards.

'Really, Mitch. You can't hold Freya Adcock personally responsible for what happened. You told me yourself. The station's budget had been slashed. Someone had to go.'

'If I speak to that woman I might lose my cool. I've never had much dignity to stand on but the bit I've got I want to keep.' What she was really thinking of was the nice shiny new tape recorder she'd pinched on her last day at the station. Her leaving present. Her bit of something after nearly thirty years in broadcasting. Freya Adcock was never going to prise that back off her.

Knowing that calmed her down.

She turned round and found herself admiring her office again; there was a fond parental look in her eye as she viewed her palm tree. 'I should have had an office years ago,' she told Tommy. 'It makes you really feel like someone. You see yourself in a quite different light. You know, go-ahead, efficent . . .'

'You never had your own office while you were a broadcaster?'

'I was never important enough and I can't say it ever bothered me. I mean, I never suspected there were pleasures in having

47

one's own territory at work. I liked being with lots of other people. Just one of the guys. Management never appealed. Still doesn't. I'll leave all that to you, Tommy. What I like is finding out. I suppose I'm just incredibly curious. I'm never happier than when I'm poking my nose into other people's business. I love learning things I shouldn't know. I suppose that's why I was a good journalist in my time. Well, onward and upward,' and she briefed him on Harry Vine and Tina Havelock.

'Is this the exception to the rule?' Tommy wondered. 'A case of don't *cherchez la femme*?'

'We're still only on day one. Then there's this clinic angle. Tina Havelock thought George might have heart trouble. But the Glick Hope Foundation is, in fact, a large private psychiatric clinic in Edgbaston. Just down the road from my place. They do take one or two non-paying patients, I believe, in some kind of research tie-up with Birmingham University. But I honestly don't know all the ins and outs.'

'So it's a pukka place?'

'Most certainly. And we can deduce, I think, from Tina's information that George went there every Tuesday after work. He could belong to one of their therapy groups or he could be having one-to-one treatment. The thing is, Tommy, why didn't Muriel Reeves tell me this? She said he stayed late at the office for strategy meetings. Then there's Harry Vine. Surely he must have known?'

'It's possible that neither knew.'

'Possible, I suppose, but hardly probable. Especially in Muriel's case. But as it's Tuesday today I'm going to push on down there this evening. It does seem a bit drastic . . .'

'What?'

'Abandoning your wife and therapist in the same week.'

'Unless, of course, he's killed himself. If he has been having psychiatric treatment that ups the suicide option, doesn't it?'

'I think it must,' said Mitch. 'Though that flatly contradicts what Tina told me. She said he was more cheerful than usual.'

'Is he undergoing psychiatric treatment at all? Hardly sounds the sort of thing a cheerful man would do.'

'Well, Tommy, it is just possible that the treatment was

48

working. George's tears were turning into smiles. Unlikely, one may think. But on the cards. Anyway, if we look at it from that angle what's a cheerful man doing going AWOL?'

Tommy was tapping his chin with a forefinger. 'If the treatment turned George into a new man he may very well feel in need of a new wife to go with a new lifestyle.'

'Or has an honest man turned into the dishonest sort of chap who sticks his fingers in the till and does a bunk? Three billion is rather a large honeypot, Tommy.'

'The jackpot. In anyone's language.'

'Well, however it is, I'm taking the rest of the afternoon off. I've a long cold night on look-out in front of me.'

'Do you really think he'll turn up?'

'I don't suppose it's all that likely. But if he were a member of a group the rest of them would turn up, wouldn't they? And if he's been going some time I expect they'd know more about George than his Maker.'

'I see what you mean. But you have to jump over a few ifs to reach that point. I mean, we don't even know yet if he's a patient there!'

But Mitch was already thinking about something else. 'I ought to go and get my hair cut. But it's too cold and anyway everyone seems to want to try and make me have a scrunch.'

'What on earth's that?'

'Hard to describe really. Sort of bursting interior sprung mattress. As that's my hair's natural starting point I immediately run into difficulties. I need to be tamed, sweetie. You know, put in rollers and stout hairnets. But rollers have suddenly become old hat. How am I going to regulate my wilder bits?'

Tommy's finger moved up to tap his bald head. 'I can recommend it. Cheap, neat, as worn by Buddha and other sages.' And he began to clear up the tea things.

Mitch put her head into his well-buttoned stuffed-hide lair before leaving. 'I'll just pick up some literature on car phones,' she told him. 'Absolutely no harm in that, I'd say. One isn't committed. What you need on the wall behind your desk, Tommy, is an oil painting of the Mitchell and Orient founder. One of those impossibly dreary dark things. You know, a chap

49

with a baleful eye and a pair of mutton-chop whiskers. That'll put a hundred years of respectable trading behind us in an instant. I'll ring an ex-boyfriend of mine. Josh Hadley'll find us just the thing for under fifty quid.'

'Wonderful idea,' said Tommy, not looking up from the pile of letters he was wading through. 'Just the ticket.'

Does he know that I'm having him on and is he having me on? Mitch wondered. The day I get to the bottom of Tommy Hung is the day I'll sprout wings and fly.

But she whistled as she went to collect her TVR from its multi-storey parking slot. When she heard the noise she was startled. She hadn't whistled for . . . no, it was no use. She couldn't remember.

I'm happy.

Good Lord, she marvelled and stifled the urge to pretend not to be. No jealous god was listening and getting envious. No god of any sort was going to strike her down. She was an atheist. Remember?

Such hard work, being a non-believer. And that was in spite of the fact that much of what went on right under her nose was beyond belief.

Now she was singing. Out loud, in the street, while absolutely sober. Out of tune, certainly, but there was a hell of a good rhythm in there. 'Strawberry fields–'

'That's it, ducks! Luvly juvly!' An old fellow laughed and raised his laden Tesco shopping bag in salute. An eyelid with more folds in it than a festoon blind winked over a beady eye.

An hour later, a bunch of brochures to hand, Mitch was in her kitchen phoning to find out if car phones came in pastel shades. 'Not pink. Or blue. Though I can see an azure blue. Something with sunshine in it. Yes.' And she squinted as she concentrated on the exact shade of blue she had in mind. 'What's smart about black, one asks oneself? Christ. It's the colour of a crow. Or a hearse. So dead, darling. I'm not averse to a two-tone if you do a line in those. Certainly not beige. When I had a mother-in-law she wore a lot of that.'

Hooking the receiver back to the kitchen wall she caught a glimpse of the corner of her cork notice-board and saw a picture of herself and Digger Rooney photographed at a Radio Brum outside broadcast. Taken last spring? Certainly after Josh Hadley had ditched her for Miss Rocket Launcher. God, oh God, the pains of getting older. Even one's faithful, not to say staid, lovers suddenly grow a pony tail and designer stubble and go whooping after the young lovelies. And then she was smiling for she was remembering Charlie Collins, the lover who had bounded into her bed after Josh had departed.

'You're crackers,' she said aloud. 'He saw you as live bait and dead meat!'

Still, it had been good having a young and vigorous lover. Someone, she thought, to really get your teeth into. She wondered about this new CAT position which was apparently all the rage in America. Reading about it, it had seemed more likely to her that you'd peak out on a slipped disc. That shows you're getting old, she grumbled to herself. When you worry more about your health than an orgasm.

Oh for a well-muscled lad. A shining leaping lord to pop your peel, taste your juices. And she found herself roving by the kitchen and dropping a piece of Mars bar in her mouth.

And as she wandered around her house, sucking her sweetie, the pain eased. She'd lived in Bristol Road for fifteen years. She and her husband Max had bought the terraced house when their daughter Cassie had been seven. It was a Georgian-style villa built on a bank above the road in the 1840s. A large conservatory had been added on to the back in Victoria's reign. Ever since Max had died ten years ago she'd promised herself she'd sell it. It was too big, too expensive to run and the dual carriageway at the bottom of the drive, one of the main arteries into the city, made access a nightmare.

When her daughter left England to study in America she had got as far as calling the estate agent. But the truth was she loved the house. The elegant rooms, the white-painted conservatory, the small glass cupola through which, as she lay in her bath, she could make out the shape of the stars. They were often paled by the night glare of the city, but they were there, aeons of heavenly bodies.

'Where else in this city can I get a house with a view of

the universe?' she asked Cassie, the ping on the satellite punctuating the sentences, when she and her daughter had last discussed the matter.

'But mummy, you've just been moaning about how hard up you are. That place has four bedrooms, six if you count the two in the attics. No wonder you need to practically take out a mortage to pay the gas bill!'

'Well, I'll just have to make up my mind and sell,' and Mitch's sigh bounced off the satellite and into the ear of her daughter three thousand long miles away.

'Yes,' said Cassie. 'After all, people are more important than houses.' As soon as Cassie had left her childhood behind her she'd taken to lecturing her mother. She lectured Mitch most about her driving, which she considered downright reckless, but she often waded in about the house in Bristol Road.

Both enjoyed these exchanges. I've got a grown-up daughter, Mitch thought, absolutely amazed that she'd apparently done a not-too-bad job in bringing up a kid.

Mother is hopeless, she could hear Cassie clucking to herself. I try my best but she's got absolutely no idea about anything. You'd think by the time you'd reached that age you'd have your life organised.

But, far from organising herself out of her house, Mitch had relegated the issue to the back of her mind. It was so far back that she'd been pricing new carpet for the stairs. 'I'm only toying with the idea,' she'd told the salesman. The acid lines of martyrdom had bitten so deeply into his face they were practically through to the bone. She'd been unrepentant. After all, there were many other jobs in this world that a guy could do.

When the phone rang, interrupting her pacing, she glanced at the clock and thought it might be her daughter on the line. In Washington it would be mid-morning, just about the time of day Cassie liked to tumble out of bed.

'Digger,' she said, when she heard his voice. 'I've just been admiring a photo of you and me together. In the service of Radio Brum.'

'You make it sound pornographic,' said Digger Rooney. 'And if you're thinking along those lines I simply couldn't oblige.

52

One is always holding oneself in reserve for the troops. Our boys come first. Sailors especially.'

'Thanks a bunch. Anyway, what do you want?'

'It's what you want. Do you remember asking me about Daisy Sharpe? The actress? Well, pin back your lug-holes. I've got me an invite to a bash at her boyfriend's abbey or mansion or whatever it is. I'm allowed a chum. Tomorrow night at seven. Aren't I all that's nice?'

'I only said I might need to get to know the lady–'

'Balls! You–'

'I'm delighted all the same. Truly. How did you manage it?'

'If you'd heard my show today you'd have known she was on it. She's trying to raise money for that charity of hers. You know, that Brazilian thing. Save the street kids from the Squadra dei Morti. The terror squads who murder young children because they say this clears the streets of crime. She's hoping to raise enough to fund an orphanage.'

'Really? One would never have thought Daisy the type.'

'Good for the image. I may be Miss Nasty Knickers on telly but really I've a heart of gold. That sort of thing.'

'My God. What a cynic you are.'

'I try not to be. I try to keep my thoughts on lovely things. Mr Heseltine, for instance.'

'You're joking. You can't have fantasies about him.'

'I even had fantasies about Mrs T, for God's sake. I do so adore power figures. Whip-er-oo yum-ee! Oh well. My psyche's never been all that it should be.'

'Whose is? See you tomorrow.'

6

The Glick Hope Foundation was just off Priory Road in Edgbaston, one of Birmingham's affluent suburbs. In a city where around a million souls rubbed together, people were less in evidence here than the hibernating grey squirrels.

Mitch had given up trying to negotiate her ice-ridged drive-way. She'd parked the TVR in the mouth of a small close on the opposite side of the dual carriageway. She left the house just after six, well padded up, a flask of black coffee in the pocket of her duffle coat. Though the evening rush hour was past its peak, she had to walk to the traffic lights before she could cross the road. The wind had dropped, the skies had cleared; the warm wisps of her breath turned her well-wrapped head into a gently steaming pudding.

Before she climbed into her car she scraped the ice off the windows and eased the wipers free. She ran the engine for two or three minutes before setting off down Bristol Road. She turned right into Priory Road and, after passing Edgbaston Golf Course, nosed down a lane by the side of a convent. It led to the pillared but gateless entrance of the Glick Hope. Her wheels bumped over humps of traversing ice as she let the car glide gently down the hill to the floodlit Victorian mansion which housed the psychiatric clinic. The car-park was directly in front of the porticoed entrance. There were a dozen other vehicles beside her own, but none, she quickly saw, answered to the description of George Reeves' green Golf. But had she really expected him to turn up?

She backed up carefully and then let her headlights play over the parked cars. Among the Volvos and Mercedes there were two or three vehicles almost as old as her own. That surprised her. Treatment at the Glick Hope, so she'd heard, didn't come cheap.

She let the car roll forward into a position which gave her a clear view both of the entrance and the other cars. She eased on the handbrake and got out. The cold hit her, stinging almost as much as a slap in the face. She pulled up her scarf a¹ ove her nose and looked at the mansion. The William and Mary gabling stood proud against a bumpy snow-clad roof. There was an Italianate tower at the west end and a large glass conservatory ran from front to rear on the eastern side. In between, Gothic windows shone dully in the wash of neon light. The building was a mass of disparate styles and yet, sitting four square in its setting of icy parkland, formed a harmonious whole. Driveways circled both the tower and the conservatory. Half-way up the hill beyond were the lights of another building, though she could not make out its size because it was only partly visible.

Banging gloved hands together, Mitch walked to the entrance. Twin caryatids supported the portico which sheltered the massive oak entrance doors. Beyond, shallow sandstone steps climbed to more doors and a huge reception hall. Delicate wrought-iron columns rose two storeys before they branched to support a glass-domed roof. Walls and floors were covered in richly patterned Moorish tiles. To Mitch it so much resembled a Victorian Turkish bath that she found herself expecting billowing steam to sidle from under the numerous doorways, rising up to bead the tiles with vapour.

It took her some time to locate the reception desk. It was beyond a jungle of potted palms, to the left of a tastefully robed marble woman whose feet were very firmly planted on her pedestal. In her hands was a book she was reading with sightless eyes.

The reception area was presided over by a large grey-suited woman who was looking at her over half-rimmed spectacles with very different eyes. Mitch was reminded of a famous dog trainer she'd once interviewed in her local radio days.

'I've just come down from Darlington,' Mitch said, surprising herself more than the receptionist. Where the hell *is* Darlington? she wondered. 'I set off early expecting to be delayed by the weather but I've actually made very good time. I'm here to meet someone . . . I mean, after their . . . you know, their . . . well, session, I suppose you'd call it?'

'One of Dr Gatting's group, yes? Our last one-to-one finished half an hour ago.'

Mitch chanced her arm. 'A chap called George Reeves.'

'Just a minute Miss – er, Mrs?'

'Flower,' said Mitch, staring at the *diamanté* petals on the brooch which pinned the receptionist's cream silk scarf to her suit.

She turned to her VDU. Mitch tried to read the monitor over a well-tailored shoulder but the machine was so cleverly sited that this proved impossible. 'Yes, dear. He's one of Dr Gatting's evening people. But they won't break until seven thirty. You're in for a jolly long wait.'

'Is there a pub near here?'

'We do have The Friend to All near the Q E. Sorry. The Queen Elizabeth Hospital. But it's dreadfully tucked away and you're a stranger to the area?'

Mitch nodded.

'You could stay here.'

Mitch looked round again and saw a scattering of green Dralon-covered seating. Only part of one banquette was being used. A muscular ginger tom with half an ear missing was stretched out, whiskers gently rising and falling as it slept.

'Thank you. I'll perhaps go into town and come back later.'

'And you made good time from south Durham? It just shows you. You can never tell. It took Dr Gatting an hour and a half to get in. And he only lives at Bideford on Avon.' She shook her head in wonder and turned to pick up the telephone.

Mitch went back out, checked the still-deserted car-park and then toured the outside of the mansion. The drives which rounded each side of the building joined beyond snowy terracing and led up to a second building. It was signposted as Mary Golding House and was a long two-storey construction with a butterfly roof. It was built, Mitch guessed, in the early seventies. There was a car-park to the side; six or seven vehicles were illuminated by both floodlighting and the glare of neon from overlooking windows. Though Mitch searched, she could find no second point of access to Glick Hope's facilities. All visitors who came or went used the same entrance. Satisfied, she walked back to the main car-park.

She'd just settled back to wait in her TVR when she heard a car's engine. She was momentarily blinded by lights and then she saw a cream-coloured Porsche whisper to a stop in front of the porticoed entrance. A small man in a Russian-style fur hat bounced out. As he rounded the bonnet the neon lighting began to define him.

Mitch drew her breath in.

Arno Czinner?

Yes. She was sure. She had seen more than one picture of

56

him in the papers, usually shepherding a glamorous lady – of late Daisy Sharpe – to some glitzy function. What had an industrialist called such women? 'Arm pieces.' Yes. That was it. She scanned the car. Tonight no one was with him.

After he'd gone in the clinic, she swung the TVR round into a better position because the Porsche partially obstructed her line of vision. She was now side on and had a clear view of the apron of stone under the portico.

Five minutes passed, ten minutes, and now the cold had penetrated through her boots and gloves. Using some of the passenger seat, she tucked her feet up under her bum, opened a cord fastening on her duffle coat and thrust her hands under the sweaters she was wearing. Five minutes later and she was so cold she wanted to cry.

She was about to get out of the vehicle when the oak doors opened. Arno Czinner came out, followed by a woman who was a head taller.

My God, is he in a strop about something, thought Mitch, as he bounced towards his car. The woman was visibly restraining herself from twittering about his heels. She jammed her limbs together as he turned on her, arms locked over her heart. He swung forward like a boxer. The woman involuntarily flinched but her feet didn't move. No. She was not to be shifted, though the loose flesh which seemed to have slid down her long and bony face to her neck quivered slightly. As he opened his mouth she drew herself up, commanding more height from which she could look down on him. He shut his mouth without speaking, took off his hat to her and then, with shocking, unexpected savagery, bit into it. His eyes never left her face. He very carefully replaced the hat. Just before he got into his car, his back turned towards her, he waved. He opened the engine to full power, an almost deafening sound in the crystal clarity of the night. He rode it down to a whisper. He swung the Porsche round gently and eased the vehicle back up the drive. The thinnest haze of snow droplets came up from under the car's wheels.

Mitch heard her heart thud-thud-thudding and realised the scene had frightened her.

The woman freed her locked arms, and put her hands to her ears, fingers forking through a frizz of haloing grey hair. Her head and trunk rocked. Suddenly she pulled back her shoulders, breathed deeply and went back indoors.

When she was sure no one else was coming out, Mitch opened the car door and began to untangle her limbs. She levered herself upright on to the snow, her body squealing as she straightened out. She hopped from foot to foot as pins and needles shot up from her feet.

Leaping and mincing she rounded the car-park, banging her arms about her chest. You can't get frost-bite sitting in a car, she assured herself. That happens to climbers caught out on Mount Everest.

Back in the car, numbed hands went about unscrewing the top of her flask of coffee. The cold hurt, the hot coffee hurt. She looked over at the clinic. What I really need is a shrink, she thought. I have to be crazy. How could I let Tommy Hung talk me into being a detective?

Another ten minutes went by, the first half accounting for an aeon, and then she amused herself by deciding which man, in the whole of the United Kingdom, she'd have to keep her warm. Naturally, she needed to see them undressed. Her circulation picked up and then went a lot faster. Soon it was going hell for leather. She forgot time.

When the oak doors opened again she was so startled her foot jerked against the accelerator. A tall bearded man came out. He wore a red woolly hat and a yellow waterproof over his anorak. He strode off up the drive, knees riding high, almost as if he were walking with a pair of swimmer's fins on.

By the time Mitch had caught up with him in her car he was almost abreast of the gates. As he moved to the side she wound her window down. 'Hello there. Are you one of Dr Gatting's group?'

He said nothing. But he did peer down towards the window to look at her.

'I'm supposed to meet George Reeves.'

'Not there.'

'He didn't turn up?'

'That's what I said.'

'But he was at the clinic last week?'

'What's it to you?'

'Hop in and I'll tell you.'

'You a prossie or something?'

'No.'

'You'll get yourself raped. Asking strange men to get into a car with you.'

'Are you going to rape me?'

'No.'

'Well then.'

'Better than walking I suppose.' He walked round the car and got in beside her.

'My name's Mitch Mitchell.'

'Colin Bell.'

'Listen, Colin, can I take you for a drink? I want to talk to you about George. Something's up. I'll drop you off home later.'

'We don't talk to people about what goes on in the group. That's one of our rules.'

'I'm sure there are very good reasons for that. Just listen to what I have to say and then make up your mind. That's all I ask. OK? You get a free drink. OK? You'll not get a better offer this week.'

'You're selling something.'

'No. I'm not. George has disappeared. I thought it just possible he might turn up here tonight. But obviously he didn't.'

'Are you telling me he's left that shitbag of a wife?'

'It could be more serious than that.'

'I drink whiskies,' he said. 'Doubles when I'm not paying.'

Mitch was now approaching the Queen Elizabeth Hospital. She could see the roofs of the complex below her, a spread of angel's wings in the blackness of the night. She remembered being alone in the small waiting-room, hardly bigger than a cubicle. There was a two-bar electric fire from which the plug had been removed. A threadbare track had been worn through the centre of the carpet by countless pacing feet. Her husband Max had not been wheeled back along the dimmed corridor which lay beyond the door.

It had been a very young Indian in a turban who had told her; too young to raise his eyes and meet hers. 'We did all we could, Mrs . . .' but he couldn't remember the patient's name, her name, and the embarrassment made him begin to sweat.

'Someone has stolen the plug off the fire,' she'd told him.

'Actually, I think it has been cut off. I mean, you know . . . People would keep putting on both bars. He didn't – well, there was no suffering. I can assure you of that, Mrs . . .'

In looking away from the severed cable his glance met hers and she caught him out in his lie.

'You're afraid. I mean, for George.'

'Why do you say that?'

'Oh, I don't know. Just now . . . you looked . . . I suppose you didn't go to Dr Gatting because you knew he wouldn't tell you a thing. Patient confidentiality and all that.'

'Here we are. The Friend to All. It's a bit grotty but it's the nearest.'

'My God. You're his wife. You're Muriel. You're not a bit like he described you.'

'Of course I'm not. I told you. My name's Mitch Mitchell. I've been employed by the family. They went to the police but as far as the coppers are concerned no crime has been committed so they aren't interested.'

'Why do you think it could be serious?'

'I can't find a trace of the other woman. I've talked to the people where he worked, his best friend . . . I'm afraid you're something of a last hope.' She stopped the car.

'His family think he's committed suicide? Is that it? George's not talked about that for a long time.'

'Would he have mentioned another woman? If he had one?'

'Most people talk about everything. After a while.'

'Including George.'

'He certainly talked about Muriel. But half the time I've no idea what he said. I mean, it was so boring. It is so boring. You drift off. Psychotherapy is about as lively as being stranded on platform two at Crewe. Sure, there might have been derailments and crashes and God knows what down the lines. All that's done is make your connection late and meanwhile you sit and yawn and twiddle your thumbs. Christ, it was a real no-no tonight. You're the only interesting thing that's happened. Picking me up. Just like that. You don't know me. Anything could happen.'

'It's not going to. Believe me. Hop out.' Even though it had been a short drive her feet, fanned by warm air from the car's heater, had thawed to rivet her to squealing nerve ends. 'Je-*sus*,' she wailed. 'Don't I need a drink. And don't look at me like that. My liver's as good as the next person's. Almost.'

The Friend to All had the elongated mean look of a Victorian lodging house. It stood on a street corner, the door set into the right angle of front and side walls. Part of the brickwork, perhaps used to house a billboard at one time, was painted black. Sore patches of new bricks surrounded smaller replacement windows on the first and second floors.

Inside the pub there was fluorescent strip lighting and some of the walls were panelled, sixties-style, in planks of pine. He settled himself down on a vinyl banquette before a formica-topped table, the yellow bleached away to white in places. She bought him a double whisky and herself a gin.

He carried on studying her as she put the drinks down. 'I'm only thirty-two.'

'Bully for you.'

'I wear a beard because I've got a double chin. Rather odd in a chap who is as thin as a rake. Don't you think?'

Mitch saw herself being hustled into an intellectual version of a game of Strip Jack Naked and said: 'I don't admit to any faults. At least, not to strangers.'

He smiled and it was undeniably a sweet smile, a rare smile, the sort that makes flesh good. But while he was smiling she was also aware of his unusually large canine teeth. 'I expect it is very slow of me. But I've only just worked it out. You're a private detective, aren't you? What a cheat!'

'Cheat?'

'Where's the trilby pushed to the back of your head? The cigarette? Where's Sunset Boulevard? Trust Muriel. Is she paying you a lot?'

'The normal rate.'

61

'Is she really a Gorgon?'

'Is that George's version?'

'He turned one of the women in the group into his Muriel until she got wise to his tricks. She said she kept trying to see this ogre in the seat next to her but as it was only poor old Pete she realised this ogre George saw was her! Sometimes she said she found herself becoming George's ogre, just to please him, just to have a bit of fun. It was like seeing double, she said. There was her own view of herself. And then there was George's view of her which made her feel quite frightened at times. Of herself, of her awful powers. It's all very strange.'

'Why?'

'Well, George came into the group in the first place because, though there was nothing wrong with his eyes, he was having the most awful trouble with his vision. Double vision. Blurred vision. He also kept seeing the end of his nose when he looked at things. Try it. It's very hard to do. Go on. Try and see that wrought-iron mirror on the wall and your nose as well.'

Mitch tried it. 'Almost impossible.'

'But not quite. George was doing it all the time!'

'What did everyone make of that?'

'Anxiety state. That's what Gavin Gatting made of it. Our shrink likes a nice bizarre anxiety state. I suppose it makes a change from depressives. Too many of them would give anyone the willies. You can't be out in the rain too long.'

'Did George go to the group meeting last week?'

'Not last week. The last time was the week before that.' He was thinking about it. 'And before you ask, there was something a bit different about him. I remember him making me feel quite anxious.'

'What do you mean? How was he different?'

'Hyper. Wired.'

'What did he talk about?'

'That week we were focusing on someone else. Chap who slept in the same bed as his mother and aunt when he was a boy. Interesting for once. I wonder if that's why Gavin Gatting

62

plays the tedious old sod so well? Makes people feel obliged to liven things up by dishing their dirt. Just to relieve the bloody boredom.'

'George gave no indication that he was planning to do a bunk?'

'Could hardly keep still in his chair at times,' Colin Bell remembered. 'Ants in his pants. For the last month or two he'd been on the offensive on the group. Quite aggressive at times. He'd also declared war on Muriel. So he said.'

'How did he do that?'

'Kept stuffing himself with junk food. She's a master cook. According to him. A female Escoffier.'

Mitch found herself shaking her head.

'It's absolutely true.'

'I'm not doubting you . . . the games people play . . .'

'You've got to look at it right, babs. Hell isn't other people like that stupid French prick said.' He tapped his heart. *'Moi.'*

'Muriel did know he was a member of your group?'

He looked startled. 'Well, I suppose so. I mean, it's usual. Often it's our nearest and dearest who frogmarch us through the clinic's doorway.' There was undeniable relish in his voice when he added: 'An action they often live to regret.'

'She never mentioned it to me. I found out in a roundabout way from someone else.'

'Perhaps she felt ashamed for him. Some people are ashamed. They think it's more respectable to be treated for VD.'

'Isn't the Glick Hope very expensive? How do you all drum up the loot?'

'Some patients are even paid for by the NHS. The Glick Hope is a charity, too. Lots of people are paid for out of the Foundation's trust fund. In fact, I don't pay for my treatment. I gave up my job a year ago. No excuse now.'

'No excuse for what?'

'Not writing my book.'

'Ah. I see.'

'It's not easy, you know.'

'I'm sure it isn't.'

'For instance, the word "thus" keeps rearing its frightfully

63

pretentious little bonce. No one ever says it, do they? Unless they are reading from the Bible.'

'No.'

'I keep writing it. Thus, thus and bloody thus.'

'George must have mentioned women other than his wife?'

'Well, there's mummy. We all have one of those.'

'No lady who perhaps caught his eye?'

Did he hesitate for a moment before he shook his head? Mitch couldn't be sure.

'Why do you think he's disappeared?'

'Anyone would take a powder if they were married to a Muriel. The wonder is he stuck with the bitch so long.'

'But he gave no hint in the group that that was what he was going to do?'

'None.'

'Isn't that strange? I mean, if you talk about everything?'

'Maybe it was a sudden decision. Maybe something cropped up.'

'Well, I suppose we'd better be off. Where do you live?'

'Moseley.'

'What are you writing?'

'A classic.'

'Humph,' she said.

'He could have killed himself.'

'Why do you say that?'

'He didn't like himself much. He thought he was pretty rotten.'

'You said he hadn't mentioned suicide for a long time.'

'He hadn't. But he was very fidgety the last time I saw him. As if he wished to be gone. It's always a possibility, you know. With a man like George.' His high-riding knees tangled with a table leg as he got up. 'You don't fancy me, do you?'

'No.'

'I quite took to the idea of being in bed with mummy and auntie. It certainly made an impression on the man in the group who told us about it. I've never been out with an older woman. What do you think?'

'Call on Muriel.' It was out before she could stop it. Alarmed, she looked up at him.

He was laughing. 'I suppose I asked for that.' He opened the door for her.

'You don't happen to have heard of a chap called Arno Czinner?'

'George's boss?'

'What did George say about him?'

'Not much at all. Mentioned him in passing.'

'Czinner was at the clinic tonight. Talking to a tall woman with a frizz of grey hair.'

'That would be Dr Lester. Our Ann. She's the director of the clinic. She's mainly to do with admin but she has a few patients. Everyone has to do their bit. Get their hands dirty.'

Picking her way over the icy pavement, perhaps worrying that she might, like George, have difficulty seeing beyond her nose, she carefully looked at her vaporising breath. She had an unobstructed view of it.

'And I thought this case was going to be so easy.'

'Nothing about George is easy. He's a very complicated fellow.'

7

'I wonder where she went last night. I called twice,' said Tommy Hung. He was watching Mitch, who, inspired by the jungle of fronds in front of the receptionist's desk at the Glick Hope, was feeding her office palm with liquid fertiliser. 'It was almost ten o'clock the second time. One can't call on a lady later than that, can one?'

'Muriel wasn't at home this morning, either. I wonder what she's up to? Of course, she could be staying with relatives. But why hasn't she rung to let us know?'

'If you give that plant any more food it'll explode.'

'Grow, grow, grow . . .' Mitch softly urged it, tickling the

65

underside of a paper leaf frond. 'And why wasn't she a soggy mess of tears when she told me her husband had disappeared? I can't help feeling there's something seriously adrift somewhere.'

'Do you really believe she didn't know George was going to that psychiatric clinic?'

'Who can say? It seems incredible that she didn't. But the incredible isn't the same as the impossible.'

'Perhaps he felt she wouldn't understand.'

'None of this seems to be stacking up right. We haven't come across a sniff of another woman.'

'That reminds me. I went to the Spread Eagle.'

'George's watering hole?'

'When he dropped in he was invariably alone but apparently he'd been there twice recently with another woman.'

'Really? We're absolutely sure of this?'

'The landlady was because on each occasion the woman wore sun-glasses. As she said, not many people in England use those in the depths of winter.'

'What does she look like?'

'Slim, couldn't say what colour of hair. Always wore a scarf over it. In her thirties and the landlady reckons well off.'

'Designer clothes?'

'I don't think a mauve anorak would fall into that category, would it?'

'Mauve, did you say? That woman who was coming through the gate of Harry Vine's cottage had a mauve anorak on. That clinches it. I'm going to have to drive out and have another word with Mr Vine. I've . . .' and she tried to analyse the feeling, 'I sort of, you know . . . feel uneasy . . . What am I missing?'

'I've got a Mr Shapiro to see. If we agree terms he'll be our second case.'

'Tommy! You've been holding out on me!'

'He's got a saddlery business in Walsall. He finds he's been despatching goods to a fictitious company. There were two small orders which were paid for promptly and one large order which wasn't paid for at all. It seems the villains scarpered with over twenty-five thousand pounds' worth of goods.'

'We're on our way. Don't you feel the breeze beginning

to billow in our sails? The Mitchell and Orient Bureau is moving!'

'We're certainly going to need that secretary. I've made a short-list of a short-list and got down to six names. We have to have someone absolutely top drawer. Classy.'

'If you think a Fenella is going to cross this threshold you're mistaken.'

'A girl with the right connections would be very, very good for us.'

'You're not serious.'

'Setting up an enterprise is rather like planning a military campaign. It's a question of a good overall plan. Vision. And then getting the detail absolutely right. Private investigating has a very sleazy reputation. I'm going for a classy upmarket image. That way when we're really steaming we can up the fees. Charge the earth. Class is an expensive commodity. You have to pay through the nose for sterling worth. We need a gel. Not a girl.'

'Jesus Christ.'

'Look here. If we're going to make a success of this you're going to have to overcome some of your prejudices.'

'Gels terrify me,' Mitch confessed. 'I'm always checking my knickers aren't slipping and suddenly all my northern vowels reappear and then the rot really sets in. I say advert-*ise*-ment instead of advertisement and – God please forgive me – sorp.'

'What's that, for heaven's sake?'

'It's how we say soap in Lancashire. That's where I was born.'

'You were a broadcaster, for heaven's sake! One doesn't wish to be ungallant, but shouldn't a lady of your age and experience have conquered her social inadequacies? I'm told my accent is quite as good as the Duke of Edinburgh's. And it only took me a year, my dear.'

'You only managed it because you didn't know it was impossible.'

'I managed it not only because I'd got two years' wages riding on it but so had a lot of other people. I didn't want to land up in some port with my throat slit. Another Chink carcass for the local meat wagon. The need to survive marvellously focuses the brain.'

'My God, you never told me that. That your shipmates would have killed you!'

'Bets aren't games. They're money.'

'Your friends would have slit your throat if you had lost them their money?'

'We're straying from the point. One mustn't see one's minor faults as endearing foibles. In other words, one will know one's knickers are as sound as one's advertisements.' He then waved a carrot in front of her indignant nose. 'By the by, I've been looking into this car phone thing. One can't really approve, of course—'

'You approve of computers!'

'But one can see situations where they might prove their worth.'

'You'll see. Our Brummie clients will love them. They're like me, honeypot. They love a bit of flash. Adds bite to life. Well, I must be off. By the way, did I tell you? I've been invited to a thrash at Arno Czinner's tonight.'

'That's fortuitous.'

'Fortuitous nothing,' said Mitch. 'I already have all the right connections. I don't need a Fenella Trumpington Hyphen Smythe in my life. I can come up with the goods. Any time.'

Tommy diplomatically retreated to the window. 'The sleet seems to be turning to rain. It's thawing.'

'That's snow.'

'The BBC man said rain.'

'God mustn't have caught the bulletin.' Mitch joined him and looked over the canal basin. 'Snow.'

Her telephone began to ring.

'We need a secretary to field the calls.' He was already on his way out of her office. 'An A1 priority.' The door closed with a sharp click. As she picked up the receiver she could hear him whistling as he walked downstairs. An old-fashioned British military air.

68

'The number works. So you really do have an office in the Gas Street Basin.'

'Oh ye of little faith.'

'Well, you must admit that, as hare-brained schemes go, yours takes the cake.'

'Listen Digger Rooney, this show is really working. We're going to hit the ratings in a big way. I've got a producer in a million.'

'You mean the scrumptious Tommy Tong?'

'Hung.'

'He's a darling but can you trust the yellow bastard?'

'I don't know.'

'I believe they don't just eat snakes. They eat doggies, too. I worry for you.'

'So do I. But as far as I know they don't eat ex-broadcasters.'

'I'm checking in about tonight. I'll call around seven and we'll use my car. One is always conscious in that TVR of yours that one's bottom – and therefore one's most precious parts – are only six inches off the tarmac . . .'

'That's an absolute lie!'

'. . . and the hole in the floor is getting larger. One day, sweetie, all your heavenly bits are going to be run over by your rear wheels.'

'Really, you do exaggerate. What shall I wear?'

'None of that tacky jewellery you're so fond of. There will be real diamonds there tonight. A froth of titles, so I hear. A bit of the other, too, in the form of an ex-boyfriend of yours.'

'I can't remember when I last had one.'

'Don't bleat.'

'Why not? You do.'

'Josh Hadley. Wasn't there marriage talk about you and him?'

'That was before he lit out with Miss Rocket Launcher. I wonder what he's done to get himself invited? He's hardly big on the social scene. I suppose there could be some connection through weaponry.'

'How's that?'

'Arno seems big on antique armour. Josh used to deal in that exclusively in his early days but now he runs a general antique business.' Mitch sighed.

'Is that a catch in your throat I hear?'

'I fancied him rotten at one time,' Mitch admitted. 'And to think. All that's left is the useless things I know about chainmail and halberds.'

'My dear. One's been there. The exotic things I now know about high finance . . .'

'Which *amour* was that?'

'Worked at the *Birmingham Sentinel*. Financial pages. Now he's a name on a national. All my chums are overtaking me. Isn't it frightful? And I'm still marooned in Toytown radio.'

'There's no justice in this life.'

'True.'

'I even remember a time when most people had morals and principles. It's a fuck-you-for-all-you've-got world now, Digger.'

'Are you on the menopause?' he asked suspiciously.

'No. I'm not as it happens. What made you think that?'

'I'm told it makes women take a dim view of the world. It certainly turned my mother into an old bat.'

'Thanks for that little vote of confidence. By the way, what is this thrash in aid of?'

'It's Daisy Sharpe's birthday. She says she's thirty-one.'

'What do you say?'

'One wouldn't, blossom. Not for the world. Too unkind,' and he put the phone down.

Mitch looked out of her window again. That's certainly snow, she decided and wrapped up accordingly before she left the office.

All the lights were on in the city, sullen on wet and slushy daylight pavements. She picked up her TVR, found she needed to switch from side to headlights, and turn the wipers up to fast to deal with the spray kicking up from wheels. She took the A38 at the Minworth Roundabout.

Tooling along, warm because the heater had plenty to work on now, she began to wonder about Tommy. She'd thought of him many times before in the last few months and had still

70

not reached any conclusions. He'd started out in a shack in Hong Kong and worked for the Royal Navy for many years as a Chinese laundry boy.

What she didn't know was how he'd made enough money to set himself up in a nice little flat off Sir Harry's Road in Edgbaston with a lounge like a reading-room in a gentlemen's club and enough left over to fund the Mitchell and Orient Bureau.

What she didn't know was what made him tick. Any more than she would know what made a little green man from Mars tick.

She'd tried to come up with one or two theories.

But who has any experience of a Tommy Hung?

As she was finding out, the unique has no track record. No point of reference. None of the building blocks theories need to get them up off the ground.

For a start, weren't Chinese men brought up to regard women as inferior beings? Weren't women supposed to work in the fields besides providing a Jeeves-style valet service for their masters? And yet here she was, his equal partner in the firm he'd founded.

Once or twice she'd wondered if Tommy had fallen for her. But there was no sign of it. He toted an array of other women along to the CBSO concerts he was so fond of. They were though, as far as Mitch knew, all Englishwomen. Perhaps he didn't go for the more demure home-grown types? As far as she knew, he'd never been married.

Of course, he could be a quasi-homosexual and fancied Anglo-Saxon women because their aggression turned him on.

She found herself laughing silently. But that was the thing about Tommy. Nothing you could think up was as bizarre as the man himself. And that did make for a slipperiness at the centre of their relationship, an ill-defined queasiness, certainly on her part. Thank God she'd bought that palm tree. What a nice simple relationship that was going to be. She watered it and ordered it to grow and it did as it was told.

Five miles before Burton-on-Trent she took the Barton-under-Needwood turn-off. She switched to sidelights and, just before reaching the cottage, cut her lights. The sun was coming out. And it was getting warmer. A glaze was forming on the snow; spirals of refracting light formed then disappeared in the unsteady sunlight.

Locking the car, hoisting her shoulder bag over her navy duffle coat, she stopped mid-turn. There were three sharp cracks. Shotgun fire. Echoing in the valley below the cottage. And, a long way off, church bells began to peal.

She opened the gate and made her way down the twisty snow-covered steps. She was about to toll the ship's bell in the porch when she saw the note tacked to the door.

No milk until further notice. Called away.

The note couldn't be seen until you were in the porch itself. Still. A good note for a burglar, and as she tut-tutted she wondered how she might steal into the cottage.

She backed out of the porch and made her way round to the lounge window, almost up to her knees in a drift of snow. She peered in. The fire hadn't been lit last night. She could still see a debris of burnt paper towards the back of the grate.

Heaving herself up on a small retaining wall, clear of the drift of snow, arms out, she bi-planed round to the gable end of the cottage and scrambled through the snow banked between the wall and a Calor gas storage tank.

Gasping, digging snow out of the top of her boots, she straightened. She realised now that the cottage was built into the neck of a spoon of land towards the top of a steeply descending hillside. The pond the cottage was named after was in the base of the spoon and from there the land rose to a rim before falling away again. Looking over the crusty top of a hawthorn hedge, she could see the bottom of the valley. She found herself confronted by the marbled stare of an iced river. On the far side of the water, a wide strand of snowy meadowland rose to plait itself into the surrounding hilltops.

By the time she'd worked her way round to the kitchen door most of the view had been blocked out by hedges and rising land. Here much of the snow had been roughly shovelled away and piled on the bank of the pond. Some had fallen in and broken ice which floated in large pieces in water warmed by the sun to shades of blackberry.

Called away. The cleared area seemed to confirm what the words suggested. The summons was unexpected. Or why bother shovelling snow?

She turned to peer through the french windows into the kitchen. She looked at the dresser, at two cakes left on a plate on the table, at the scatter of unwashed crockery. A hurried departure? Could that also explain why the bottle of pills and the repeat prescription had been left near the draining board? Amiodarone, she remembered.

Amiodarone. That distant ring of a bell again. Where had she come across it before? A story she'd done in the past? Had Harry Vine got some socially undesirable disease; the kind journalists did pieces about?

She shook her head. She'd done thousands of stories when she'd worked in the media and was left with a litter of useless detail, from the 2,000 toilets and 30,000 toilet rolls provided for Pope John Paul's visit to the Midlands in 1981 to the fact that the average height of the British had increased by four inches in two generations.

Looking at the bottle again, she made a mental note to check out the drug. She thought of the paper which had been burnt in the grate. She wondered about the woman in the mauve anorak. Harry Vine's mistress? George's? Just a friend?

Now don't go into a blue funk, she told herself. You're going to break into that cottage and take a look round.

Mitch was a lot more timid than she liked to think she was. The decision was making her knees tremble. Stamping her feet briskly, shaking her nerves back into line, she opened her handbag and took out a meat skewer. She'd used this once before to successfully break into a place and after that she'd overcome self-consciousness to practise from time to time. In this case she thought the stable-style kitchen door would be more vulnerable than the french windows.

As she probed through the bottom of the upper section of the door a lump of snow fell off the lintel on to her upper lip. She sucked it inwards and then drew her lip between her teeth as she

73

concentrated. The skewer hit the metal bolt. She leaned inwards, increasing purchase as she moved the skewer sideways as far as it would go. She repeated the action, working slowly, patiently, feeling the bolt beginning to slide. Two minutes later she'd freed the door. Stepping out of the way as the upper section swung towards her, she bent to unlock the bottom half.

Sitting on the doormat she pulled off her boots, wiped her gloves a little drier on her duffle coat, and stepped in. She went into the lounge first, making straight for the grate. She opened her bag and sorted out an instrument, a folded British Telecom envelope, unpaid bill inside. She poked among the ashes. All she could clearly make out from a fragment of unburnt paper at the bottom of the pile was three letters, apparently the beginning of the name of something for the sequence started with a capital G. Gan . . . She dropped the scrap into the envelope and then pushed the burnt paper back into its heap with a poker. Feeling pleased with herself, she rocked back on her heels.

'Gan . . .' she said aloud. 'A place-name? Christian name?'

Suddenly she heard a sound. Gerr-bub-bub . . . Skin cringed over vertebrae.

The refrigerator, she realised, switching itself back on.

She rose, aware of anxious itching in her feet, the need to be gone. You're too old to get caught breaking and entering, she told herself. Christ. The last thing you need at your age is being remanded for social reports.

But though her feet were urging her towards the back door, her mind marshalled quaking flesh and drove it up the open-tread stairway.

There were two bedrooms and a bathroom. In the main bedroom she found the duvet half off the bed. Folded on the chair next to it was a navy blue and orange herringbone-patterned jersey dress with a pair of knickers and a very large bra folded on top. A necklace of white plastic beads nestled between giant sized cups. Tights were hanging over the back of the chair.

'I've simply got it wrong.' Speaking aloud, astonished, shaking herself, as if that would make the pieces fall into a more believable whole.

74

'I wonder where she went last night. I called twice,' Tommy Hung had told her.

Oh no, she thought.

How can I believe it?

If she brought a change of clothes surely she must have intended staying the night?

Still shaking her head, she went back down into the kitchen to check the spelling of the drug. It was after she'd written it down that she noticed again the cakes left on the table. They sat in an oaty crumble of grains.

Tempted beyond her powers to resist by one of Muriel Reeves' Stanhope Firelighters, she picked up a cake. Her mind reeled as she ate the evidence – of what? Adultery between Muriel and Harry Vine? Was she really the *femme fatale* at the centre of this case and not some elusive Mercedes-driving lady in mauve?

If only, she thought, people would do what's expected of them. Stick to the rules. Play the game as it's supposed to be played.

And why would she leave a dress here, her dirty knickers, for God's sake?

Because she expects to be back to collect them after a couple of away-from-it-all nights with her joy boy?

Why did she employ me to find George if she and another bloke are having it away?

Mitch felt a headache coming on.

8

Mitch chose to believe that, though Tommy Hung played games with himself in all the rooms he lived in, it was here, in his kitchen, that a little of his soul was exposed. The 1970s flat-roofed block of apartments he lived in, off Sir Harry's Road, Edgbaston, was set in lawns seeded by floodlights. The perimeter was defined by great beech and chestnut trees which lost their summer voices with their leaves in the autumn; now they sighed or sometimes roared out in their frozen shrouds.

There was snow in Tommy's kitchen, too: a snow-white tiled floor and walls, and white units surrounding the stainless steel sink and fitments. Here all Tommy's meticulousness was revealed in absences. There was no friendly clutter of objects. A place for everything and everything in its place; a small, galley-shaped operating theatre. Tommy's kitchen made her worry. There was, she thought, fanaticism behind this extreme orderliness. Cooking was not an abstract occupation. It cost animals their lives.

But why did it seem more natural to encounter untidiness in the lair of a flesh-eater? Why jib at all this whitened order? Wasn't this just a quirk of her occidental mind? Wasn't white the colour of sacrifice in the East?

And yet she couldn't help worrying that she was heading for trouble if she really let herself trust a man who maintained such a kitchen. Mitch had been betrayed more than once and now picked her way through life with extreme caution. The truth is, she thought, I'm no nearer to deciding what I really feel about Tommy Hung than when I first met him during the Jon Stanton investigation.

The plain white blind was drawn half-way down the kitchen window. As she waited for the kettle to boil, she raised it a little and peered out. Though it was not long after four in the afternoon, the floodlights had been switched on, bathing the car-park and grounds in depthless light. The snow, which seemed so rigidly to cover the scene, was nevertheless on the move. A large chunk suddenly descended past the window, pounding the path outside, sending up a mushy splatter, some hosing the window. The thaw is really beginning, she thought, as she turned back to the white porcelain on the black tray.

Tommy was in the bedroom packing.

She carried the tray into the lounge. In here Tommy was playing the patrician English gentleman. With tongue in cheek? She couldn't be sure, but probably not. Though none of the 1970s architecture had been altered, Tommy had contrived a room in an exclusive male London club. White's? Boodle's? Too dignified for the Drones. It was not likely he'd ever entered such doors; he'd probably based his notions on spy films. And yet he

76

had so spookily caught the essence of such a place that Mitch sometimes found herself listening for the arthritic click in the knees of a manservant moving at snail's pace or the bubbling snore of a snoozing member.

The book shelves told other tales. They were packed with detective stories. Here was a trove of barely remembered names like Ethel Lina White and A E W Mason rubbing covers with Agatha Christie and Dorothy L Sayers. Recently there had been additions to the American section. A new author, the only one extant, sat next to Chandler. An alligator on the cover introduced Elmore Leonard's *Maximum Bob*.

Tommy had once told her that he'd first had a burning desire to learn English because another of the laundry boys on ship had retold such stories for free drinks and packets of cigarettes. 'But his stock ran out, my dear. Can you imagine?'

Mitch had found she couldn't. The whole thing seemed incredible to her. It wasn't that she disbelieved Tommy. It was more that, viewed from – as she now saw it – the narrowness of her own life, a life like Tommy's really was beyond belief.

As she prowled round the room now she thought that if she were ever to get to grips with her new partner she was somehow going to have to grow through that narrowness. Expand her horizons.

'I'll take my wool-lined mac. Rain is forecast for tomorrow but I've no doubt it'll remain chilly. Especially on the east coast, my dear. It's most dreadfully bracing at the best of times.' Tommy put a small canvas suitcase by the lounge door. 'I've only been to Great Yarmouth once. To be frank, I never intended to repeat the experience.'

'You're sure Mr Shapiro is on the right track? That the gang who swindled him out of the goods operate from down there?'

'I couldn't fault the chap's logic. He's a very sharp man. Luckily for us, he's also a very angry man. I've already banked his cheque for our initial two days' work. He also gave me an advance on expenses. We seem to hit it off quite splendidly.' He sounded surprised.

'I should think the goods will have been passed on by now.'

'In that case he wants his pound of flesh.'

She gave him a cup of tea. 'I've every faith in you, Tommy.'

'Have you?'

She laughed. 'A man who can learn to speak English like the Duke of Edinburgh in a year!'

'The difficulties involved are very different. It is wise not to be too optimistic. You seem to have a natural flair for the work.'

'I wish that were true–' and she was about to discuss the latest developments in the case when he put his hand up.

'First I must give you some messages. I don't want to forget. There was a call from the stockbroker Willie French. The upshot is I've arranged for him to take you to lunch at Mr Bunter's tomorrow. If it's not convenient you're to ring up his secretary in the morning.'

'What's that all about, do you think?'

'Oh, Czinner Enterprises. He's after information but he could be very useful to you.'

'But how can I be of use to him? I don't know anything which could possibly interest a stockbroker.'

'Don't you? You'll only find that out when Willie French has eaten his way through to his dessert. In a market where millions of pounds change hands on rumour, hard information is at a premium.'

'Millions bet against rumours? You're kidding.'

'You've a lot to learn about the stock market, my dear. They get up to all sorts of shenanigans if they see the colour of money at the end of the trail.'

'Such as?'

'Well. Take the structure of the market itself. Speculators can manipulate that to their own advantage. England has a two-week account system. Any deals struck are only settled after that span. So you can sell shares you don't own on the first day of the account and buy those shares so you can deliver them on the last day of the account.'

'How can you make money doing that?'

'You sell the shares you don't yet own at a high price. Then you and your fellow bear raiders get rumour-mongering. The share price drops. You then buy the shares you need to close out the deal at this lower price. You can make a killing even though you've never put up a penny of your own money.'

'What if it comes unstuck? Say the price doesn't go down? Perhaps the firm concerned lands a huge order in America or suddenly announces a windfall? What if the shares actually go up?'

Tommy shrugged. 'If you're a gambler you expect to drop a packet now and then.'

'Is there evidence that someone has been trying to manipulate the Czinner share price?'

'Not that I know of. But it could be that Willie French senses a whiff of something in the breeze. These chaps are hunters, my dear. They simply smell money instead of meat.'

'And you can make a killing out of a falling share price as well as a rising one,' Mitch said thoughtfully. 'I shall certainly keep my date with Mr French. Even if it comes to nothing Mr Bunter's puts on a very good meal. The other message?'

'Ah. You have a summons. Mr Czinner's secretary rang. Mr Czinner wants to see you at Aston Clinton. I said you'd ring. I also mentioned in passing that you were going to this party of his as a guest of Daisy Sharpe. I think this is shaping up to be an altogether bigger affair than an errant husband. Don't you?'

'To be honest, the more I look into the matter the more baffled I get.' And she told him what she'd discovered at Harry Vine's cottage.

'You broke in?'

She nodded.

He thought the matter over. 'I don't feel I can reproach you for your methods. They yielded such new – not to say unexpected – information. I only ask you to remember that should you be forced to appear in court you place the Mitchell and Orient Bureau in the dock with you.'

'I know, Tommy. I gambled and this time it paid off. I still find it hard to believe. I was under the distinct impression that Harry Vine didn't like Muriel.'

'He either deliberately misled you or your dislike for Muriel coloured your impressions of what he said.'

'Do I really believe a man like Harry – an attractive man, worth

79

more than half an eye, I thought – is shacked up with the likes of Muriel Reeves?' She was asking herself more than Tommy.

'Well, when you saw George Reeves' photo you thought him an attractive man. And there seems no denying he's been married to Muriel for twenty-odd years.'

'It's not all that rare to find Beauty and the Beast marriages, I suppose, though the role of Beast is usually a male one. And the chap compensates for it by having lots of cash. In George's case it looks like he has personality problems. But how did the woman entice a man like Harry Vine between her sheets? I mean, honeypot. Women like that go out with shopping trolleys.'

Tommy began to laugh. 'You're jealous!'

'Too right,' said Mitch. 'Here am I, permanently on a diet, slapping on a mud pack when I get half a chance, never, never buying Crimplene or nylon overalls and does a Harry Vine fall for me? Not on your life. And I'm not expected to give a toss? Not many.'

'You're a very attractive woman, Mitch.'

Mitch was brooding. 'Can one be attractive at fifty?'

'You can, my dear. You are.'

'Fifty is a terrible age. One is neither fish nor fowl. I keep thinking people are seeing the old boot I'm about to become.'

'You had a bad experience when you were investigating the death of young Stanton. That's what all this stems from. Not being fifty.'

'Perhaps you're right.' She sighed. 'But to get back to Muriel Reeves. All right. There is evidence. I saw it with my own eyes. That I find it incredibly hard to believe, I could put down to my prejudices. But if she's having it away with Harry Vine why is she paying me to find her husband? I had to stop thinking about it. It gave me a headache. I mean, it's seriously weird.'

'It might seem so. But there will be logic – at least of a kind – behind it.'

'A smokescreen? She's bumped off Georgie boy but to the outside world she's busily establishing how concerned she is that he's missing? How much she cares for hubby? Why, she even paid a private eye to find him?' Mitch considered it. 'Well, I suppose she's cocky enough. But it doesn't fit.'

'Why not?'

'Does it really seem likely? No. There's a lot more to this than a man and woman fouling it up. Don't you feel? Why, for a start, does Mr Midas himself want to see me? And don't tell me a man like that is just concerned for the deserted little wifey.'

'There is the woman in mauve. It's still possible that this is a more straightforward case than it appears, my dear. Never a good thing to look for complications. In my experience truth is simple.'

'Well. I'll bear that in mind.' Mitch began collecting their cups. 'I must be making tracks. I've a hair appointment in ten minutes. I've simply got to dragoon myself into some sort of shape for this bash at Czinner's. When I know I'm looking a mess I go all sort of gauche and timid. It's twice the effort to go out into the wicked world and perform. But with my hair half-way decent, a bit of eye-liner on and decent rags on my back – why, that's when the juices flow and the brain starts to motor.'

'One never realised eye-liner was an IQ raiser.' Tommy was looking at her with a child's wonder; he might have been seeing his first giraffe in a zoo.

'Most research is directed by the male of the species. They don't know the half . . .' Mitch grinned at him and fastened the toggle of her duffle coat. 'Ring me with your number when you find a hotel.'

'You did have another call, Mitch. Just before I left the office.'

She groaned. 'Don't tell me. Freya Adcock.'

'She's starting to sound a bit grim. If you don't ring back you're likely to find her camping out on your doorstep. You haven't been up to anything, have you?'

'What could I get up to? She was my boss and she fired me. Well. Didn't renew my contract. The effect is the same. Besides, all that's history now.' But Mitch found she felt distinctly uneasy. She suddenly realised that whatever Freya was after it wasn't the tape recorder that had accompanied her on her exit from Radio Brum. Freya would have got one of her hirelings to retrieve that. Oh my God, she thought. I'm not going to find myself featuring in some libel suit? Who did

81

I interview on my show during those last few days? What did I say?

Or is she setting me up to carry the can for something another broadcaster has done?

She shook herself as if trying to get Freya out of the creases in her clothing. All that was in the past. Gone. No plastic-bangled arm was going to rise up from that grave and grab her by the scruff of the neck.

'Got to be off, Tommy. Happy hunting. Make sure the bugs don't bite.'

'Watch out for Mr Czinner,' Tommy was shouting after her. 'A man who thinks he can walk on water is going to drown. When he does anyone too near will go down with him.'

Mitch turned to blow him a kiss as she went out of the door. She was still thinking of Freya. She determinedly steered her thoughts away from that Medusa-like figure and concerned herself with what she was going to wear that evening. In the end she decided on her black silk culottes with matching jacket embroidered on the back with rose and cream chrysanthemums. Under it she wore a cream silk blouse, but, heeding Digger Rooney, no jewellery.

How she'd loved to slap on the make-up when she'd been younger. Now she liked to believe she was a serious woman of the world. No more glitter on the eyelids, only a whisper of blusher on the cheeks. Oh, come on, she told herself. You've got to have a bit of fun. What about false eyelashes? They're not really unserious. Are they? And she delicately picked up an eyelash with a pair of tweezers.

Mitch would have liked to have been tall and slender and age in a dignified way – she felt she had the soul of a *grande dame*. Unfortunately, her genes had not provided her with the right equipment. She was short and bouncy with hair that tended to rise on end and wave about a lot, usually in the wrong direction. She also – and this is why she favoured pants for evening wear – had too much calf muscle. But as she was always telling herself, when it came to waists, God's truth, cross your heart and hope to die, she curved. Really curved.

So why the hell is a woman who has all the charm of a fully

82

loaded oil tanker getting her grappling hooks into all these men? she asked her mirror. What's Muriel Reeves' secret?

She looked into the mirror again and told her face that in ten years' time it would be sixty. Not good news, especially as she was as randy as she'd ever been. Perhaps if she dyed her hair grey her hormones would get the message?

When the door bell rang she was relieved. Contemplating her ageing body, she thought, was like feeding her ego rat poisoning.

But here was Digger saying all the right things. 'You're really socking it out tonight. You look great.'

'You look pretty nifty yourself. But where's the ear-ring?'

Digger lifted his chubby finger and rubbed his ear. She saw it was swollen. 'I'm allergic to gold.'

'No one is.'

'You can't believe how pissed off I am about it. One of my dreams has always been to have a Rolex watch with an absolutely amazingly vulgar gold strap. When my ship comes in. You know. One always hopes . . . And now I find I'm allergic to gold.'

'You could always wear the watch over a white glove. You could start a fashion.'

'Just wear one glove? Could they arrest you for it?' he asked as he ushered her out of the house and down the drive to his car, which was illegally parked on the pavement.

They were through the Queensway tunnel and riding towards Spaghetti Junction when Mitch asked him about Daisy Sharpe.

'Well, I expect I told you. When it comes to acting she's worse than me. But she's always had two great advantages. She knows exactly where she stands in the talent stakes so she's never been tempted to take on more than she could cope with. And – this is the real plus – she's a superb saleswoman. In this case, of course, the product is herself. But I heard a very strange thing a couple or more months ago which frankly I didn't believe. No way. But I heard it again just today. They say that Daisy told the men in suits she's not going to sign another contract.'

'She wants more money.'

'I heard she wants to check out of *Motel*. Period.' He shook his head. 'Doesn't sound like my Daisy. Anyway, you know that *Motel* has got this new producer chap? It seems he and Daisy get on like Fergie and the Windsors. They say she's about to be terminated before her contract runs out.' He shook his head again. 'What the hell does she think she's playing at?'

'Perhaps now she's got Mr Czinner's money to play with she wants to jack it all in? Perhaps all this is preliminary to marrying him.'

'I hear things about that. Like he's looking over the field again.'

'Really?'

'Forget the marriage-to-Daisy scenario. Every now and then he likes to rove and pick himself out another piece of young meat.'

'Don't they all. One does get a tad fed up with grinning and bearing it.'

Digger was shaking his head again. 'Daisy's going to have to look to her knitting. And sharpish. She loves money. She'll tell you herself that she finds it a real turn-on. A chap wearing a Porsche swells all her girlie bits. Where the hell is she going to find another billionaire? They're not exactly thick on the ground. Anyway, I think Daisy was dreaming if she ever thought this Czinner guy would marry her. She'd have certainly been a very different number from his first wife. She, apparently, was his business partner and the brain behind much of his early expansion.'

'What happened to her?'

'She went into academia when they split. Daisy's many things but no one could accuse her of being an intellectual. And you know what they say . . .'

'A man who has a second wife is still making his first mistake.'

'I've never heard it put quite like that. But it is surprising how many guys marry the same type of woman again and again.'

'Of course, one could change,' said Mitch, thinking of George Reeves. 'I mean, there's always psychotherapy.'

Digger looked at her in surprise. 'That's a bit drastic. Not to mention that in my experience when people change they do it for the worse. I don't think it's possible. To change for the better.'

'Why not?'

'Well, for a start people who change are pushed into it. They don't do it voluntarily. Usually something hideous happens. That's what precipitates it. They are completely pissed off and start trying to make other people's lives a misery too.'

'Whatever happened to suffering being good for the soul?'

'Pull the other one, sweetie. I'll tell you one thing. If the rumours about Arno and Daisy's affair are true I for one will steer clear. That little kitten has got tiger's claws.'

'I think, Digger, we're a bit at cross purposes here. I was talking about psychotherapy. Change. Not reaction to adverse circumstances.'

'Balls. What is all this, anyway? Why this sudden interest in shrinks? In Daisy? In Czinner? When are you going to tell me what this is all about?'

Mitch looked at Digger's cherubic face and then at his new butch hair-style; a sly choirboy beneath a head-banger's thatch. 'I wouldn't want to make your hair curl. It would spoil the whole effect.'

9

> There was a young lady of Riga,
> Who went for a ride on a tiger;
> They returned from that ride
> With the lady inside,
> And a smile on the face of the tiger.

The old rhyme drifted down to Mitch from her childhood, perhaps not just put in mind by the way Arno Czinner was contemplating the nubile creature he was talking to. Hadn't she first read it in a Victorian tome not unlike those that filled the shelves in the library where Daisy's guests were having drinks?

Three interconnecting rooms at Aston Clinton were being used for the birthday party, all of them off the broad corridor she'd walked down on her way to interview Tina Havelock. The library opened on to a long ornate drawing-room furnished in blue and apricot. Arno Czinner dominated this room from a painting hung in the central panel of a ceiling-high chimney-piece. The portrait was not large and at first glance seemed flat, almost two-dimensional; latent in the planes of paint was the glitter of gold. Latent too, around childlike lips, was Czinner's tigerish smile. A David Hockney? Mitch had wondered, but had not been close enough to decipher the painter's signature.

The double doors at the far end of this room led into a large dining-room where a buffet supper had been set. Here there were some touches of the deep blue used in the drawing-room, though the main theme was aquamarine and yellow ochre. The interior decorator – perhaps influenced by the painting in the drawing-room – had also introduced hints of gold.

The three reception rooms were glossily professional and, Mitch thought, glossily vulgar. Though she didn't mind a bit of tartiness, too much, far from being fun, made her cringe. She agreed with Digger who'd once said: 'Only a small amount of bad taste is correct.' But at the time she hadn't let him know that. She'd told him: 'You're not just a snob. You're an impossible snob.'

The suite of rooms lay on the opposite side of the house to the car-park and entrance. Great swags of damask curtaining were undrawn. Snowy statues and shrubs were revealed not only by oblongs of illumination cast by sets of french doors but by beams from artfully placed terrace lights.

Mitch, having filtered through the rooms and found her bearings, had returned to the bar in the library for another gin and tonic. Looking at Arno Czinner now she was sure he had deliberately decided to confound his more conservative business associates and upstage some of Daisy's theatre guests. Under his pin-stripe suit he wore a T-shirt and on his feet were a pair of soft red leather boots. He was shorter, by a good two inches, than the girl he was talking to, but, by taking up an inordinate amount of space, he appeared larger. Sweeping gestures sometimes exploded into staccato bursts; his whole body punched upwards. It reminded Mitch of the way some politicians rocked up to their toes to thump home a point in a key speech. Though he was not an attractive man, it was a measure of his dominance that you saw him first and not the girl, for she was beautiful. Her hair was shaved to above her ears, leaving a thick lick of blonde tied back in a pony tail. Remarkably large nipples budded from her tiny breasts, boldly displayed through the seventies crocheted tunic she'd obviously bought from some Oxfam outlet. She wore it with cream bell-bottomed pants.

'That kid looks familiar,' Mitch said to Digger who had found her side. 'The one with Arno.'

'She ought to. That's the girl Josh Hadley left you for.'

'So it is. I didn't recognise her with that Indian brave hair-do. And, of course, I've never seen her nipples before. Amanda – yes, Amanda something. What the hell does she see in Josh? He's even older than me.'

'I used to fall in love with daddies myself once,' said Digger. 'But one usually grows out of it. Daddies are always ordering one about. When I chucked my last one out he quite literally landed in – well, over, actually – the dustbin. Sadistic buggers, daddies, until you let them have it.'

'How's the job-hunting going?'

'Don't ask. But I've got to find something quickly. The station's budget has been cut again. More of us for the Old King Cole. And there's no doubt I'm on the next hit list. I can't open my mouth on air without that shit of a programme organiser's balling down my cans.'

'Cheer up, Digger. You haven't been given the boot yet. Anyway, getting fired isn't that bad.' A lie. Mitch had found the experience devastating. But she wasn't going to let Digger or anyone else know that. Show your wounds and some bastard was liable to rub salt in them.

Mitch began looking round for Josh Hadley but she couldn't spot him. She did see Daisy Sharpe in a chestnut silk corset which she was wearing over a matching skirt artfully shredded round the hem. Fingerless grey gloves, in knitted lurex, almost reached the top of her arms. They reminded Mitch of those worn by the rent collector who had called at her childhood home every Saturday morning. Daisy was apparently quite indifferent to the fact that her lover was paying court to another woman. She was hooked into a tall, muscular man with a fully shaven head; something of an intellectual Mitch supposed for, though his shirt was buttoned to the collar under his Italian suit, he wore no tie. 'There's Daisy's lover getting stuck into someone else and is she worried? Not on your life. She's grappling with Mr Baby Buddha! And where the hell is Josh?'

Digger laughed. 'What an old square you are. Some people like their love', he pronounced it 'lerv', 'to be complicated. They have to work bloody hard for their thrills. And don't look at me like that. It's not my scene. I'm straight down the line. A nice little number with a tight bum. Preferably one who can whip up a decent *halvas tis rinas . . .*' and he smacked his lips.

'I seem to have gone off love altogether.' Mitch sighed. 'The flesh is willing but the spirit is appalled.'

'That's because you've recently had bad experiences.'

'What with one thing and another I've been going through what the Chinese euphemistically call interesting times lately.'

Digger squeezed her arm. 'Excuse me. I've just seen Black Jesus. If I could manage to get those two guys on my show . . . after all, it was me who first played their demo disc . . .'

'They look unglued.'

'Oh no. They're very anti-drugs.' Like a tennis player loosening up before a serve, Digger wound his shoulders back, coughed, swung to his toes, and went off after his game.

Arno Czinner, Mitch's quarry, was still chatting up the fair Amanda. Not wishing to be tangled up with another party-goer if the opportunity arose to collar him, Mitch turned to the shelves behind her and pulled out a tome. It was a bound volume of the *Windsor Magazine* dated 1895.

She was about to dip into it when a voice behind her said: 'Long time no see . . .'

There was a scampering in her heart; a rat in the wainscoting.

'Josh! Digger told me you were on the birthday girl's guest list. I'd no idea you knew her. Or him.'

'Daisy's been a good client of mine for a while now. You're looking particularly eatable–'

'And I see you've still got your pony tail.' She looked over at Amanda, in thrall to Arno Czinner. 'A him and her act? Do you measure tails? Who has the biggest?'

'And claws as sharp as ever, I see,' smiling, shaking his head. When they'd been lovers the growing of his pony tail had been a source of friction. 'It makes you look like some grotesque old reprobate. It's out of character,' she'd protested. But it wasn't. Almost immediately afterwards he'd slipped out of her sheets and into Amanda's. The kid was the same age as Mitch's daughter. Looking at him now, though, she thought the pony tail rather suited him. Josh Hadley might confine his activities to land, but – in spite of his tortoiseshell glasses – he was as much the buccaneer as any lateen-sail-hoisting raider.

'I didn't quite like the way you were sizing up our Arno, Mitch. That man comes with a health warning.'

'That doesn't seem to be deterring your girlfriend.'

'That's been over for a while now. Didn't you know? When she heard Daisy had invited me she asked if she could tag along. She's opened an art gallery and wants to meet the right people. I told her Arno wasn't one of them.' He was looking round. 'Though, to be honest, one or two people here would be very good clients to have. She's selling what she calls good modern art.'

'What's that?'

'What the dealers decide is the in thing. Usually some young kid they think they can make a killing out of. The art market makes the antique business look as innocent as a kiddies' tea party.'

'Well. Amanda certainly hasn't taken your warning seriously.' Arno's hand was getting stuck into the girl's bottom. Her finger was moving down his lapel, and because she was taller than him her neckline spooned open as she stooped.

'She's made it very clear to me that she's a big girl now. Perhaps it's time she realised that this is a wicked world.'

'You're not indulging in a little ill-wishing are you?'

'You're right. One must guard against one's vindictiveness.'

'Was she worth it?'

'Oh yes.'

Mitch was aware of a pang, a stirring of old pain, old grief.

He said: 'I've heard you've opened a detective agency with that eccentric little Chink. I suppose you're here doing work for a client? Do be careful. The Arno Czinners of this world cause a hell of a sight more grief than the Jack-the-Rippers.'

'The woman who needs a word in her ear is your ex-girlfriend. Not me!'

'Amanda's a strong-minded young lady at that wonderful age when she knows more than God Almighty. But I'll try.'

'You shouldn't have let her talk you into bringing her.'

'How the hell did I know that Czinner would make a beeline for her? He's supposed to be shacked up with Daisy Sharpe. Do you want a refill?'

'I'll stick with this.'

'Well, I'm going to top up.' She watched him go, a tall, rangy man who didn't, she thought, age so much as weather.

'Was she worth it?' she'd asked him.

'Oh yes.' And the tone of his voice had told Mitch more than his words.

A sudden jolt of anger almost lifted her feet off the floor. And I was worth dumping for a little bitch who has only got an eye on the main chance! Hold steady there, she told herself. I mean, this kid Amanda does have a pair of suction pumps for tits.

And whoever said love was easy?

Unless you intend to curl up and die in a gin bottle you've got to hang on to your seat and play your hand, she told herself. She was always having to give herself these little lectures.

The trouble was her appetites had always exceeded the amount doled out on the plate set before her. Supply-side problems, she thought they called it in the business world.

Czinner certainly seemed to be well on the way to solving his. He was saying something and Miss Bitch's nipples – Amanda, remember? – were standing to shocked attention.

She replaced the bound volume of the *Windsor Magazines* and as she turned back she saw Toby Trubberman, curls of blond hair falling into arctic blue eyes, broad red braces over blue

90

and white pin-striped shirt, his sleeves rolled over elbows and forearms glistening with sweat. He was disturbing the air at the doorway. The Finance Director was making signals, none of which Czinner saw. Trubberman ploughed through the room.

Czinner, turning, also abruptly turned off the girl. When the pair of them left the room, Trubberman was three feet behind Czinner and falling back a little further. Surprisingly it was Daisy Sharpe who rescued the abandoned girl. With a swish of her artfully shredded hem, she scooped up Amanda and introduced her to the man with the shaven head. Daisy's hand then linked through the girl's, the hem, like a tail, swished again and she called: 'Food, my sweeties!'

'C-C-C-caviar, Daisy!' a voice shouted from the back of one of the groups.

'C-C-C-caviar!' A catch-phrase, their catch-phrase, Daisy's free hand rising to the ceiling, rallying her friends.

'C-C-C-caviar!' sang the chums as they all surged out of the library.

The exit of Arno Czinner seemed to have the same effect on Daisy's guests as the pulling of the first champagne cork.

'I say, Daisy, can we have bike races down the corridor?'

'I want hide and seekieweekums!'

'You mean you want to jump in Tessie's saddle!'

'School's out,' said Mitch to Digger as he came up behind her. 'Did you have any luck with Black Jesus?'

'No one was in . . . though, like man, I knocked on the door loud enough to wake the dead.'

'I told you they were zonked.'

'So you did, blossom. Are you and Josh Hadley going to be an item again?'

'All is not as it seems.'

'Come on. Let's get at the bubbly,' and Digger was moving ahead of her.

'Not caviar. Not for me,' said Mitch.

'A taste for the cultivated only. Ow. That hurt.'

'Be nice to me then.'

They had just filled their plates and were moving from the buffet table when Mitch turned to see Toby Trubberman, collar now open, tie loosened, steam through the door. He came alongside Daisy Sharpe's skin-headed companion and towed him briskly away.

'Something's up,' said Mitch.

'A deal's come to the boil? Doesn't it look sexy? All those hairy men dripping sweat and dominance?' Digger popped a stuffed olive in his mouth. 'I just love Mr Thunder Thighs.'

'The skin-head? Who is he? I marked him down as an intellectual.'

'With Daisy? Are you kidding?'

'Well, he has his shirt buttoned to the collar and no tie and the Italian suit. Isn't that the male way of saying my brains have got bigger balls than yours?'

'Adrian Cain's the Czinner gofer. The errand boy.'

'Really? I wish people wouldn't steal each other's uniforms. So confusing.'

'You don't have to tell me. Just the other day I saw a lad who wasn't a policeman wearing policeman's shoes. I made my play. Do you know, the bloody kid turned out to be straight? I almost got my head stoved in. It's a dangerous world when you can't rely on the evidence of your own eyes.'

'By the way, you haven't introduced me to Daisy yet. I've not thanked her for letting me come to her bash.'

'If Daisy wants an introduction she'll make herself known. At this performance you're strictly an extra. One of the crowd scene.'

'But surely one should observe the decencies? One can't drink the bubbly of a stranger. Not at twenty quid a bottle.' She took a sip from her glass. 'Forty? Even fifty?'

'Throwing money away on the likes of us shows the rest of the world you've got so much you won't miss it. Not the kind of statement ninety-nine point nine per cent of us can make. And when you think about it, Czinner gets what he pays for. Mega dick status.'

'Sometimes, Digger, I think you're even more cynical than me.'

'You just don't know much about money games.'

'Money and me don't do well together. It's a bit like my love affairs. The relationship is always going sour.'

'Czinner is some operator. They say he's a debt billionaire.'

'A what?'

'It's better than being a billionaire. It's so cheeky. It's being a billionaire with two fingers up. When you owe that much the banks daren't pull the rug out from under you. Think of the black holes it would throw up in their balance sheets.'

'You're making my head whirl. How do you know all this?'

'I told you. I was on terms of endearment with a financial journalist. Believe me, in that world pigs can fly and do every day of the week. Another glass of bubbly? Yes? It seems that Czinner's bankers can afford us.'

She and Digger had wandered into the blue and apricot drawing-room and when he'd gone to refill their glasses, Mitch found herself being haunted by Arno Czinner's two-dimensional smile. She moved closer to the portrait. I've eaten better meals than you, those lips seemed to tell her. Jesus. You should be proud I've elevated you to my table. Proud to have me feed on you.

The groups of people in the reception rooms were thinning out. In the corridor there were great shouts of laughter. The distant hammer of disco music, possibly from the basement, also drifted through the opened doors.

'Miss Mitchell, OK? Right?'

Mitch swung round to face Arno Czinner.

'I had my secretary ring your office this afternoon. Your associate told her you were coming to Daisy's little jolly. Surprised me. I didn't know she knew any private eyes.'

'A friend of a friend.'

'So Daisy tells me.'

He then stood before her, not saying anything, perfectly at ease. She resisted the need to break the silence, relieve her growing feeling of anxiety. She sank back on her heels; digging them in, she realised, surprised.

Eventually he said: 'I understand you're working for Muriel Reeves.'

She nodded.

93

'I got her on the blower and we had a little natter. The day before yesterday. Tough titties, eh? I don't see why she should bear the burden of your costs on top of everything else.'

'Are you warning me off, Mr Czinner?'

'No. No. Not at all. Not on your life. I want to pick up the tab. And she's very happy to have me do it. By the way, have you two been in touch with each other today?'

'No. I went round this morning but she was out.'

'We couldn't raise her either.'

The silence lengthened again as he waited for her to question him. But she was beginning to realise he wanted something from her. She thought she'd like to make him ask for it. Nicely.

'For a woman who used to earn her living by chatting into a microphone you certainly know how to hold your fire, Miss Mitchell. Yes, I admit it. I had someone check you over. I like to know who I'm dealing with. I'm told you were the woman who saved the Chancellor's life last summer, right? In that terrorist affair. I like a cool operator. We could do good business together, Miss M.'

'What do you have in mind?'

'This George Reeves thing seems to be developing in unexpected ways. I'd like to mull things over a little longer, OK? Look at all the angles before I brief you. No point in firing a gun at the wrong target. I wonder if you could see your way to spending the night here? Then we could get cracking first thing tomorrow. A working breakfast. Yes? We may take time thinking about a problem, Miss M, but when we're ready to go we like to see jet fumes coming out of bums. OK? Daisy can provide you with all the things you'll want. You need have no fear. If people do a good job for me they earn top dollar. But this is my creed, Miss M. Only a good workman's worth his hire. The rest can go get stuffed.'

'The job *is* related to the disappearance of George Reeves.'

'Haven't I just said? What else, for Christ's sake?'

'I'd have to check back with Mrs Reeves first.'

'You got it.'

'Then I'd like to take up your offer and spend the night

94

here. There are one or two minor problems. I came here with someone. I'll need transport back to Birmingham tomorrow.'

'We'll take care of it. I breakfast at seven. If you want to join me and one or two associates in the gym at six you're welcome. OK?'

'That's kind of you. But I won't take up the offer.'

'You've got to keep yourself fighting fit.' He threw two mock punches. 'That's a fucking jungle out there. Decency, honesty, playing the game, level playing fields? Forget it. Shylock rules, OK? In fact, Miss M, Shylock would look like Mother Teresa compared to some operators. And then there are shits who bite the arms and legs off those who feed them. You wouldn't believe . . .' and he shook his head. 'We may play hard here at Czinner's but we play fair. Anyone who goes for this greed is good crap has a rock where his brains should be. We say so loud and clear. Loud and clear. OK? That's a crusader at our entrance. The genuine article. Czinner Enterprises fights armed with Christian principles, Miss M. No fucking around.' He'd ridden to his toes. Mitch practically saw the sword in his hand. 'The good guy's got to win. Right? That's why I'm in the gym at six o'clock every morning, Miss M.'

They both turned as a huge wedge of snow crashed by the french windows. A wave of slush rose, obscuring the panes.

She looked back at him. 'I'll see you in the morning then.'

'Then we'll get into gear.'

10

'That shade of blue, darling, is you.' Mitch, with her dark brown hair and eyes, never wore blue. That was for the good girls, the blondes. But she found, much to her surprise, that Daisy Sharpe was right. 'Royal blue. You can wear vivid colours. So few of us can.'

Mitch had been taken over by Daisy as soon as Digger had gone to collect his coat. But how she'd been summoned, from what region she'd appeared, was a mystery. The attention she'd been paid was flattering. Mitch was allotted a bedroom with connecting bathroom next to Daisy's, found a matching satin nightdress and dressing-gown, very forties, very expensive – the kind of gear which Mitch felt so good in her shoulders glided back, her breasts lifted and her bum rotated effortlessly – and given her pick of the oils and unguents from Daisy's own dressing-table. If this was how the actress charmed all Arno's guests, Mitch could quite see how they'd come back for more. And more. How wonderfully corruptive total attentiveness to one's needs could be.

But the question still remained. What did Arno Czinner really want of her? What percentage was in it for him if she tracked down Muriel's runaway husband?

How did she figure in his scheme of things?

Not a comfortable question that.

It was beginning to look as though Georgie boy had been as enterprising in his own way as Czinner Enterprises and done the modern equivalent of blowing the office safe before he took to his heels.

Of course, from what she'd learned about George he wasn't the type to do any such thing. 'He has principles,' Harry Vine had told her. 'Everything by the rule book. He never looked beyond that.'

But perhaps, during those long – and according to Colin Bell boring – sessions in the psychotherapy group, George had relieved his tedium by looking over the top of his rule book. Had he seen – how had Harry Vine put it? – 'that the rules were made up by the bastards out to get and keep the lion's share.' And then acted according to new lights?

And if George had skipped with a bundle of loot this might explain why Muriel and her boyfriend were so anxious to find him.

Yes?

Not a bad bit of theorising, she decided.

But was it true?

Meanwhile it was one o'clock in the morning, early yet as far as most of Daisy's guests were concerned. From the top of the

Pre-Raphaelite staircase Mitch could hear the sound of music and merriment coming from various parts of Aston Clinton, some of it from the corridor directly below her. Mitch was in the middle of a plan in which she hoped to deceive the actress into giving her the key to her bedroom.

Twitching up the hem of her dressing-gown with her hand, she descended the heavily carved stairway. Her nightwear, the setting, the anxiety set up by her nefarious errand, gave her a sense of unreality.

She found Daisy riding on the back of a stalwart young man who was tearing down the corridor on all fours. The two couples behind them were being well beaten in the race, mainly because the women on these mounts faced backwards.

Shrieking with laughter, none of them saw Mitch for a while. She stood there like a policeman at a fountain during New Year revelling. Embarrassed, sanctimonious, impatient and with a ridiculous desire to shout "ere 'ere!'

But now Daisy was off her gasping mount and all concern.

'I'm so dreadfully sorry,' Mitch told her. 'I've left my handbag in your bedroom. It wouldn't matter but the damn thing contains my medication.'

'Sweetie, no prob. Justin, darling, over there!' and she pointed flashing fingers to her bag, on a stone window-sill.

'Can't we swim?' Justin asked, picking up the small bag by its gold chain. He then used it for a partner in an old-fashioned waltz: 'Daisy, Daisy, give me your answer do . . .'

'No drunks in the pool. You know how strict Arno is. Dead bodies, darling, are bad for his business.'

'I'm jolly well not drunk!'

'Pissed as a newt.'

'Where is Mr Czinner?' Mitch asked.

'Making absolute millions,' said Justin. 'He never stops, does he, Daisy? That's a fucking jungle out there. But he makes all the other horrid beasties hop. Right? Shylock rules . . .' His voice suddenly sang out, a hymn-chanting bass: 'Shylock drools, Shylock fools the balls right out of your boxer shorts. OK there?'

'Cut that out, Justin. Shut up. Here you are, Mitch, it's the gold-coloured one.' She handed her a bunch of keys. 'Better bring them back down again. Arno doesn't like keys lying around.'

'The ceiling's like the sea. Going in and out,' said one girl absently.

All three men became alert. 'You need a bit of fresh air, Nicky. Come along with Peterkins.'

'Hey! Wait for me!' Justin cried, trotting after them.

'I bagged her first.'

'The ceiling–'

'We know, darling. A nice little lie-down, eh?'

'Shouldn't you . . .?' Mitch paused.

'Oh, Nicky loves entertaining the troops,' Daisy told her. 'As long as they don't go down to Arno's gym. He's very particular about his equipment.' She turned to her depleted band. 'We need reinforcements, *mes enfants*. Search party deploy!'

She watched Daisy go, leading the way, hand raised. When Daisy moved the hand straight out in front of her they all broke into a trot.

Mitch found herself shaking her head. The actress was well past thirty. How could teenage games still amuse her? Perhaps those pubescent years had been Daisy's best years and, like a woman who would not relinquish the hair-style she'd had in her salad days, she would not let them go.

Daisy's bedroom revealed a very different woman. It was like no other room Mitch had seen at Aston Clinton, so she must suppose the actress herself had created it. The carpet, walls, curtains and bedcover were cream, the furniture light wood Biedermeier, and there was a yellow Tibetan tiger rug on the floor. Four paintings by the thirties woman artist Gluck decorated the walls. A group of three small oils of flowers, perhaps painted when Gluck was friendly with Constance Spry, were grouped over the bed. A woman in a hat, a cigarette holder protruding from sensuous lips, looked down from over the mantelpiece.

Mitch, turning and studying each painting, revelled in Gluck's sense of design. She wondered whether they actually belonged to Daisy or were lost in some labyrinthine Czinner deal.

She opened a bird's-eye maple wood door which led to a short corridor. On one side of this was Daisy's all-white bathroom, at the end a working actress's dressing-table and off to the right a walk-in closet and storage.

What had surprised Mitch when Daisy had gone into the closet to get her some nightwear was how few clothes the actress had, and only a handful of those were from famous houses. Mitch guessed Daisy patronised fashion students from one or two local colleges. Looking at the rack again, she also guessed that Daisy had disciplined herself to hang only the clothes she knew she would wear on a regular basis.

It would be wrong, she further realised, to dismiss the actress as a lightweight. She might act the part of of a billionaire's arm piece to perfection, she might love to indulge in horseplay and drink bubbly, but there was also an organising intelligence there. Why think that odd? Mitch asked herself. To run a successful career as an actress today took a lot more than dramatic talent.

Mitch began to walk her fingers through the clothes on the rack. At first she couldn't see what she was looking for, what she had earlier had a glimpse of from behind Daisy's back. There it was. A mauve anorak.

But this hardly conclusively proved Daisy was the woman with George in the Spread Eagle, or the woman Mitch had seen leaving Harry Vine's cottage.

She remembered the mauve skin-tight balaclava. Spotting hats on the shelf above the closet rail, she began to finger through them. Her hand hit something solid. Her fingers fumbled along the outline of a circle. A knob? She stretched up on to the pads of her toes and carefully edged the object from under a woman's trilby. It thudded into both hands. Unbalanced, she fell back, a shoulder blade jarring against the wall. 'Shit!'

She looked at the object in her hands. A radio receiver? Not the sort which would pick up the BBC, she immediately realised. She studied the row of buttons, the large central dial. My God. Bugging equipment.

Carefully restoring it to its place, she leaned back against the door, running her hands through her hair.

Who had Daisy been bugging? George? Harry Vine at his cottage?

Arno Czinner?

She started to search through the hats again. The balaclava was with a pile of scarves.

Stealing out, she went into the bathroom and collected the handbag she'd purposefully left behind her earlier.

She caught a glimpse of herself in the mirror over the wash-basin.

Well, go on. Take a good look. A detective. You? You didn't even recognise a piece of bugging equipment when you saw it.

I did.

Eventually.

'Oh shit,' she muttered and turned her back on her image.

Everyone has to start from scratch when they switch to an entirely new career, she told herself. Anyway, what is detection? Persistence.

Pray God.

Just that.

'It's got ellipsoidal lights.' Justin, half unzipped, was strolling by the bottom of the stairs. 'Three point five litre engine. Develops over 280 bhp . . .' He ran the zip back to full mast. 'That's better.'

'Justin!'

He looked up, blinking. He didn't recognise her.

She threw down the keys. His hand was too slow. They fell to his stockinged feet. 'Return them to Daisy for me, would you?'

'My shoes have gone walkies.' He was surprised.

'Leave them on, old boy,' said Peterkins. 'I do when I'm bonking. A lot of leverage in a shoe.'

'Daisy's keys,' muttered Justin, grovelling on the floor for them.

Mitch stared at them in some disbelief before turning to go back to her room. Though the lights were off, it was partially lit by the floodlighting illuminating the car-park which lay beyond a broad gravel path and a narrow belt of shrubbery. Hearing a gentle but irregular pit, pat-pat-pat, she went to the windows. Rain? Melting snow? She couldn't quite be sure.

Small holes were beginning to appear in the covering of snow.

She drew the curtains and switched on the light. It was a black, white and mauve room; great mauve satin bows tied linographs to the black and white striped walls, the woodwork was done in faux marbling, the wrought-iron taper-stick lamps had candle-shades and there were a lot of purple pansies on the quilted bedcover and the curtains. The pansies had also found their way on to the sanitary wear in the bathroom, which was boxed in mahogany and supplied by brass piping.

The rooms had dimmer switches, which Mitch used.

She had a bath, fiddled with her hair, paraded up and down before the long mirror in her expensive nightwear, got into bed, turned over and lay on her stomach, then her back, tried her side, pushed a pillow away, plumped the other, purposefully shut her eyes and then opened them again. It was no use. She was far too restless to fall asleep. She remembered the bound volumes of the *Windsor Magazine* and decided to go downstairs to get one.

Closing her bedroom door softly behind her, she could still hear the distant thump of disco music and, nearer, loud shouts of laughter, but she saw no one as she went down to the library. She'd just reached down a volume and was about to return when she heard voices in the corridor.

'Who told you to come fucking back? Listen, dickhead, you stay there. Right? OK? I don't care if you're there all night. All the next day. You stay until I tell you to move. Got that? Until your nuts drop off if necessary.'

'Sorry, captain–'

'Cut that crap. Captain! I want roots growing out of your feet. And I want you to keep in touch. Got that? Adrian, Adrian, we could have big problems here. And I don't need you fucking around. I need to rely on you to do as you're told. Got that? By the way, you worked in with the Development team, didn't you? With Vine and Reeves?'

'Until you pulled me out.'

'You ever heard of a set-up called R E Ganymede Sons?'

'Never.'

'Jumping Jesus . . .' Mitch, tucked behind the library door, strained to hear more but they had now moved too far down the corridor.

When the coast was clear she sidled round the door and back up the stairs. Her heart was pumping furiously. Something really was up. It seemed as if she might be right about Georgie boy lifting some cash before doing a bunk. How much? Mitch's mind reeled.

Arno Czinner was a billionaire.

She thought about what she'd heard. Had Adrian Cain been told by Arno to keep observation somewhere? At Harry Vine's cottage? No, no, more likely at Muriel Reeves' house.

Ganymede.

Gan, she remembered. The fragment of charred paper was still in her purse.

But she must not jump to too many conclusions. There was a whole telephone directory full of names which started Gan.

Back in her room, she crossed over to the window and peered out. Drizzle misted the panes, but she could make out figures in the car-park, a man, Josh Hadley, she suddenly realised, helping a very drunk Amanda into his car. They had driven off when she saw Adrian Cain appear, trench-coat collar pulled up about his shaved head, loping along the path which cut between the shrubbery on his way to the car-park. She waited until he had driven away before she let the curtain fall.

What role does Arno Czinner see me playing in all this? she wondered as she climbed into bed. If he had decided, she'd already know, she thought.

He'll certainly see me as expendable. A pawn to throw away in his pursuit of what?

No doubt about it. Money. That was what Arno Czinner was about.

She opened at random the tome she'd taken from the library.

She read: 'When I was first taken to Blanktown Gaol I travelled very much like a gentleman in a low-wheeled cab, at my own expense . . .'

Mitch yawned, read a little further and yawned again.

A crash shook her awake. She started up. She was aware of the light from the lamp and the bound volume, open, spine towards her, on the rug by the bed. The noise must have woken her when the book hit the floor. She looked at her watch. It was five o'clock.

Yawning, she clambered out of bed and headed for the pansy-spattered lavatory. On her way back, she stopped at the window and twitched back the curtain.

The car-park was practically empty. Large areas of tarmac patched the snow. It was then she became aware of the motorised roller she'd backed into with her TVR. It was side on to her, under the arthritic arms of an old oak tree. Something appeared to be sticking out from under the back roller. A complicated pattern of shadows.

Mitch's palm rose to cover her widening mouth.

Fingers?

She was already turning to find her dressing-gown.

The only thing she could hear as she stole through the house was her own panic, the yammer of her heart, a sudden gulping squeeze in her throat.

Fingers?

Whispers of dread goosed her ankles as she passed the cannon and heaps of cannon-balls in the long corridor. Entering the silence of the two-storey hall she paused under the flags and banners of ancient regiments. Smashed corpses reeking amid the vibrating rip of petards. Bleeding flesh rendered artistically in the dark areas of canvas over Aston Clinton's reception desk.

Mitch shut her eyes, swaying a little.

So Georgie boy has been dead all along, she found herself thinking.

She jerked herself together.

You don't know that.

Back straight, heel-toe, heel-toe, marching steadily, keeping her nerve, she crossed the black and white marble floor and shot the bolt back on the inner oak doors. A side light had been left on in the vestibule. The long shadow of one of the suits of crusader armour crossed her path. She descended the short flight of Portland stone steps and released the deadlocks on the outer door.

Though it was early morning, it was still dark and that darkness was full of the sound of water, gushing, dripping, gurgling. It was only when she stepped out that she realised she'd not put her shoes on, but the gravel was well . . . her mind reached for the word 'rollered' and then rejected it in horror. Snatching to lift her skirt, she found herself running across the gravel and on to the paved way between the band of shrubs which separated the car-park from the house.

As she came off the path she could see the back of the motorised roller, the horizontal cylinder of water mounted above the crushing weight of the iron wheel, the boxy fuel tank, the protruding steering wheel with its levers. What she could not see was a hand. Relief loosened her limbs, set up a tremor in her joints. Walking more slowly now, she skirted a puddle and a patch of snow and then she circled to the other side of the roller.

The hand was wearing a wet Fair Isle glove. Also visible was a stained piece of chalk-striped suiting and a soggy strip of sheepskin jacket.

Where is the rest of him? That's what she found herself thinking, for the roller was no more than four to five feet long and certainly less than four feet wide.

Unless he were kneeling.

Or folded up in some way.

Burst, splintered, crushed.

Shrouded in snow for a week.

Just his hand left.

But there was more than that, she now realised. An indeterminate amount of splodge oozed from one side of the roller. Much of the stuff was still whitened by snow, like pastry edges frilling from beneath the weight of the pin.

The knuckles of her hand were in her mouth, teeth crunching on bone. She began to sag, knees as gooey as the stuff beneath the roller.

'Am I thinking of the right guy? He had a plump face. Right?'
'No.'
'Christ Almighty. We've got to book a cathedral or something.
We got to try and do this right. This is a man we're talking about
here. A fucking fellow human being. Anyone would think this
is fucking Italy. Fucking Mafia. This is a Czinner employee. My
man Reeves. I got to go again.'
Czinner leapt out of his kelim-covered armchair and opened
black lacquer double doors. He turned back to Mitch: 'We need
a fucking priest. Not the police. Doesn't anyone say their prayers
any more? People are crap, Miss M. One hundred per cent
unadulterated shit,' and he hastened off to the lavatory.
Mitch took another large gulp of brandy. She was sitting on
the edge of a plush Knoll settee in the suite of rooms Arno
Czinner reserved for his own use. Everything in his study,
the terracotta walls, the Persian rugs, the Doric ceiling cornice
picked out in white, seemed preternaturally bright. She took
another gulp of brandy. She was hoping the alcohol would
fudge the edges a bit.
Arno came back, not quite teetering on his feet, but far from
properly balanced. He was making darting thrusts about the
room. On one he picked up a twelve-inch statue of a female from
the white marble mantelpiece. 'Miss Daddy Longlegs,' he said.
'I don't like too much flesh. When you're down to bare bones
everything's a hell of a sight clearer, right? It's a Frink. I never
acquire crap. Crap's a bad idea, Miss M.' Tucking it into the
crook of his arm, as though it were a baby, he was tracking back
to the window. Mitch heard the car engine and joined him.

Daisy Sharpe was standing on the broad gravel path in front of the entrance to Aston Clinton, watching a taxi driver load suitcases into the boot. There was also a huge flattish parcel wrapped in pink newsprint.

'That was her fortieth birthday last night,' said Arno. 'You can't kid the kid.'

'Should she be going? Won't the police want to question everyone?'

'You said it yourself, Miss M. That body was put there at the beginning of the snows. Christ. How long ago does that make it?'

'The day he actually disappeared. Thursday. Perhaps sometime during Thursday night. Pretty soon after he died. Rigor sets in after three or four hours. You'd have to bend him to get him under the roller. Unless the body was chopped up. But why go to the trouble of putting the remains under a roller in the first place? To make identification difficult? But no one else is missing. Only George.'

'You're supposing he was dead before he went under.'

She looked at him and then away.

'We can't lay our hands on the wife, either. She's certainly not at home. Adrian Cain has been parked outside her house all night. No sign of her. What the hell is going on here? I thought this guy Reeves had lit out with another woman. He'd got his hands on a good pair of jugs, two juicy pears with a tight little entrance hall and the door's open. Tast-ee. And I sympathised. I really did. But there are ways of doing it, OK? You tell your wife you're hitting the road. Any ape knows that. You have a little respect for all those years you've spent in the same bed. I tell her we'll pay to find her hubby for her. You've got to square accounts. Parting's a big thing. Am I right?'

They were watching Daisy climb into the taxi.

'Daisy was like my first wife,' he said. Mitch noted the past tense. 'A lot of human stuff in Daisy. That kiddy has raised a hell of a lot of cash for that charity thing of hers. Helping those Brazilian kids those death squads go popping for.'

Daisy pulled the taxi door shut. She looked straight ahead of her.

106

'You go off people. OK. It's only natural. But that doesn't mean the time you spent together is shit.'

'Daisy doesn't look forty.'

'She told me she's been planning *her* exit for more than six months. Will you get that?'

They watched the taxi go and then the exhaust fumes evaporate in the raw dawn light.

'Got it all marked down for the morning after her fortieth birthday party. That's an actress for you. Makes a performance out of shit all.'

'Did she say why?'

'Who cares why?'

'It's an odd thing to do. Make up your mind to leave a guy but not for six months.'

'Oh God, let me be good. But not just yet. Right? Daisy'll have her reasons.'

'You don't seem to mind. It doesn't worry you one bit.'

'No. Well. I admit I've been getting restless, Miss M. Fresh fields and pastures new. What's life without a few new beginnings? And you can't have those without a parting or two. Oh Christ. Got to go to the john.' He paused just long enough to restore the statue to its place on the mantelpiece.

Mitch was unaware she'd shifted slightly, that from her new vantage point by the window she could see round the azalea which had been partly obscuring her vision of the car-park. Snow had retreated far enough from the motorised roller to reveal more of the stuff which had oozed out from under iron rims. It didn't look like pastry any more. Her eyes were still widening as she turned away. Feeling stiff, almost splintery, she carefully moved to the Knoll settee and just as carefully picked up her brandy.

She turned to see Arno leaning against the ebonised door post. He was still hitching his combat green track-suit bottoms higher. He looked up at her. His skin had a slimy shine, like going-off cheese. 'It was the smell. The smell of that thing,' he said. 'It's turned my bowels to water.'

'I don't remember a smell.' But she was remembering other things. Shutting them out, she said: 'It need not have been done to confuse the issue of identity. After all, the Fair Isle glove tells all in that respect. It would seem. Do you think, Mr Czinner, someone has sent you a warning? You know of no one with a grudge against you?'

'A whole raft of them, toots. A whole damn army.' He was back in the room, picking up his glass, tilting back his head. 'But who the hell minces up a fart of a clerk because they've a grudge against the boss?'

She'd already jumped to another line of thought. 'I wonder if it's anything to do with the loot?'

'Loot. What loot?'

'What was all that about during the party then? Why did Adrian Cain spend all last night outside Muriel Reeves' house? Most people yell their heads off when they've had something stolen. Why are you being so bloody coy?'

'You don't understand, Miss M. We've a rights issue coming out.'

'What's that?'

'A method of raising capital for our businesses on the stock market. In effect you issue more shares and ask the institutions and punters to buy them – usually at a discount to the quoted share price. If it gets out that someone has stolen a bundle right from under our fucking noses, where are our famed tight financial controls? Investor confidence could evaporate. The share price could drop below the rights issue price. No bugger on this earth then buys and effectively – even though the issue is underwritten by merchant banks and you get your cash – you are right up shit creek. We are in the process of raising half a billion, Miss M. We can't afford to have anything happening that will rock the boat. Anyway, we're not sure yet that money has gone missing. It's gone walkabout. That's pretty sure. But is it still in the company somewhere? Christ only knows. As yet. We're jumping through accounts like the computer's got St Vitus dance.'

She was staring at him, hardly able to believe what she was hearing. 'Isn't a body being found under a roller in your car-park worse for investor confidence? Wouldn't you say?'

He had turned to study her. 'We can't have you popping off

your mouth like some loose cannon.' He put down his glass. 'I was going to employ you anyway.'

'To do what?'

'Initially I was going to fund Muriel Reeves' investigation.'

'I never quite understood that. Why? Is it because George has run off with a wheelbarrow full of cash?'

'We're not sure any cash is missing, Miss M. I keep on telling you that. I can't seem to drum this into your head. Here we have principles. We know what's right. Those are crusaders at our entrance. Sure, we might fight with the gloves off but we are the good guys. We like to help a little lady in distress. We're tough bastards. Too true. But we've got good Christian values. Those crusaders were tough guys, too, weren't they? They had to be to beat the Turks.'

Mitch found herself sitting down again. She was aware she was in a state of shock, that her brain wasn't functioning as it should, but even so there were times when listening to Arno Czinner was like being turned upside down on a ride at the fair. I think it is because that crook actually believes he's basically a good man.

Well, the men of affairs must believe it too. They must think he's sound. Why else would they open up the bank vaults, show him round and promise him another half-billion to go with whatever other mountains of money they've already given him?

She stared at Arno. So great was her sense of unreality that she found herself on the edge of panic.

'Steady there,' Arno said. 'It hits you now and then doesn't it? That – out there.'

'Yes,' she gulped.

'I don't quite yet know how we're going to handle it. But no cathedrals, right? No big noises? Eh? Something nice and quiet and respectful. Low key. No one needs to be in a cathedral to pray for that poor guy's soul. Right?'

Mitch found her right hand gripping the arm of the settee, hanging on.

'This is a hell of a thing. Just another two weeks and we'd be free and clear. Rights issue squared away. All done and dusted.'

'Why put him under that roller?' She was again trying to climb on top of the situation, find a reason for such a bizarre act. 'And why here? No more than a few yards from the entrance to Aston Clinton?'

'That's what I'm going to employ you to do. Get to the bottom of it.'

'The police will do that.'

'I doubt that. Have you ever taken a look at the crime clear-up rate? Quite an eye-opener, that. Those who actually get caught are so few they're practically an endangered species. Not to mention the times the boys in blue get a bit too desperate and gaol the wrong guy.'

'You do have a jaundiced view of British justice.'

'A police force is there to act as a deterrent. Someone to call in. Someone to make you feel it's safe to sleep in your bed at night. They're not very good at catching criminals. You've only got to look at the figures.'

'You really think I'll have a better chance?'

He tapped his head. 'You've the right sort of stuff up there. You'd like to think you're straight down the middle but you're not. You've not got a copper's mind. You've got an investigator's mind. Devious. Slippery. Persistent. Am I right?'

What a con man, she was thinking. Can I really afford to fall for his lies? All he wants to do is control my tongue, make me keep my speculations to myself. But she knew she couldn't give up the case now, any more than a bloodhound who'd caught the scent.

'Five thousand pounds up front. If you crack the case, the same again.'

She watched him as he went round to his desk. He took out a cheque book from a drawer before sitting down.

She almost salivated because, she realised, it was expected of her. He was wafting pork sausage under the nose of a dog. 'People are crap, Miss M. One hundred per cent unadulterated shit . . .' That was what he'd just told her, that was what he believed; no doubt with the aid of his cheque book he'd proved the point many times.

He did not pick up his pen but a Corinthian helmet which was

110

being used as a paper-weight. 'It was made five hundred years before Christ,' he said. 'Some little Greek guy's head was in this. Some guy as hot as Hades, pissing fear, trying to disembowel the other guy.'

'Nothing changes.'

He put down the helmet. 'Too right.'

'Five thousand . . . that's a lot of money.'

'A lot of faith . . . in you . . .'

'The police are bound to ask you,' Mitch said. 'They'll ask you if money went missing when George did.'

'But I don't know if any did and nor do you. Certainly it's not a fit topic for press speculation. Wouldn't you say? Those guys have got enough anyway. I don't suppose there's any way we'll be able to keep a body out of the papers. Who do I make this thing out to?'

'The Mitchell and Orient Bureau.'

'Good to have you aboard.'

His hand did not reach far as he proffered the cheque. She had to really lean over to collect it. She studied the date, the amount, the signature, folded it and put it in her dressing-gown pocket. She said: 'It might be a good idea to check out Harry Vine's cottage too. Though I don't think we'll find them there.' And she told Arno Czinner what she'd discovered at the cottage.

He whistled. 'Will you get that? She's the one who is doing the dumping? Christ, was I wrong about her.'

'But if they killed George why the hell did Muriel Reeves employ me? Do you kill a man on Thursday and on Monday morning employ a detective to find him?'

'Still, if those two have really flown the coop . . . Excuse me . . .' and he picked up the telephone. 'We'll get someone out there. Make sure the cottage is empty.'

While he was issuing his instructions, she was wandering round the room. A hand went in her pocket to make sure the cheque was still there, that he'd not in some way magicked it out.

When he'd put down the receiver, she said: 'The police are certainly taking their time in coming. Did you tell them someone

111

was dead or someone was murdered? They might think it a heart attack or something.'

'We don't really know anyone has been murdered. Not yet.'

'Squashing a body with a motorised roller seems to indicate foul play.'

'One would never want to say too much. A minimal approach is usually the best in tricky circumstances.'

'Is the roller always kept in the car-park? I mean, when it's not in use?'

'It was brought in for a specific job. We're making some new gravel paths beyond the terrace at the back of the house. But when the snows came the work was temporarily halted.'

'The thing was hired?'

'Yes.'

'So using it was likely to be a spur-of-the-moment decision. And the only people who are likely to know it was in your car-park are people who work here.'

'Lots of people come here. We control a raft of businesses from here.' He got up and walked back over to the window. 'It won't be long before our people start turning up. What will happen? What are the police going to do? I mean, out there.'

'I should think they'll seal off the car-park and then secure a route to the body.'

'What does that mean, for Christ's sake?'

'They decide on the line of a path to the body and then they get down on their hands and knees and do a fingertip search of that ground. After that's done, they then fan out to search the whole area. They mark finds. They're photographed by a stills man and then they're videoed.'

'It's going to take a long time then?'

'Right.'

'How long before they move that . . . him?'

She shrugged.

'What a fuck-up,' said Arno Czinner. 'A love triangle, eh? Oh hell . . .' and he made off again through the ebonised doors.

Mitch, hearing the distant wail of a police siren, went to get dressed.

12

'I wondered, Digger, if you'd ring News Information and get someone to send what they've got on Arno Czinner?'

'Did you?' His voice was grim.

'Oh, come on. It's only a phone call away.'

'Look here, will you? I'm not a junior partner in the Mitchell and Orient Bureau. It may have escaped your notice, but I already have a job. Here. At this radio station.'

'You're not mad at me for staying at Aston Clinton last night?'

'Of course I'm not. But do you realise, Mitch, the only time you get in touch with me is when you want something? It gets boring.'

'Oh Jesus. I'm sorry. I'll take you out to lunch next week. Push out the boat. The Plough and Harrow? Lots of bubbly. You know I love you really.'

'This request of yours doesn't mean you're thinking of working for that crooked little wanker?'

'He's given me a cheque. It's all up-front.' She could hardly keep the wonder out of her voice. 'Cash in advance.'

'In advance of what? What's he got in mind for you?'

A mean draught lifted the roots of hairs at the nape of Mitch's neck. What if the cash was for something other than trying to silence a loose cannon's guns? What if Arno had other plans for her?

Digger said: 'I hear a body was found in his car-park this morning. The kids in our newsroom are out there now trying to stitch together the story. You're crazy. You know that?'

113

'Come on. Why would Czinner dump a corpse in front of his own front door?'

'All I'm saying is that if you become a victim of your new employer's friendly fire you can be sure of one thing. It was intentional.'

'Sure. This fellow's a shady deal-maker. I'll buy that. But murder? He's got too much to lose. Con men don't kill. It's strictly verbals.'

'You're nuts.'

'Look, we need the money, Digger. We're only just setting up. I promise you I'll keep my back covered.'

'This isn't Mitch Mitchell deep in some whacky enterprise. The only thing you'll be deep in is shit.'

'Daisy did all right.'

'Going after money gives Daisy an excuse to indulge her taste for masochism. Anyway, even she has limits. Far from marrying the bloke, she's thinking of getting out.'

'Got out. The taxi came this morning. She had it planned for a long time apparently.'

'She's scared. I tell you that in confidence, Mitch. I tell you so you'll stop arsing around with Mr Genetically Improved Rattlesnake. Send that cheque back.'

'Need the money. Got to pay the phones and the electric. You know how it is. What else did Daisy say?'

'Nothing I'm going to tell you.'

'Look . . . you're way off if you think Arno is tied up with this body. I was with him just after it was found. He was really shaken. He was in a hell of a state. His bowels had turned to water.'

'Are you sure it wasn't indigestion? Swallowed the kill too fast and got a pain in the guts?'

'Oh, Digger . . .'

'Laugh if you want. I'll get you that stuff from News Information and I won't set our journalists on to you. But make sure you book that table. Digger wants to feel his friendship is appreciated. I sometimes wonder why I put up with you at all. The trouble is that this new lot at Radio Brum seem like Martians. Christ. They don't smoke. They don't drink. They run round working their arses off. Deadly serious. Deadly dull. They make Bill and Ben the Flowerpot Men look depraved.'

'Oh come on, Digger . . .'

'Oh well. I'm for the chop when they make these new staff cuts. God knows who'll employ me. It's a hell of a thing, Mitch, but the truth is that homosexuals are about as interesting as housewives these days. Blacks are all the rage now.'

'I rose initially on the novelty value of being one of two women journalists in a newsroom of sixty.'

'Prehistory.'

'So it is.'

He sighed. 'I suppose that's what I'm about to become. A note to the archives.'

'I'm *not* a note to the archives. No way. Stuff that for a game of soldiers,' and she slammed down the phone.

Oh well. Oh hell.

She phoned back to apologise.

'Leave being smarmy to insurance salesmen,' Digger advised. 'They do it better.'

She slammed down the phone again.

Well, I don't care, she thought. She drew the cheque out of her pocket and examined it again for error. She could find none. Somebody loves me. Even if it is a genetically improved rattlesnake. Better get *you* to the bank straightaway. She kissed his signature. Before you bounce.

She went upstairs, stripping off her evening wear in her bedroom before putting herself under the shower. She hoped the water would clear her brain.

Did Georgie boy do the equivalent of clear the office safe before he was killed? It was a good bet. Did someone who knew he'd done it and wanted the loot kill him? Daisy Sharpe had been bugging someone. She could have found out. She certainly timed her exit from Aston Clinton. Then, of course, there were the prime suspects, Muriel Reeves and Harry Vine. Apparently they'd also exited, but clandestinely.

Then there was Arno Czinner.

But if it were Muriel and Harry why had Muriel employed her? And if it were Arno why had he planted the corpse

115

outside his own front door at a time when investor confidence was all?

Daisy loved money. She'd planned to leave Arno for the last six months. Had she delayed her departure in order to line her pockets first? She had been seen with George at the Spread Eagle. Had she teamed up with him and then killed him when he'd prised the loot out of Czinner's coffers?

It was too early to suppose that Harry Vine and Muriel really were missing.

And Daisy a murderer? Would she be strong enough to put the body under that roller?

Why put it there?

Am I missing something here? Out of all these people, Arno is the natural villain of any piece.

He's got to figure. Hasn't he?

But instead of feeling fresh after her shower she was becoming drowsy. She didn't want to think. She didn't want to see the soggy hand-knitted glove, a strand of wool unravelling from the thumb.

Shocked, she realised this wasn't the first dead hand which had reached out through the dark to her. There was her first case. There was that other hand.

'It was the smell,' Arno Czinner had said as he'd come through the ebonised doors again. His dark brown eyes had not been larger but they had seemed it for his sweating skin had shrunk to cling on to his skull. In that moment she had known of the bond that had been forged between them; they had both looked on those remnants and seen their ending. The difference was that Mitch had experienced it before and knew what to suppress. She hadn't smelled dead flesh.

It was only after the police had arrived that her grip on the reality of the situation loosened and she found herself taking part in something which seemed to be happening a long, long way away. She watched a second self walking about and apologising for being in evening wear and drinking coffee, her real self taking care not to be there at all but here, deep inside, at a very safe distance.

Yet she had jarred together again; it had happened when

she'd been put out. She had supposed herself to be the chief witness. Hadn't she discovered the body? But it wasn't the superintendent in charge of the case who had interviewed her, or even a sergeant, but an out-of-uniform constable.

Thank God, she thought now, for the pettiness of human nature. If it weren't for my smallness of mind how would I get through the largeness of events? The truth was I felt peeved at my lack of importance. That shook me back together again.

Poor Georgie boy.

But I can do something for him. I can help nail his killer. If I manage to keep myself in one piece. Operate competently.

She fed herself coffee and half a slice of toast before setting off for the office. It was now getting on for eleven o'clock. The people of the city, those brash and big-hearted Brummies, were mincing along like a lot of camp comics as they negotiated slush and puddles underfoot. Some of the arterial roads were awash as parts of the drainage system backed up. Dirty spray surged intermittently over the TVR's bonnet. All the city's lights were on, souring the thin grey winter light.

Much to her surprise and relief, she found a parking space in Gas Street. As she bent to feed the pay and display meter she felt a splash on her neck, spreading to slither over the knob of her spine. Looking up and stepping back from the dripping converted gas street light, she saw the sign on the wall above the folded-back canopy – THE BEST BAR NONE. She experienced the inward little nod which told her that territory which had been alien only a day or two ago was now familiar. Her patch.

She walked down the alley which led into the canal basin. Here the snow hadn't quite turned to slush, but there were a lot of black footprints in it; some had formed into a ribbon of path. The canal waters were steely grey, shot at the edges with the darker reflections of the surrounding buildings.

Turning left to her office, she saw the eyeless holes in the building erected on a bridge spanning the canal; roof ribs rested in the skyline like the carcass of some dead animal. This end of the basin, right in the heart of the city, had not yet been redeveloped. Beyond a clock tower, behind vulnerable young branches doused in sodium light, were the grey elevations of an office block which were bisected with dark lines that gave a raffish, latent thirties feel to a picture dominated by abandoned Victoriana.

Soon, Mitch realised, she wouldn't notice any of it; soon she'd be quite at home.

The girl was a little way down from the office, sitting on the step of the curio shop. She had been hidden from sight by the shop's bay window. A slight kid, her straight black hair tied back in a plaited pony tail, a fringe touching her eyebrows. She wore a cheap wine raincoat over a good wool check jacket and straight navy blue skirt. She got up when she saw Mitch coming. 'You aren't with the Mitchell and Orient Bureau, are you?'

'Mitch Mitchell.' She found herself being studied by eyes so squeaky clean and clear it almost hurt to look in them; small, Celtic blue.

'I want the job.'

What job? Mitch found herself wondering and then remembered Tommy's advert.

'I've been waiting since nine o'clock.'

'You must be frozen.' The kid's face had been rubbed bright pink all over.

'Oh, I've tramped about a bit. It's a very interesting place.' There wasn't a noticeably Brummie accent, but the city was there, all right, in the speech rhythms. She wasn't going to say 'babs' or 'ta-ta-a-bit' but there was nothing of the gel about her. Tommy would not approve. Mitch found, to her surprise, this bothered her.

'What's your name?'

'A J Evans.'

'A J?'

'I'm sure you can see how awful Amanda Jane is. It makes me feel like an old-fashioned doll. You know, before Barbie and breasts and bikinis. When dolls were babies and not sex objects. I tried Mandy but that made me think of a munching Jersey cow. All udders and doe eyes.'

'Names are hell,' said Mitch who certainly wasn't going to remember the unspeakably awful Christian name she'd got landed with.

118

'I like A J. I think I can do something as A J. I don't feel tied down any more.'

Mitch noticed that the brown leather on the uppers of the kid's boots was patched with the sort of deep stain which appears when there is a large hole in the soles.

'What is the something you want to do?'

'Be a detective.'

'We're looking for a secretary, A J.'

'After taking my degree I did a business studies course. I can handle all that stuff.'

'You'd be much better off joining the police force.'

She shook her head. 'All those men and all those uniforms. I'd be starting off with my ankles tied together, Miss Mitchell. It's a male-dominated culture with male ethics and values. I'm not saying that's wrong. But I'm female.'

'Well, you better come on up before we both freeze. I don't suppose, A J, you've got a ruling-class accent in your locker somewhere?'

The girl looked at her with astonished and astonishing eyes.

'Tommy Hung, my partner, has. And he was born in the arse-end of Hong Kong.'

She was quick. 'Your partner wants someone who's posh?'

'He thinks it will be good for business. He wants to try and remove the sleazy image detective agencies have. Make going to see your private eye as respectable as going to see your bank manager or lawyer.'

A J stared at her again.

'Class always comes dear. And Tommy is only too happy to up the rates.'

'Oh dear. It isn't as if I can't see he has a point. And, of course, he is Chinese. They believe in spending on face.'

'How do you know that?' Mitch was surprised.

'One of my brother's university friends comes from Hong Kong.'

'So he's just Anglicised what he'd do naturally, anyway? What is thought to be a good business ploy?' Mitch was thoughtful.

She let them both in, collected the post from the mat and took A J up to her office. She made some coffee and offered her a shortbread biscuit. 'You might as well know that Tommy has had at least fifty letters in. Not counting what's in this lot.'

'I knew you'd get masses. That's why I decided to come down this morning. I hoped to jump the queue.'

Mitch was thinking it over. 'I can't offer you much hope. As I said, hiring's Tommy's department. But right now we're in a bit of a fix. Tommy's working on a case in Great Yarmouth and a small investigation I'm doing has suddenly blown up into something very big and nasty. We certainly could do with a pair of extra hands at the moment. Someone to help mind the shop and do some basic research. I can offer you a week's employment. After that, you take your chances.'

A J didn't even ask how much she'd be paid. 'OK.'

'Do well, kid, and Tommy could change his mind about his gel.'

'I don't think I could ever manage to speak with a plum in my mouth. It can't be easy.'

'The only thing that worries *me* is your boots. I'll pay you a hundred pounds for the week and I'm going to give you an advance. Buy some decent footwear. You're going to be doing a lot of leg work. You'll get expenses, of course.'

'Great! I mean . . . thank you, Miss Mitchell.'

'Mitch. Hang on a minute and then we'll get down to it.' She picked up the phone and dialled the office of the stockbroker Willie French. She confirmed her lunch date and then gave A J a crisp account of the investigation so far.

'Just before I left Aston Clinton one of Czinner's employees rang to say there was no one at Harry Vine's cottage. There's no sign of life at Muriel Reeves' house either.'

'Perhaps Mr Czinner's reasons for being so cagey about whether money had been stolen had nothing to do with this rights issue. At the moment, what would his motive be for murdering George? If a lot of money has gone missing . . . Are you happy about being employed by this man?'

'I'm happy about being employed by anyone.'

'Yes. I see,' but she didn't sound convinced.

'Look at it this way. Defence lawyers are always representing criminals – sometimes murderers.'

120

'What if you found out anything incriminating?'

'There's no way we'd aid and abet wrongdoing. We'd turn him in. It's hardly a matter of principle, A J.' Mitch's voice was dry. 'If we don't, we could land up in the dock ourselves.'

'Yes. Yes, I do see.'

'Whatever my private opinion of Arno Czinner may be, he's regarded, you know, as a very respectable businessman. The sort of chap who'll very likely get a knighthood in the near future.'

'Oh well . . .' and her brow cleared. 'That's all right.'

'Let's get the show on the road. First of all I want you to find out all you can, officially and unofficially, about the actress Daisy Sharpe.' Mitch thought for a minute. 'I've quite run out of credit with Digger. Try and get the unofficial information from Woody. I'll give you his number. J J Woodward is a retired newspaper man. He worked for the *Birmingham Sentinel*. If he can't give you the information, he knows who can.

'Then, we have to make a start on the money. That's where the key lies. I mean, we're talking billions. That's a monster honeypot in anyone's language. I'm seeing this stockbroker chap at lunch and I want you to take a look at Czinner's Finance Director, Toby Trubberman. A very pretty boy and so young! I got a copy of his personnel file before I left Aston Clinton this morning. But what we're after is not on any file. Have you a car?'

'A VW Beetle. It's my brother's, really, and not very reliable.'

'Toby lives in a little village called Chorley, near Lichfield. That's a plus for us. Ask around at the local. See what kind of lifestyle he has. You can pretend to be a newspaper woman. After all, a chap on his staff has been found killed.'

'OK.' The kid's eyes were gleaming.

'There is one thing I want to make crystal clear. Out in Czinner's car-park there's a human porridge which was walking around on two legs last week. Just as we are now. If I have to worry for one moment about your safety you've blown it. You're out on your ear. You are not to talk to Daisy or Toby Trubberman or any of the principals. All I want from you is some good background research. The emphasis is on background. You do understand?'

121

A J was nodding. 'Honest.'

'Good. When I've looked at the post and taken the calls off the answering machine I'm off to Mr Bunter's, that restaurant just off Burlington Passage. I'm dropping into the library on the way back. I've got to do a little research on a drug.' As she got up, she said: 'I know why I want to see this stockbroker. But what I can't understand is why Willie French wants to see me. Money,' she guessed. 'He's going to use me to make some. And how the hell is he going to do that?'

13

Mitch had left the office early for her appointment. She wanted to detour to the Bureau's bank in Waterloo Street before going down to Burlington Passage. She didn't even consider taking the car. Even if she found other parking spaces, dicing with city-centre traffic would take as long as walking.

Away from Gas Street Basin, the last of the slush had washed away leaving eddies of mud, pushed into changing patterns by thousands of feet. Water dripped off buildings and trees, sprayed up from wheels.

But it always cheered Mitch, being out and about in these streets. Unlike London, this was a spruce city, a city its proud fathers liked to wash and brush and shine. The paving stones she was now crossing formed white and pink rings round the memorial to Joseph Chamberlain. It more resembled a folly than anything, she thought – two clock towers without a clock, one of the towers a reflection in the circular pond lapping the memorial's foundations. Still, they hadn't stuck public lavatories under their famous son, as they had in other cities.

Lengthening her stride, she turned the corner by the museum and art gallery and sauntered into Victoria Square. This had recently been pedestrianised and patches of pinky herring-bone paving brick bled through snow. The square itself was dominated by the floosie in the jacuzzi. There she was, oh the tart, monumental legs wide apart to the knees before lolling to cross at the ankles, her big greeny grey bottom sunk into a delicate rosy lotus blossom afloat in water which cascaded down flights of steps to another pool. This was presided over by a pair of much smaller statues, naked lovers who were so prim and proper they looked as if they were sitting staring at each other over a bridge table, not a fountain. Perhaps they were making up for that great floosie raised high above them who perpetually showered them with spitting silver jets.

The city fathers had tried to make their goddess respectable. Round the edge of her pool were words by T S Eliot, lines about the lotus rose, spelt with two 'o's for added gravitas; about her being out of the heart of light. But it was no good. The Brummies had her measure and named her accordingly.

Mitch loved her. My God, this was a lady who let you know she performed and undoubtedly in many more positions than dreamed of by mere mortals. That the city had the sheer nerve to put the spouting bitch of creation bang in its bull's-eye made her want to let out three cheers. Let other municipalities nervously nod in the direction of the cool beauty of minimalist kidney-shaped benches topped with asphalt or glass and steel cabinets significantly stuffed with discarded clothes, ashtray and plastic cup. She was all for the splendid vulgarity of the floosie in the jacuzzi. Hip, hip, hurrah!

Victoria Square, named for the old Queen and now subverted by her open-legged sister, led into more imperial ways of which Waterloo Street was one. It was full of the solid, established architecture favoured by banks and building societies, thick stone walls, stout doors, lots of granite steps announcing you were going up in the world when you crossed over such thresholds.

Certainly Mitch, mounting the steps of her bank, always had the impression she was moving to a higher plane even when her bank balance pointed entirely the other way.

'Lovely day,' she told the clerk.

He looked at her in astonishment.

But who cares what the weather is like, she thought, when

123

you are paying five thousand pounds into your bank account? Mitchell and Orient Bureau. In the black. (Fingers crossed.)

Mr Bunter's was a fashionable eatery in what had once been cellars used for storing spices. The large open space was light and airy, spanned by brick arches supported by handsome pillars.

'Mr French is expecting you,' said a boy with a ring in his ear and a butcher's striped apron over his jeans. 'He's by the bar.'

Willie French's face was like a pot-bellied jug, stout handle turned towards her. All his flesh had been expensively made, out of Scottish salmon, undercut steak, lobsters and oysters; he was jolly and well and jolly well satisfied with his place in the food chain. Conservatively tailored, no jewellery, no body lotions, his thick black hair neatly trimmed. Shrewd of eye, firm handshake, an attentive host.

He was a man who was relaxed enough to wait. It was not until he had chosen collegiate pudding and she'd decided on crème caramel that he guided the conversation round to Czinner Enterprises.

'They announced their five hundred million pound rights issue last Wednesday.'

'Yes. So I heard. To tell you the truth, I'm on pretty shaky ground when it comes to shares. I'm not even sure if my idea of what a share is . . . well, if it's correct.'

He did not seem at all put out and nor did she feel patronised when he explained.

'A public company, in theory at least, is owned by its shareholders. Let's make it simple. A company issues one hundred five-pence shares. That company grows and prospers. A shareholder wants to sell his shares on the market. The next buyer now might have to pay five pounds for that five-pence share.

'Say this company now needs to raise more money to expand its business. It could go to its bankers but the money it raises from them will be expensive. It could find a lot of its profits going out in interest payments. An alternative might be to have a rights issue and get much cheaper capital. The company issues more shares – making its original hundred into a hundred and fifty. It then asks its current shareholders and the market to buy those shares – and if all goes well the company raises a lot of money much more cheaply. They only have to pay out – say – four per cent interest on that money, in the form of dividends.'

'There must be snags.'

'Sure there are. For a start, you have to persuade a merchant bank to underwrite the issue – that is, take up unsold shares at the rights issue price.

'Normally shares in a rights issue are sold at a discount to the actual market price. Now, say the rights issue goes badly. None of the existing shareholders want to add to their holding in the company. The share price plummets. The rights issue price is five pounds a share – a price the merchant bank has undertaken to pay for each unsold share. But the market price for that share is only three pounds fifty. On each share the merchant bank stands to lose one pound fifty.

'Conversely, if the market reacts well, the bank might sell the shares not taken up at a fat profit.'

'It's a gamble?'

'The bank lays off its gamble. Other institutions, insurance companies, unit trust managers, usually undertake to pick up a chunk of the stock. A rights issue is an orchestrated event which only gets off the ground if banks and institutions feel good about a company. Think that it will do well for them. Ah!' And he picked up his spoon before his pudding had been set before him.

'Of course, the merchant bank gets a fat fee for all its trouble. In practice, they try to talk a company up, get a band-wagon rolling. Thank you. That looks excellent,' he said to the waiter, and turning back to Mitch: 'A rights issue is very much about timing. In a recession you're very unlikely to get many of them away. Everyone's running scared. They've probably already had their fingers burnt and if not are afraid they're going to. When things start to pick up a bit everyone starts to see blue sky ahead. When that happens, they take more risks.'

'So when you need cheap money desperately to see you through a recession you can't raise it? When you don't need it half so badly you are in with a chance?'

Willie laughed. 'Isn't that life?'

'But whatever happens now Czinner gets his money? The merchant bank has to pay up?'

'Unless the rights issue is pulled. And that happens very, very rarely indeed.'

'But it could happen?'

'If a combination of adverse circumstances hit the stock – well, yes, it could.'

'Five hundred million is an awful lot of loot. What will Czinner do with it?'

'He says it's to make acquisitions – buy other companies.'

'What do you think?'

'I think he needs to repair his balance sheet. Right on the eve of the 1990 recession Czinner paid way above the odds for two companies. The Jane and Jarrod chocolate company – not too bad a mistake – and a huge engineering company based in Preston. That was disastrous. Profits fell off the graph paper but the bankers always got their interest payments. I must say at one time the haemorrhage looked unstoppable.'

'That's the time Czinner got the reputation for being able to walk on water?'

'And it's why the City is backing him now. They think the man's nothing short of a miracle worker.'

'But you feel it's too good to be true? That's why you're having lunch with me today?'

'Shortly after I'd talked to Tommy Hung I met a friend of mine who is concerned with the Glick Hope Foundation. They've been heavy sellers of the stock ever since the shares started to rise back last June.'

'What is the significance of that?'

'You don't know? Their director is Dr Ann Lester. She's Czinner's ex-wife and in the first place helped him build up the business. When she divorced him she picked up her medical career again and became a psychiatrist. The settlement left her with a big stake in Czinner's which she deeded to the Foundation.'

'Presumably, then, she's behind the selling?'

'Presumably. But the Foundation may be selling for quite

126

mundane reasons. They might want to reposition their portfolio, perhaps switch more funds into fixed interest paper or bonds.'

'What's your interest in all this, Mr French?' She was now remembering what Tommy had told her about how to make a bundle on a falling share price.

He said: 'There are four partners in our firm. We act as a team in the management of pension funds of some smaller West Midlands companies and we have the funds of one or two charities under management as well. Three of us are bulls of Czinner's stock. I'm bearish.'

'Meaning you expect the shares to go . . .' and Mitch turned her thumb down.

'It has to be more than sentiment. I have to give my partners good reasons for shifting their stance on the stock.'

'I don't know what you regard as good reason. Have you listened to the news on the radio?'

'Not since breakfast time.'

She shook her head. 'It wouldn't be on then. Too early. A body has been found in Mr Czinner's car-park. Crushed under a motorised roller.'

Willie French whistled softly. 'But I hardly think that Czinner would go in for a literal killing. He's far too sharp a chap. That's not his style at all. Do we know the identity of the victim?'

'It seems probable it was George Reeves. He worked in the Finance Department. His boss, Harry Vine, was called a Development Manager. But he was sacked a couple of months ago.'

'The Development Manager is the chap who looks at targets – you know, businesses which it might be worth while taking over. Czinner is basically a buyer and seller of companies.'

'It would appear that Reeves' wife was having an affair with Vine and I think the police's favourite theory to date is that she and her lover killed Reeves.'

'Would they be right?'

'It's on the cards.'

'But you don't really think so? What's your opinion?'

'One doesn't have one if one's new employer is Czinner.'

'Now you tell me!' He threw his hands up.

'Anything you've said will remain just between us. I think

127

being employed by Arno might turn out to be a Hansel and Gretel situation.'

'He's fattening you up for the pot?' He raised his eyebrows.

'I'm certainly going to keep all my options open.'

'While taking his money?'

'The eighties pretty well put paid to ethics, don't you think? Anyway, they were probably a device which helped the haves maintain the lion's share.'

'So speaks a post-Puritan!'

'So speaks a lady who hopes to keep paying BT, the water companies, the electricity companies and the Poll Tax Mark Two. Not to mention the mandarins, the Queen, the royal progeny–'

'Stop, stop, stop!' He put his hand up. 'I get the picture.'

'So I should hope.' But she was smiling. 'I can see you're too much of a gentleman to remind me you're picking up this particular bill. And I'm still prepared to do the decent thing. Now and again. If I stumble across anything that might be useful to you . . .'

'You'll give me a ring?'

'As long as it doesn't compromise the Mitchell and Orient Bureau.'

'I'd keep mum about my source. I promise you. And, of course, I might be able to help you untangle one or two of the financial aspects of what's going on – or has been going on.'

'That thought had occurred,' Mitch admitted. 'I, myself, have a feeling that a very nasty can of worms is about to be opened. Is that what you mean by sentiment? Market sentiment?'

'Exactly that. Thank you, Miss Mitchell.'

Half an hour later Mitch had arrived at the Central Library in Chamberlain Square. It was not a building you could overlook. She'd always thought that if you sliced a pyramid through the middle and then turned the bottom half upside down you had Birmingham's answer to housing civilisation's written record. She had often wondered how a psychologist would interpret such an edifice. It always gave her a wrong-way-up feeling, but once she'd refocused she usually found what she wanted within this slabby piece of reinforced concrete.

What she found out about the drug amiodarone amazed her.

When she got back to the office she found a note from A J Evans saying that she was going out to Chorley, the village where Toby Trubberman lived. There had been two calls for her. Daisy Sharpe had left the number of the television studios. Colin Bell asked if she could call at his house around four. He had something to tell her.

Who the hell was Colin Bell? she wondered as she picked up the phone. And then she remembered. The chap from the Glick Hope she'd had a drink with.

'I need to see you.' When she finally reached Daisy, the actress was very abrupt. 'My God, pet, I'm in a frightful rush. Listen, I've got to go over to the opposition's studios this evening to see someone. Can you meet me in the bar there about nine and drive me back to my flat? My car's in dock and I'm not sure it's going to be ready today. Someone wants to meet you.'

'Who?'

Daisy ignored the question. 'And we keep this strictly *entre nous*. Right?'

'But–'

'Can you make it?'

'Sure–'

'Must fly, darling. Things are happening. Ghastly things.'

Mitch put the phone down. She slid her rump off the side of the desk and strolled over to the window. Her hand strayed to thoughtfully stroke the papery frond of her palm.

A J came in five minutes later. She was wearing new ankle-length boots.

'They remind me of the dainty lace-up jobs Victorian females wore,' Mitch said, walking round the kid and admiring them.

'I can bend each one double in the palm of my hand,' A J said.

'What would you want to do that for?'

'It just shows you. They're so supple. It's like wearing a pair of gloves. They're brill.'

They made tea, reopened the packet of shortbread biscuits, and sat facing each other across Mitch's desk. Mitch had tilted her chair so far back it touched the wall. Her legs climbed up

129

in front of her, heels wedged comfortably over the lip of the desk. A J's legs were hooked over each side of the arms of her chair and swung back and forth like metronomes. One hand hung over her nose and every now and then she opened her mouth and fed herself a piece of biscuit. Mitch, who often found herself groping for understanding when with Tommy Hung – I know this man is not what he seems for he's a Chinaman, not an English gentleman – found herself totally comfortable in the presence of A J. Perhaps that's because I'm used to having a daughter around. There was a tearing in her heart as if a bit of it, but not too much, had caught on barbed wire. Cassie was in America and Mitch had not seen her for several months.

Do children ever grow out from under your skin? she wondered. Or does something of them always lie deep within the tissues in which they were conceived?

She really had to try harder with Tommy. After all, he had opened the doors of this new world for her. If only I could get a handle on him. He was like tasting some new and strange-looking food, she thought. Your eyes screw, your nose wrinkles, your mouth purses before you've even spooned the stuff from the plate on to your tongue.

Well, why not? You are what you eat.

She looked at the kid again, this time noticing she had a very efficient set of teeth. She looked as if she'd make short work of anything, however alien to her normal diet. 'Right. Let's get back to business.'

A J immediately realigned her body, well forward in the chair, elbows on Mitch's desk, propping up an eager head.

Mitch restrained the impulse to drop her chair back on to all four feet. After all, she was paying. She was boss.

How about that.

A boss for the first time in fifty years.

The boss.

130

14

'The Trubbermans certainly live well. They've a three-storey Georgian manor house called Job's Hall. It's built on the site of a medieval nunnery. A hundred yards from the house itself, on the east side, there's a massive square yard with all sorts of barns and stables round, including the nuns' dovecote. The driveway splits into three branches, one to the house, one to the stable area and one to Job's Church which is more or less parallel to the back of the north side of the stable block. It's an odd kind of set-up because although the church is small, the churchyard is not only large but crammed with graves. And yet Job's Hall and a farm are the only buildings near it. There is no village or anything, just smallholdings scattered in the fields and Chorley, which is a couple of miles away.

'Toby Trubberman bought the place two years ago. He seems quite well liked. His wife apparently comes it a bit strong at times – too much the squire's lady. They have one mongol kid. She doesn't live with them but at a home in Surrey.'

'Does Trubberman play around with other ladies?' asked Mitch.

'If he does, he's extremely discreet about it. At first sight the family seem respectable right the way through. She sings with the choir at Lichfield Cathedral and does a lot for charities. He helps organise the Lichfield Festival. They run with the dry sherry and claret set. Not the G and T mob,' A J said.

'That's a lifestyle which would cost a mint to set up and service.' Mitch nibbled her thumb. 'The trouble is I've no idea what a Finance Director can pull in. No doubt there'll be bonus shares and God knows what besides his salary. Czinner Enterprises is capitalised at just under three billion.'

A J's eyebrows began to lift.

'I know . . . I can't imagine anything over ten thousand,' said Mitch.

'A hundred crispies seems an enormous wodge to me! There was something I learned which could possibly have a connection. The landlord at the pub in Chorley told me there had been a break-in at the hall a few weeks ago. Toby Trubberman himself told him and said the police reckoned it was the work of kids. One or two items were stolen, but the only thing of any value was a silver art deco compact. It was on Mrs Trubberman's dressing-table, apparently. The point is, there are a lot of quite valuable antiques in the hall and none of them went.'

'Hence the theory about kids.'

A J nodded. 'Mrs Trubberman went off to see friends in the West Indies some time ago. Her husband is supposed to be joining her for a holiday at the end of the month.'

'After the rights issue, I suppose. That's good work, A J. Did you have time to get any stuff on Daisy Sharpe?'

'Your friend Mr Woodward filled me in on her background. By the way, he asks if you'll ring him later.'

'He wants to tell me how much it's going to cost me.'

A J looked at her in surprise.

'Not in money. Now he's retired from the *Birmingham Sentinel* he does stories for trade papers. Earns a bit extra on top of his pension. He gives me info. I give him a couple of little items he can follow up. That's how it works.'

'Well, it seems that Daisy Sharpe was born locally. Yardley. Her parents now live in a flat in Spain. She never managed to get into drama school. She started out as a model and then did some television commercial work. One of the ads she did apparently hit a nerve and her face became quite well known.

'There was a child, born with a heart defect. It died soon after birth.'

'The father?'

'Popularly believed to be Calvin Price, the director of the ad which set her on the road to a successful career. Daisy's never been married and she's never disclosed the name of her baby's father.'

'But it couldn't possibly be Arno Czinner?'

A J shook her head. 'She didn't even know him then. From there she went into summer shows at the seaside and then did a bit of rep before landing a part in *Motel*. After that, of course, she became a household name.'

'And the financier? How did he come into her life?'

'She actually met Arno Czinner – so Mr Woodward says – through his ex-wife. I suppose like many actresses she's asked to attend this and that charity's fête or whatever. Anyway, the West Midlands Choir put on a carol concert for the Glick Hope Foundation. And Dr Ann Lester, who is a director of the Foundation, introduced them. But Daisy's main fund-raising activities are for an organisation which builds homes for the street kids who are targets of the Squadra dei Morti – the death gangs in Brazil.'

'Hmm.' Mitch chewed her finger. 'So Arno and Dr Lester must still be friendly in spite of the divorce?'

'I thought you'd be interested in that but the only thing that Mr Woodward could tell me was that he usually turns up at their functions.'

'I suppose keeping an eye on Dr Lester is equivalent to keeping an eye on Czinner stock? She apparently deeded a chunk of it to the Foundation. A block of shares would have voting rights, I suppose. So it would be to his advantage to keep on friendly terms with his ex-wife if he could.'

'Anyway, according to Mr Woodward, Daisy and Dr Lester ended up becoming very good friends. He thought that most peculiar. It is a bit, don't you think?'

'Rather unhealthy, I'd say. But when it comes to their own lives I suppose psychiatrists make as much a botch of it as anyone else. What interests me are all these links we're finding between Czinner and the Foundation.' Mitch thought about it and sighed. 'You can bet your new boots that if those links are important in this case – and I think they must be – they'll be so in a quite unforeseeable way. At the moment complications are piling on complications. What can the Glick Hope have

133

to do with George Reeves being found under a roller? And yet he was a patient there – and that's quite apart from the Czinner-Daisy-Dr Lester connection. You've done a good day's work, A J.'

A J turned a little pink. 'Oh . . . well, thanks . . . I . . . well, it was marvellous. I love it. Finding out, I mean.'

'Now I'm off to see a chap called Colin Bell,' and she told her about the meeting on the snowy driveway of the Glick Hope.

'There is one thing . . .' said A J.

'Shoot.'

'I don't know. It keeps occurring to me. That roller. Not long ago the pavement was remade outside our house and one was used to flatten the tarmac. It made a terrific din. Surely if that thing were used in the middle of the night or something . . . someone must have heard it. Mustn't they?'

Mitch thought about it. 'The car-park's about a hundred yards from the entrance to Aston Clinton. There's a belt of shrubs in between. I don't know. You could ring Arno's secretary. She's supposed to be getting me a list of who was at Aston Clinton last Thursday night. You might ask her for a bedroom plan so we can see exactly where they were sleeping. And take it from there. But be wary, for God's sake. No tripping over the coppers' feet. Now, I really must fly. Tommy Hung might ring. If he does, get his number, will you? I'll be back before six to lock up. You don't mind hanging around until then, do you?'

'No problem,' A J said and began to clear up the cups and saucers.

Though it was a little before four in the afternoon when Mitch left the office, it was already getting dark. It had begun to rain quite heavily; even in Gas Street Basin there was now little sign of snow.

She collected her car and threaded her way through the beginnings of rush-hour traffic on to Bristol Road. Filtering left, she picked up Pershore Road and turned past the county cricket ground towards Moseley.

Colin Bell lived on the border with Kings Heath. The small Victorian terraced houses were shielded from pedestrians by four feet of garden – most of which was cellar grating – and low brick walls topped by coping stones. Some of the brickwork was so loose tufts of grass were growing through. Sweet papers and cartons had lodged behind the wall in Colin Bell's front garden. The original front door had been replaced in the 1960s by a new one, flush, with a plastic handle, now broken. In places the orange paint had worn through to the beige undercoat.

It was a woman who answered the door. Dirty blonde dreadlocks were threaded with shells and beads. She wore a stained ex-army surplus sweater ten sizes too big for her, a pair of black Lycra leggings, purple knee-length socks and canvas trainers with holes in their toes. There was an unfocused look about her rather prominent blue eyes. Mitch wondered if it were drug-induced.

As Mitch said her piece the woman scratched her crotch and then turned and went back down the hall and stood at the bottom of the stairs: 'Bug-a-lugs!' she yelled. 'There's a woman here!'

A baby began to cry in the kitchen. 'Belt up!' she shouted before looking up the stairs again. 'Shift that arse, you lazy sod! Col! Colin!'

A door banged upstairs. First Mitch saw stockinged feet and then the rest of Colin Bell came into view. 'Miss Mitchell! Come on up. My place is on the first floor.'

As Mitch passed the woman there was a sour smell which she only slowly realised was unwashed flesh. She recoiled slightly.

The woman, perhaps aware of this, yelled after them: 'Jesus! You'll be fucking the Queen-Mum-isn't-she-lovely next!'

The baby's cries grew louder.

'Shut it! You just shut it!' its mother screamed.

Colin opened the door on the landing and, much to Mitch's surprise, stood aside so she could go into the room first. 'Don't mind Rosalie. Actually, she's doing very well. Very well indeed,' and he nodded, agreeing with every word he said.

'Is she?'

'She's a New Age Traveller. But it's winter. They tend to hole up in winter.'

'Is this a squat?'

'Not really,' said Colin.

Mitch decided it might be wise not to go further into that. Colin's room, she noted, was clean and neat. The floorboards had been stripped and varnished and the walls covered in white chip paper. There was an old G-Plan put-you-up sofa, a matching chair, a badly stained teak coffee table, shelves, on one of which was a microwave, kettle, bread and some tins. On more shelves was a very expensive sound system and neat files of records and tapes. There was a word processor on a 1930s Tudor-style oak table under the window, surrounded by typescript, newspaper cuttings, paper clips and mugs of pencils. The space underneath was used to house piles of books.

'It's too cold in winter.'

'What?'

'To do much travelling,' Colin explained. 'Rosalie is a girl with many problems. But she's doing OK,' and he was nodding again. 'Oh yes. We can say that. She's doing just fine. Would you like some cocoa? Or I've got a bottle of elderflower wine. One of my friends makes it.'

'Cocoa, please.'

He switched on the kettle and measured cocoa into mugs. 'I'm going to tell you about something which was said at one of our group meetings. If it were known I'd told you they'd sling me out on my ear and quite rightly. I want your assurance that you'll let no one know where your information came from. OK?'

'OK.'

'I gave it some thought before I rang you. But then I kept thinking of the roller ... I've got to help nail that bastard. Poor George didn't deserve to end like that. It is his body, I suppose? They said on the radio he'd been missing since Thursday. It is true?'

She didn't answer him. He was swinging towards her, his moist green eyes widening a little.

The infant had gone quiet now.

He turned back to his cocoa-making. He said: 'Mike died.'

'Who?'

'Rosalie's man. Drugs.'

'Ah . . . yes.'

'She's coming through.'

They were silent. Mitch watched him pour boiling water into the mugs. 'The Travellers buried him under a rowan tree on Cannock Chase. They emptied a couple of drums of cayenne pepper over the grave. To keep off the dogs and foxes. They don't like society's normal method of disposing of bodies. Do you?'

'I don't care what they do with what remains after I'm dead. I always like to leave logistics to others.'

They both sat on the sofa. He put his mug on the coffee table. A ring of moisture began to form round it. She quelled the housewife's itch in her fingers; she mustn't snatch up the mug and stop another ring forming. Other people's stains were their own business. 'Of course, you never knew George,' he said.

'Everything by the rule book. He never looked beyond that,' Mitch said. 'That's what someone told me.'

'Right. An obsessional. He did his little exercises every morning. He left his toothpaste and brush unaligned. It almost killed him at first, he said. He had to force himself to turn his back on the mess and leave the bathroom.' He drank some more cocoa. A froth of milk stuck to a patch of beard to the left of his mouth.

'Did he get on well with other members of the group?'

'We're not there to get on well.'

That sounded daunting. Mitch said nothing.

'People who are good at numbers are often obsessional,' Colin told her. 'You'd be surprised. Of course, a need to have everything spot on – adding up correctly – is a good thing in a bank manager or an accountant. Wouldn't you say?'

He was prevaricating.

'Look, I was a journalist for years. I've never divulged my sources.'

He got up and wandered over to the table by the window. 'You used to do consumer investigations, right? For the telly?'

'That was years ago.'

He was reading some typescript. 'How do you spell pharmacist?'

'C-H-E-M-I-S-T. That way you keep them in their place and medicines stay cheaper.'

137

He laughed and put the page down. 'Have you come across a guy called Harry Vine? Talked to him, I mean?'

'George's ex-boss?' and she nodded.

'George and Harry went to school together.'

'I know.'

'Harry raped him.'

Mitch pursed her lips. No sound came. All the different pieces of the jigsaw were falling into new patterns.

'When I listened to the news at lunchtime the inference was that Harry and George's wife had done this awful thing and then run away together. It wasn't said. But that is the conclusion anyone would draw from the way the information was given. Harry Vine was a practising homosexual, according to George.'

'What about George?'

'The young George was a highly disturbed boy. Four or five months after it happened he chucked himself out of a second-storey window. It was while he was in a general hospital being patched up that he met Muriel, though, of course, they didn't marry for four or five years. She's three or four years older than him. He was transferred to a psychiatric hospital for a while and when he came out he and Muriel began seeing each other.'

'So he's not a homosexual? Then why did he go and work for Harry when they met up again all those years later?'

'Unfinished business? I mean, of course, of a sexual nature? The reason George gave the group was that he was over fifty when Jane and Jarrod was taken over. Who else was going to offer him a job?'

'No one else has even hinted at Harry Vine's being gay.'

'Apparently the Czinner outfit is very macho. Vine felt he had to keep quiet about his sexual preferences.'

'And yet he took George on . . .'

'If anything came to light, presumably Czinner would ditch the pair of them.'

'But working for Harry stirred up all George's old anxieties? Was he gay or not? Is that why he was having treatment at the Glick Hope?'

Colin Bell didn't answer.

'Did Harry again make sexual advances to George? I mean, while they were at Czinner's?'

'Harry apparently liked younger men.'

Mitch shook her head. 'After what happened you'd think they'd steer clear of each other.'

'Gavin reckoned that neither of them had worked it through. That's why they resumed the relationship.'

'Gavin?'

'Dr Gatting. Some of us thought that George was gay and still fancied Harry. But he was having difficulty facing up to this. I mean, he actually went to his doctor complaining about his vision – it wasn't that he didn't see the nose on the end of his face, he kept on seeing it!

'Another theory bandied around in the group was that he was heterosexual and had turned Muriel into some kind of monster so he could punish himself for what had happened.' He shook his head. 'I never believed that held water myself.'

'Is he gay or not?'

'I really don't know. But I do think there was someone else.'

'Just a feeling?'

'It was when one or two of the others were talking about their affairs. And George was asked outright if he had a bit on the side. Do you know, he went bright red?'

'But he didn't say who it was?'

'I think he might have. Eventually. Anyway, the point is that Harry is gay. And that being so it is hardly likely that he and Muriel are lovers, is it?'

'And yet it appears both of them *are* missing. It seems a bit much to suppose that at the same time they both took it into their heads to disappear.'

'Could they be dead? Like George?'

'If it is George's body under that roller. Even that hasn't yet been proved.'

15

Her winker was out and she was edging the car towards the crown of the road, preparing to turn right, when she saw the back of Freya Adcock's sky blue Ford Cortina half-way up the driveway to her house. She immediately knocked off the winker and stuck her boot into the accelerator. The car behind her, which was slipping lane to overtake her on the inside, hooted in fury. She showed the driver two fingers. They shot up over her left shoulder, well away from the bounce of her black curls. Her boot was now down so hard that the old TVR's rattle became a paroxysm of shudders.

She had recovered herself enough to ease up a little as she approached the university. This time she completed her right turn and climbed the hill towards the campus. What the hell's the matter with me, she wondered. That fratricidal bitch isn't barking away at my heels for one lousy tape recorder. She probably thinks that one of the casuals half-inched it. She wants to get hold of me for something else.

But what?

Got to be bad news, she thought, though her panic was subsiding a little. She remembered her last day at Radio Brum, Freya standing at the studio door, her carthorse of a figure crammed into a baby pink Laura Ashley dress with frills of lace round the scoop neckline, her size ten feet in those kiddy bar-strap sandals she'd got it into her head were arty. 'Don't think of it as your swan-song,' she advised Mitch. 'Go out on a high. Sock it out, kiddo.'

Mitch knew why she was there. Ready to pull the plug if Mitch got out of line. Freya knew that Mitch knew why she'd be in the ops room just beyond the studio glass. But they were both friendly and beaming away at each other.

Freya said: 'We'll never get another broadcaster with quite your attack. You had such a terrific sense of style.'

Mitch hadn't screamed: 'Well, why the hell are you firing me then!' like she should have, but carried right on beaming.

Now, when she recalled the scene, she remembered that Radio Brum's manager had used the past tense even before she'd opened the pots and started the show. She also thought of all the other times she'd been fired. People were always assuring her she was a genius before or even while they were issuing the order of the boot. There had to be something wrong somewhere. Hadn't there?

She was shaking her head as she pulled into the kerb. It was probably a reworking of the same instinct which rustles up the best breakfast in the world for a man who is about to be hanged.

But if Freya isn't after me for the leaving present I awarded myself when I left her damned station, what the hell does she want with me?

You did worry at one time that she fancied you, she remembered.

Oh, come on. You don't kick out the little bit of stuff you've got your eye on.

But that was the whole trouble with Freya, she thought. She could do anything. Just glimpses of what went on under that lid of baby-soft hair, all tricked out with plastic hair slides and ribbons, would liquidise any normal person's knees. As Woody, her retired journalist chum, had once said: 'She makes Medusa look like a big girl's blouse.'

Mitch was, though, aware of the dull ache which was not localised but part of the whole of her flesh. She missed her days in broadcasting. There. It was said at last. Better that it should be out in the open.

Well, the bitch must have turned tail by now. She reversed the car down an opening and turned for home.

And she can try as she likes. Her teeth were grinding together. She's not going to get that Uher out of me.

141

She didn't let herself even think: 'What's a broadcaster without a tape recorder?'

This time when she reached her house the coast was clear. But Freya had left her calling card. On the mat behind the front door was a memo dated a week ago which told staff that in future all expenses claims would be personally checked by her. Broadcasters could only charge for meals outside the building if they were engaged in authorised outside broadcasts. On the back was a scribbled note.

'That man of yours is useless. I'd get someone else to take your messages if I were you. I have a business proposition to put to you which should be right up your street. I've told my secretary to slot you in at nine tomorrow morning. Please ring and confirm. Cheers. Freya.'

Mitch ran a hand through her hair and then lifted a chunk of it on end. My God, she thought, astonished, she wants to employ the Mitchell and Orient Bureau. It was something which had never crossed her mind. Well, if the Bureau can work for a genetically improved rattlesnake it can work for that baby-faced Medusa. Beggars can't be choosers. She rang Jilly Jones, Freya's secretary, to confirm the appointment. Jilly rang back an hour later with a change of venue.

'Can you make it her flat, Mitch? There's been a hiccup. She's got to catch the ten thirty train to London.'

'Sure. Can you tell me what it's about?'

'Haven't a clue. All I know is she's been pretty foul-tempered about not being able to reach you before. Make sure you turn up or my life won't be worth living.'

Probably some poor devil she's fired is making menacing phone calls, she thought. Or sticking live rats through her letter box. Or has kidnapped that fearful cat of hers. She went upstairs to run the bath water. With some effort, she put Freya out of her mind. She needed to think about the case in hand. She'd only just climbed out of the bath and towelled herself dry when the phone rang.

'I've just sat down and opened the evening paper,' Josh Hadley told her. 'God Almighty. What a shock. I thought I'd better ring and see if you're OK.'

'That was nice of you. I'm fine. Honestly.'

'I hope you're not getting yourself tangled up in all this. It implies in the paper that the wife and lover are the chief suspects. But nothing remotely connected with Czinner is as it seems, Mitch. That man would make a corkscrew look like a railway line.'

'You think he's somehow involved?'

'Sure as eggs.'

'You could be right. But I can't see him leaving a mashed-up corpse practically on his front doorstep. Financially this is a very sensitive time for him. His fortunes literally depend on a good clean respectable image.'

'You go for this lovers-dun-it theory?'

'No.'

'If they didn't do it and Czinner didn't, who the hell did?'

'There are other players.'

'Do you think they got the wrong man? I mean, if anyone was going to get done in you'd think it would be Czinner.'

'Well, if it is George Reeves under that roller I think it will be one crime Czinner isn't guilty of. Even if it turns out that Czinner has a very good motive.'

'Listen . . .' He hesitated. 'Look, I know it's been . . . well, it's been some time. Would you care to have dinner with me? No strings. No . . . well, you know . . . just nice nosh, nice wine, nice chat. I've missed you.'

'You've a hell of a way of showing it.'

'Oh, come on. Don't hold grudges. Say Chez O? Next Monday at seven?'

'OK. As long as you promise to flirt a bit. I'm beginning to think I might have changed into a Dralon curtain. The ultimate in invisible background material.'

Josh laughed. 'You're about as invisible as a nude sitting on a traffic light. Cheer up. Life may not be easy but it can be a lot of fun. Anyway, it's no use getting the jitters now. You're more than half-way through your performance – and I, for one, think you're the hell of a good show.'

'Remind me to give you a cuddle.'

'Love to.'

'Listen, do you think you can get me an ancestor? We can't afford more than a hundred pounds.'

'I deal in Chippendale tables, poppet.'

'A picture, idiot. A portrait of a Victorian gentleman in his topcoat looking frightfully grim and full of sterling worth and respectability. Mutton-chop whiskers would be rather nice. And a top hat. He can hang in the Mitchell and Orient Bureau's reception area and be our founding father.' She was marshalling some of Tommy's thoughts. 'One really must have a pedigree, don't you think? Give the impression of coming from the right background. Being made of the proper stuff.'

'Are you crazy? You only set up shop a few days ago!'

'I shall have a little gold plaque under him. Col. H R H Mitchell and his dates. I don't quite know why his initials will be H R H. But to me they sound frightfully grand.'

'So I should think. His Royal Highness. Listen, are you winding me up?'

'Of course not. Tommy wants the bureau to be the height of respectability. Coming to us, he says, will be the same as going to your lawyer or your bank manager. If that's the image one wants to present to one's clients one must have a revered founder. Don't you think?'

'Oh, I see. You're winding poor old Tommy up!'

'You said it yourself.'

'What did I say?'

'One must have one's fun.'

'I didn't quite say that!'

'I don't know what you're getting so upright about. Tommy will love his ancestor. You see if I'm not right! The frame has to be one of those really heavy gilt jobs. Lots of substance. If people don't know the artist – and they certainly won't know this one – they'll judge the picture by its frame.'

'You shall have him.' Josh was laughing. 'If I have to turn this city upside down and inside out you'll have your ancestor. You might have to spend more than a ton.'

'No. I won't. Not if you're crafty.'

'I'm supposed to be crafty on my own account! Oh, all right. If it will cheer you up.'

144

'You'll find us just the ancestor we need. I'm sure of it.'

And Mitch, putting down the phone, began to smile to herself. A date, another client for Mitchell and Orient, and a respectable ancestor. Things really were looking up.

She finished dressing and was helping herself to an acceptably large gin when the bell went. The man on the step seemed much too big for the doorway. Mitch felt like the doll in dolly's house being peered at by someone's daddy.

'Miss Mitchell? I'm Superintendent Ball. May I come in?' and he was over the threshold and she was backing away as he was saying it. 'This is Sergeant Smith.'

In her former career as a broadcaster, Mitch had come across the likes of Superintendent Ball before. She dubbed them Testosterone Tommies. Though she was physically intimidated, backing off as the policeman pushed his way down her hall, still in full retreat when he took command of her sitting-room, she was mentally invigorated. As long as Testosterone Tommy had no access to instruments of torture, she felt pretty sure of being able to hold her own.

'Would you like a drink, Superintendent Ball? I'm having a gin.'

'No.'

'Would you care for a seat?' She sat down and waited until both policemen had settled themselves before she got up to collect her drink from the trolley. She crossed the room again and leaned against the side of her large Victorian mantelpiece.

The superintendent looked up at her.

She smiled as she looked down on him. 'What can I do for you?'

He had rather prominent blue eyes with a large amount of white showing, and this, she thought, explained why he appeared to glare. He took his time about unbuttoning his raincoat. The plaid wool lining showed. As he placed two heavy hands carefully on his knees she found herself left with the idea that he might place them elsewhere, probably round her neck. No doubt that was the impression he wanted to give her.

'Miss Mitchell, have you been in touch with your press contacts? I hear you were a broadcaster before you became a . . . an . . . I'm not sure how to describe you. How *would* you describe yourself, my dear?'

'Private investigator.'

'I see. Yes. Well. We've got us a private investigator here, Sergeant Smith. Let's hope, with all her experience, she'll be able to give us a tip or two. Eh?'

'Certainly, Inspector. I'll do all in my power to help you.'

'Superintendent, my dear. We must get our facts straight, mustn't we? The media seem to have taken it into their heads that Muriel Reeves and a laddie called Vine have run off together, leaving the body of hubby behind them.'

'I haven't been talking to them.'

'Who has?'

'I imagine it must be Mr Czinner. Or his press person. A company that large wouldn't motor along without lots of public relations people riding on the back bumper.'

'Why would he wish to put a story about like that, Miss Mitchell?'

Mitch was already finding his voice wearing; everything he said had an enormous weight. If he announced he was going to the lavatory, she felt it would sound like a trump on Judgement Day.

'I'm told Mr Czinner's firm is trying to raise five hundred million on the stock market. If he can find someone to blame for the corpse in his car-park he feels he can emerge with his credibility intact, which is tantamount in this case to getting his cash.'

'I understand Mr Czinner is employing you?'

'He is.'

'Why do *you* think he needs a private detective, Miss Mitchell?'

'You'll have to ask him that.'

'Why would Czinner get it into his head that Vine and Muriel Reeves have run off together?'

She gave him an edited version of what she'd found at Harry Vine's cottage. 'Have either of them turned up yet?'

'No.'

'Of course, you're looking for them.'

146

'Yes.'

Suddenly Mitch found her Nonconformist northern upbringing letting her down. It often – and unpredictably – reared its prissy head-prefect head. She was then pitchforked into doing the right thing even if that was likely to be very wrong for her own well-being. 'I've since heard it rumoured that Harry Vine's a homosexual.'

'Is that right?'

'I don't know for certain.'

'And which little birdie told you that?'

'You are going to have to make your own enquiries, Superintendent Ball. However, I'm told it is not common knowledge. The Czinner organisation has a very macho image and, of course, Vine worked for them up till a couple of months ago. You noticed, I'm sure? All those suits of armour and axes and things?'

'You are saying that Vine had very good reason to keep dark about his sexual preferences?'

'One would think so.'

'But you obviously believe your source? Who told you Vine was gay?'

'I'm very willing to help you, Superintendent, but–'

'May I remind you it's your duty, Miss Mitchell. This is an enquiry into a suspicious death.'

'But not yet a murder enquiry? I'm only asking you, Superintendent Ball, to consider the overall picture. During my years as a broadcaster I built up a very wide range of contacts in this city. People talk to me because they know I never reveal my sources. It would be a shame to make an issue of it because in the end, you know, you'll find I won't be able to accommodate you. Tell you, in fact, anything at all.'

Superintendent Ball rose, ostensibly to twitch back the curtain and look out of the window. He turned to her. Mitch could not pretend other than that he was very large, very intimidating and that he frightened the hell out of her. She even supposed this might be a good thing in a policeman. There was no doubt about it. You'd certainly feel safe if Superintendent Ball was on your side.

But he wasn't on hers.

She turned herself into a rock. Every surface of her was impervious. She wasn't going to be swept away.

'Well, well . . .' he said. 'We're going to play at being silly beggars, are we?'

Sergeant Smith coughed.

The superintendent sat down again. 'And what else have your sources been saying?'

'There is perhaps another piece of information you might find helpful,' and she told him about the bottle of pills in Harry Vine's kitchen. 'I think you'll find that he hasn't taken the pills with him.'

'What is all this leading up to?'

'The prescription was for a drug called amiodarone. It is quite often used in a condition called hypertrophic cardiomyopathy. It's a disease of the heart muscle which carries a significant risk of sudden death. Amiodarone is an antiarrhythmic drug. Of course, I don't know if Vine had this condition but in the circumstances one might want to check his medical records.'

'Harry Vine could drop dead at any time?'

'So it would seem.'

'And yet he didn't take his medicine with him when he left.'

'There is the fact, too, that in the first place it was Mrs Reeves who employed me to find her husband. Why would she do that if she'd killed him?'

'Hmm. Is there anything else?'

'I don't think so. I suppose there's no doubt it was George under the roller?'

'I don't know yet who the unfortunate man was. Or even if he was murdered. We don't know anything yet, Miss Mitchell, do we?'

His attitude towards her had changed and in such a way it made her even more wary. The overt aggression was gone. Now Testosterone Tommy was letting her pass through his lines into his camp; he was trying to fool her into believing that he thought her good enough to be his ally. It was a pretence, she felt sure; he was one of those men who knew all women to be inferior. They had none of the right bits.

She finished her gin, went over to the trolley, and poured herself another one. As they weren't drinking, she was aware that her act was aggressive.

'I don't even know why Mr Czinner is employing you.' He had come back to it. 'He's hardly short of detectives. Off-duty chaps have been pulled in by the dozen. He can hardly take a piss without falling over another Sherlock Holmes.'

'You'll simply have to ask him, Inspector Ball.'

'Superintendent. I shall expect your full co-operation, Miss Mitchell. And make absolutely sure you don't get under our feet, my dear. A private eye, eh? Well, well. I'd hardly call it a job for a girlie.' He shook his head. 'It's a nasty old world out there. You're liable to get your head stoved in. Scum. That's what we deal in. And they're all twice your size. If not more.'

'So are you, Mr Ball.'

'Ah. But we're on your side. The strong arm of the law, eh? Don't make a nuisance of yourself. We don't want things to get nasty between us, do we? There's a good girl.'

16

Mitch showed her security pass to the man on the gate. She should have surrendered it when she left Radio Brum but, thinking it might prove useful, had kept it. The guard waved her through and she parked her car behind the seven-storey broadcasting complex. Irregular blocks of light had turned it into a crossword puzzle in a shifty night sky.

The bar – sometimes discreetly referred to as 'the hospitality facility' – was not in the main building, but three minutes' walk away, across a footbridge and behind some trees. It seemed to have been built with the specific aim of discouraging any attempt to be merry or even sociable. The architecture had a lot in common with an aircraft hangar and the grey and blue décor could have been created for any airline; the whole impression was of being about to depart for other places. Now.

Mitch, in all her years as a broadcaster, had rarely used the place. She wondered at the ambiguity of an organisation which could spend hundreds of thousands of pounds providing a facility with the apparent intention of making sure it was never used.

About thirty people, some by force of circumstance, others blind to any of the surroundings they might ever find themselves in, arranged themselves about a space designed to take two hundred. All were looking a little liverish in the inhospitable lighting. Mitch spotted Digger Rooney talking to a man with a face like those twists of salt tucked into the crisp packets of her childhood. There was no sign of Daisy Sharpe.

She waved to Digger and then approached the barman. 'Ah. There's a message for you,' he said in answer to her question. 'Something's cropped up. A last-minute change of plan. She asked if you could meet her at ten o'clock. Her flat. I wrote it down . . .' He dived to the back of the till and produced a piece of paper. 'It's one of those blocks of flats in Gas Street Basin. We're not an answering service, you know. If you try this on again you'll be well out of luck.'

'It's really very kind of you. Let me buy you a drink. Mine's a gin and tonic.'

'I'll have it later,' he said and gave her no change from two pounds.

She retired to a table on the other side of the bar, sitting near a rubber plant for company. Seems to be my night for changed venues, and the thought brought Freya to mind again. Her head was filled with a vision of her ex-boss garrotted by some of the station's yellow leader tape. Not bad enough, she decided. Maybe fried alive on some nice naked wires? The trouble is, she thought gloomily, radio really *is* getting to be wire-less these days.

'You look truly ferocious. Not a pretty sight.' Digger Rooney had a gin and tonic and a double whisky in his hands. He put them on the table. 'Don't I need a drink. God protect us all from fucking farts of programme organisers.'

150

'That chap with a salt twist for a face? He's the new chap, is he?'

'I've just got to get out. Take today's show. I've six items on the menu. The only one he said he liked went down like a lead balloon. Some dick from the Town Hall talking about the conference centre. God, God, God . . .' and he drove fists into his eye sockets, but not too hard.

Well, thought Mitch, perhaps Freya made the right decision for me. After all, they do say there is only one job in life worth having. The boss's. And now I am a boss. 'You've got to ride with it. Your contract still has a few months to run, hasn't it?'

'Four months,' said Digger. 'After that . . .'

'You don't know for sure.'

'Anyway, I'm sorry I was so shitty on the phone this morning. Christ. I'd no sooner come in and he was getting up my jacksie. You know the scenario. The master boots the dog. The dog bites the cat's head off. But I've already made it up to you. I did send for that stuff on Czinner from News Information. But that will only be the garbage everyone else gets. So this afternoon I got hold of Brett Baker Brown. He used to write for the financial pages of the *Birmingham Sentinel*. He's doing the same for a national now.'

'I think I remember him. A tall skinny lad with a Black Country accent.'

'That was four years ago. He's shrunk his vocal chords and bought a couple of thousand-pound suits since then. God. Has he left me behind. And I looked like the go-goer when I first met him.'

'You're just feeling low tonight, Digger. You'll put it all back together again.'

'Will I?' He looked at her gloomily. 'Or have I reached *that* time in life?'

'What time?'

'You know it well. When you start to go backwards.' He sighed. 'I'm thirty-five next month. Anyway, that's enough whingeing for one day. Brett did tell me something which may come in useful, though it all happened about two years ago.

151

Czinner was rigging the stock market at the time. That's what Brett reckons.'

'Was he? How?'

'Listen, all the world knows I'm no financial genius. I can give you the gist. If you want the "t"s crossed and the "i"s dotted you'll have to get hold of Brett.'

'Finance always tends to give me a headache,' said Mitch, fortifying herself with a large sip of gin.

'Are you sitting comfortably? Well, here goes. There was a theory in the eighties that you could build up your business on the basis of debt because inflation would increase the value of your assets which would in the end reduce your debts.'

'Like house prices? You took out a mortgage to buy a house for forty thousand. Five years later you sold the house for eighty thousand and pocketed a profit of forty thousand?'

'Something like that, blossom. Though, of course, you have to take into the reckoning the money you pay back month by month to the building society. The interest you fork out.'

'God. You're right. One never thinks of that.'

'People like Brett do. When you think about things like that long enough you can afford thousand-pound suits. Where was I?'

'Losing me if you're not very careful,' Mitch warned.

'Sit up and keep paying attention then. Czinner was as keen an advocate as any of this theory. He bought businesses by the bucketful in the eighties – the last two at huge prices on the eve of the recession.'

'I know about those. Jane and Jarrod, the chocolate people and some huge engineering concern in the north.'

'The recession hit. Not enough money coming in to pay the interest on the Czinner debt mountain. He tries to sell a few companies to raise cash – but every other billionaire and his dog are doing the same thing. Prices of assets plummet. He actually does sell off one or two companies he bought at the beginning of the eighties for a tidy profit. But eventually that source of revenue dries up. The institutions, seeing his problems, begin to sell his shares. The effect of that is that his share price begins to drop. With me?'

'Hanging in there. You're remarkable. I never realised you knew your way around financial matters.'

'While you were learning about antiques from Josh Hadley, I . . .'

'You and Brett Baker Brown?'

'It was sweet while it lasted. Anyway, where were we? Oh, yes. Czinner's share price is tumbling because people believe his debts are larger than his assets. At that stage of the game Brett reckons Czinner's assets were worth around 1.6 billion and his debt 2.8 billion.'

'Think of the good a billion could have been doing. It's criminal.'

'If you're going to go all ideological on me I'm going to shut up. It's not like you. In the eighties it was greed that was *good*. Let's face it. We all like a bit of bunce in our pockets.'

'That's one way to look at a billion pounds, I suppose.'

Digger laughed. 'Don't let it worry you. You and me, kid, we'll always have pockets to let. Here comes the harder bit.'

'The rigging of the stock market?'

'The thing to *grasp* is that Czinner shares are being used as collateral against some of his huge debts. They are the securities against which the banks have lent the money. When the share price goes down and keeps on going down that security begins to evaporate. The banks clamour for more–'

'Which Czinner hasn't got?'

'What he must do at all costs is drive his share price back up. Otherwise it's curtains.'

'And that's what he does? And your friend Brett thinks he rigged the market to do it?'

'A series of huge share deals and put options are put into play. They effectively shored up the price of Czinner's shares. The banks no longer called for extra security. Czinner squeaked by and six months later his share price had stabilised.'

'That must have been when Mr Czinner got his reputation for walking on water. But the money must have come from somewhere.'

'There were all sorts of rumours at the time. It was even suggested at one point that Saddam Hussein provided the cash. At least two shell companies in Switzerland and some Liechtenstein foundations bought an estimated two hundred million pounds' worth of shares.'

'If he had access to huge funds why didn't he pay off his loans?'

'Two hundred million – and that is what the share support operation is estimated by Brett to have cost – is nothing compared to a total debt shortfall of a billion. Listen, you know I'm no financial genius. Here's Brett's number. If you need more, you ring him.'

'Actually, you've done marvellously well, Digger. My God. What a can of worms. I mean, doesn't any of this rigging business show up when company accounts are audited?'

'Creative accountancy seems to have been specially designed for crooks and con men as far as one can judge,' said Digger. 'At least that's Brett's opinion. He reckoned that the only danger signals investors get are external ones, like the chairman driving a Rolls with a personalised number plate or paying Lord Snowdon to take the photographs which appear in the company accounts. Winning the Business Brain of the Year Award is reckoned to be on a par with being given the Last Rites. Associates start choosing the coffin.'

'You're joking.'

'No. I'm not. The real laugh is it's true.'

'But there must be something in the balance sheet one could pick up on.'

'The language itself defends the entrance to many a black hole. Brett's favourite is "accumulated deficit on goodwill reserve".'

'A line like that could certainly put a whole nation to sleep. You do pick interesting lovers, Digger. I'd never thought of pillow talk in educational terms before. It gives night school a whole new meaning.'

'One has to do something when the fucking's over. Don't you find?'

'Chance would be a fine thing,' said Mitch. 'And chances start running short when you're pushing past fifty.'

'I've fifteen more years of getting stuck in? The trouble is, blossom, one can't be *abandoned* any more. Think of the risks.'

'Abandoned? You? Admit it, Digger. The only thing that has ever really seduced you is a sponge pudding.'

'I do have a weakness for them,' he admitted. 'And custard made the proper way. With eggs. However, sex has not been entirely without its moments.'

'I'm glad to hear it.'

'What the hell are you doing meeting Daisy Sharpe in a morgue like this? Don't look like that. I was ordering a round when Sunny behind the bar took the telephone call.'

'I'm not. I'm meeting her at her town flat. It's quite a coincidence. Her place in Gas Street Basin can't be far from our offices.'

'The opposition's television studios are only five minutes' walk from her. I remember her getting that flat. Not long after she landed the part in *Motel*. I couldn't believe her luck. She's worse at acting than me.'

'So you've said. More than once.'

'Believe me, I was pretty much the pits. Though when I was a kid I did look rather fetching in a pair of tights.'

'But her face had become known, Digger. There was that ad.'

'God, here I am, still plodding around in Toytown radio. What a week. We had this Human Resources bitch down from London. Do you know what she told me?' His bum started to rise off the fake leather seat. 'I'm getting to be chronologically challenged.'

'What's that?'

'Old.'

'If you're chronologically challenged already where does that leave me?'

'Not so much up shit creek as under it.'

They both laughed. 'You've got to face it, Digger. There's always been a bias against employing grown-ups in radio and television. It's a trade for kiddywinkies.'

'But what can I do? No one is going to employ me to do their detecting. And I'm not going back to summer fun shows at holiday camps. I'd rather my bones were used for fertiliser.'

'The last thing I wanted to be was a detective,' said Mitch.

155

'Now I'm beginning to think it rather suits me. It's like one of those awful dresses you see on a rack. You know you'll look terrible in it. But nothing else fits and in sheer desperation you try it on. And there you are, by God. Transformed.'

'The only thing I'm likely to be transformed into is a lavatory attendant in a men's bog.'

'One would think, Digger, for a chap like you that could be heaven.'

He looked at her and they both laughed. 'I am putting some feelers out for you.' She hadn't yet, but she promised herself she would do the first thing in the morning.

'Try all your connections,' he begged. 'Don't give up on me.'

'Of course I won't. By the way, you haven't come across a chap called Harry Vine?'

'In what connection?'

'I believe he could be part of your world. Until Christmas he was employed by Czinner.'

'Gay?'

'Yes.'

He frowned. 'Something rings a bell. In connection with that young actor?' He was asking himself. 'The guy who works on *Motel* with Daisy? Bit part.' He thought about it and shook his head. 'I've probably got my wires crossed.'

'Look, I'll buy you a second lunch at the Plough and Harrow if you come up with any information on that one. Don't look at me like that. You know you love being bribed. Especially by sponge puddings.'

They looked up as a man bawled: 'The negation of technology is not sought by its transcendence in the metatechnology of hi-tech! Nor the katatechnology of deconstruction! Jesus wept. The negation – the negation, listen, will you? You could learn something here! The negation happens by the mere displacement of the material by the conceptual!'

'If you're going to be horrid, Jason, I'm going! Now!' A blonde was jumping up from her chair. 'I've had it up to here! Meta kata balls to you!'

'I see the old place doesn't change,' Mitch said to Digger.

'I suppose it *is* high time I left the place and joined the real world,' sighed Digger. 'Though one isn't frightfully keen on becoming a grown-up. Not really really.'

17

Mitch walked out of the bar into a new world. Banks of mist had drifted into the city; the few remaining lights in the broadcasting complex were vaporising at the edges.

Just before getting into her TVR, she looked back at the building, her heart contracting a little. Leaving broadcasting had not been as easy as she'd made out to Digger. She'd spent many years of her life within those walls, working in television and network radio when she was younger and local radio just before she left. It was a strange thing. She'd never looked back when she'd left print journalism for broadcasting but now . . . now . . .

Why was it harder to put the past behind you when you got older? Too aware of all the things that can and do go wrong? Too aware of how much energy is burning away getting up the nerve, the damned cheek, to go out there and try to make it all happen? Too aware period, she told herself. Youth is as blind as a new-born kitten.

But I don't regret this change of career. Do I? Really?

When you come to the end of the line what can you do but get off the train? Look round at the terrain. See if you can get something new going for you.

Sighing, she climbed into the driver's seat. She turned the mirror towards her. She scanned her face and then began to wield her lipstick. To Mitch making up her face was always as decisive as strapping on a pair of six guns. Ready for action, she turned on the engine and moved into gear.

The mist thickened to fog as she took a short cut past the Accident Hospital. As she turned into Holliday Street she was down to twenty miles an hour. She parked the car at the bottom of Gas Street.

People, laughter and light tumbled out of THE BEST BAR NONE. Steps echoed in the yellowish gloom as youngsters clattered towards Broad Street. She turned down the passage which led into the basin. The fog oozed up out of the canal waters, sidling across towpaths, gathering about mooring posts. Puddle Dock, Daisy Sharpe's city base, was on the opposite side of the basin to Mitch's offices.

The footbridge rose greasily over dank water; she felt her foot slipping. Treading more cautiously, she headed down to the spar which divided the basin in two. No lights showed in the long boats tied up on each side of the brick walkway. The sweetish odour of alcohol drifted towards her as the doors of the pub on the far side of the basin opened and closed.

Reaching the apron of terrace before the doors, she turned towards the towpath and made her way past new buildings, their red, black and yellow Legoland porticoes and external stairs fuzzily illuminated in sodium lighting. Further down, towards a bend in the canal, were the Puddle Dock flats, earlier buildings with wrought-iron balconies stitched in large loops to chunky brickwork. Daisy Sharpe lived on the fourth floor, her balcony sheltered under the wings of a low pitched roof.

The wide entrance hall was covered in polished light and dark grey vinyl tiles. Fixed concrete planters were built under windows on either side of the ribbed glass doors. Rubber plants, looking as though they needed a good spray of starch, limped across ceiling tiles held in place by strips of steel. A man in a grey cardigan sat behind a plastic reception desk. He didn't look up from the pages of a racing pink as Mitch went over to a bank of lifts. There were more grey vinyl tiles in the upstairs corridors. Wrought-iron holders were lined with plastic tubs. Dusty fake leaves sprouted from moulded plastic stems; all trembled in twitching light. One of the fluorescent ceiling strips was faulty.

Mitch found number eighteen and rang the bell. There was no reply. She rang again and then looked at her watch. It was already four minutes past ten. She rang a third time and then leaned against the wall. From a flat further down the corridor she could hear the jabber of a television set.

Under her feet was the muted whine of a washing machine in spin mode.

It was fifteen minutes past ten and Mitch was thinking about pushing off when Daisy Sharpe, with a little wave, came down the corridor towards her. She was wearing a cream three-quarter length coat over black Lycra leggings; swaying along on high wedge-heeled shoes. Real diamonds glittered in her ears; real, Mitch deduced, because they were so small. There was something funny about her eyes and when she came nearer Mitch saw she'd lost one of her false eyelashes. Not only that, there was a smear of dirt running from cuff to elbow of her jacket and her hair was escaping from its pony tail. 'Darling. Such a fuck-up. You would not *believe* the day I've had. And now Ann is giving me the run around. Whisky. Whisky. Whisky. Otherwise I'll just curl up my fingers and scream! It's too bad of her. Oh fuckie fart!' She'd dropped her keys. Picking them up, she wrenched the door open. 'Make me a strong one. With soda. No ice. The trolley's in the lounge. I must check my answerphone. Oh God. Who could believe all this shit?' and she disappeared ahead of Mitch down a short corridor, tearing off her jacket as she went.

Mitch shut the door behind them and went into the lounge just in time to see Daisy disappearing into another room. She looked about for a drinks trolley. The room was cream; walls, carpet, leather seating and curtains. There was a black pop art rug by the sofa and, against the wall opposite, a 1920s amboyna art deco cupboard, the doors decorated with geometric designs outlined in ebony stringing. Above it was a 1930s Karoly Patko oil of hefty-thighed girls cavorting on a beach. There was no sign of the Glucks although Mitch was pretty sure they had been in the huge pink newspaper parcel the taxi driver had manhandled into his vehicle when Daisy left Aston Clinton.

She went across to the glass and chrome trolley and mixed Daisy a strong whisky and soda. She poured orange juice for herself. She'd already had too much gin that evening.

Daisy wasn't long and when she came back her hair had been reassembled and she was wearing the right number of eyelashes. 'There's no message from her. I really don't know

159

what to make of it, darling. Ann Lester – Dr Lester – asked me to arrange a meeting between the two of you at my flat. But first of all she wanted me to do a little sounding out . . . she wasn't sure if you were still working for Muriel Reeves. That was the first plan–'

'You are talking about the Dr Lester who is a director of Glick Hope? She was thinking of employing me?'

'Don't look so flabbergasted, darling. Why shouldn't she think of employing you?'

'You didn't know? This morning Arno Czinner asked me to work for him.'

'Arno! Well, he told me he wanted to keep you on ice until he'd time to pick your brains. My dear, he never employs women. At least, not above the rank of secretary. Not since he divorced Ann. How extraordinary. To do what, may I ask?'

'Surely you've been questioned by the police about the body in the car-park?'

'Yes, but Superintendent Thingy's dealing with all that, isn't he? Mr Super Dick. Why on earth would Arno employ you?'

'There could be other reasons,' Mitch admitted.

'Well, if you can work them out you really are in the same class as Sherlock Holmes,' Daisy Sharpe said, finished her whisky and poured herself a stronger one.

'But why did Ann Lester want to employ me?'

'As things stand, sweetie, it would hardly be politic to tell you that! What worries me is where the hell is she? As you'll have gathered, there was a change of plan. The garage did manage to have my car ready on time and something very urgent had cropped up I wanted to talk to Ann about. It was arranged I should collect her from her house when I left the studio – around half-past nine – and talk to her on the way over here.'

'Before I arrived at ten? You wanted to discuss your split with Czinner?'

'Not at all, darling. I'd made up my mind to do that months ago. It was nothing to do with him. If you must know, it was about something happening at work. It's been simmering for a few months and now it's come to the boil. I don't suppose it matters, really. One had one's plans all cut and dried in any case.' She stopped and looked at Mitch. 'The point is, when I got to Ann's the house was in darkness. No one was there. I know she said I was to pick her up there but all the same I went to the clinic just to make sure she wasn't there. She wasn't. I called again at her house on the way back. Still no joy. I've checked the answerphone. She's left no message.'

'You're getting worried?'

'It's quite unlike Ann. Absolutely out of character. She's a stickler. She would never let one down.'

'Anything could have cropped up.'

'But she hasn't left me a message. Look, I'll make no bones about it. I'm worried.'

'Why?'

'Oh come off it, darling. You must realise that if she was thinking of employing you she had a lot to worry about.'

'And Muriel and Harry Vine have already gone missing . . .' Mitch said, more to herself than Daisy Sharpe. 'We'd better ring the police.'

'Hang on a minute, sweetie. She could still turn up at any minute!'

'What do you suggest we do then?'

Daisy Sharpe drank her whisky while she thought about it. 'I'll tell you what. I'll check out her house again – have a talk to her neighbours. I know Violet who lives next door. Could you go down to the clinic? Check there again. There's that in-patient facility at the back. I never thought of asking there. I'll leave a key to the flat with Bill down on reception. Just in case she turns up while we're gone. If we get back here and . . .' She spread out her hands showing the emptiness between them. '. . . then we'll think of the police. We don't want to call them unless . . . God, what a mess. Where the hell can she *be*?'

'Why was Ann Lester thinking of employing me?'

'Well, she didn't elaborate to me. Something about money. It always is when it comes down to Arno.'

'Did she ask you to fix this meeting up before or after the body was discovered in Arno's car-park?'

'After. But what could that have to do with it?' Daisy was obviously considering this for the first time. 'Oh God. I've had such a day I've never had a moment to think, sweetie. All hell broke loose down at the studio. I know it doesn't matter. Not now. But I was so . . .' Tears had come into her eyes. She shook her head vigorously. 'No more of that. Look, you don't mind checking out the clinic do you?'

'You really are worried?'

'Yes.'

'OK.'

Daisy finished her drink. 'Where the hell did I put my coat?'

'You were pulling it off when you went to take the messages off your answerphone.'

'Where the hell is she?'

Not here, thought Mitch, as she drove into the deserted Glick Hope car-park thirty minutes later. She switched off the lights and climbed out of the TVR. The mist had cleared a little and moonlight flickered over the mansion's William and Mary gabling. The only lamp burning was under the classical Greek porticoed entrance. Then she realised it wasn't classical at all. The twin caryatids supporting the roof were not the Hellenistic figures she'd imagined them to be. Now they stood out from the darkened building, thrown into relief by the light shining behind them, she realised that what she'd taken for Grecian drapery was in fact mummy wrapping. Dual representatives of the Egyptian god Osiris, the weigher of souls who reigned over the kingdom of the dead, guarded the doorway to Glick Hope.

Mitch, staring at Osiris, Lord God of the Cemetery, felt whispers of cold thread through hairs of skin unsettled on bones.

The two figures, not so neatly wrapped up as they should have been, far too much muscle and vitality evident beneath their grave clothes, crystallised for her something she'd been denying since she'd discovered the remains under the roller.

She was terrified.

Now she admitted it she could feel her cold turning to sweat, was aware of a peculiar butterfly beat somewhere between her thighs. Her knees juddered together.

Drained, she leaned against the door of the TVR.

Perhaps, after all, Ann Lester was here.

She straightened up, pushing her way back through terror. She'd mastered it before she passed between the mirror images of the Lord God Osiris. She tried the double doors. They were securely locked. As she stepped back she almost walked into a plastic crate filled with empty milk bottles. She found herself clutching this everyday image to her, almost using it as a spell to guard her from the power of the gods set up here.

She turned and walked down the driveway to the Italianate tower at the west end of the mansion. As she rounded the corner she saw a car parked on the drive. It was pulled well into the wall, giving vehicles going to the in-patient facility behind the building plenty of room to manoeuvre. She tried the handles. The car was locked. Just in front of it, recessed into the wall of the tower, was an arched doorway.

Taking a small torch out of her handbag, she played the beam over the door. In the stonework above was a carving showing a star growing out of the roots of a tree. Mitch liked her motifs to be clear cut, knives, forks and cups of tea on motorway signs, stick ladies with skirts on over the appropriate lavatory. Life was quite mysterious enough without mumbo-jumbo.

The worst of it was how mumbo-jumbo kept making a fool of her. While reason discounted any such thing, she knew in her bones that the door to the tower would open. The torch beam began shuddering in nervous fingers.

The door wasn't even on the latch. It swung wide easily.

She shone the torch across the threshold. She could make out a Moorish tiled floor and part of a huge wrought-iron lantern.

She became aware that she was sniffing.

'I don't remember a smell,' she'd told Arno Czinner as he had leaned against other doors.

The tower was square, though the tiles shifting in the beam resolved themselves into a circular pattern. At their centre was a spiral staircase with stone tread and revolving wrought-iron banisters. On the far wall was another door which, she was sure, would lead into the main part of the building. A framed fire regulation notice was screwed to the back of it. She crossed the threshold. The click of her heels on the tiles brought her up short. She bent down, took off her shoes, and stuffed them into her handbag. She had taken two more steps when she heard it.

Heard what?

She looked up, snapping off the torch.

There was the noise of a branch soughing against stonework. The click of cooling or cold central heating piping.

Talking?

Not that . . . a mumble?

A groan?

No.

But there was somebody. She was sure. Up on the floor above her.

Somebody had heard her push open the door, heard the click of her heels, heard her switch off her torch.

One minute, two minutes, standing in the darkness, her heels not quite on the floor, paused for flight.

Corpses make noises after death, she found herself thinking. Corpses talk as gases escape and fan over their vocal chords.

Her mouth began to open; suddenly she was terrified she'd scream out. Marshalling her bones, she determinedly crossed the tiles and took hold of the banister. She drove herself up the stairs, quick, brisk steps. The loudest noise of all was made by her heart. She thought it would batter its way through her ribs.

She stepped off the stairway on to the first floor. Now her eyes were used to the dark she could make out a replica of the entrance below. Here, though, the door set into the far wall was ajar.

She found herself looking round. For a weapon? Her grip tightened on the strap of her handbag.

Itchy feet. An almost overwhelming desire to run for it. Teeth firmly clamped together, she directed those itchy feet across the tiles. She pushed the door open and peered into the gloom, head well forward, the bag with the shoes in almost crushed to the shape of a hammer. Sighing, she leaned back, making herself relax. She momentarily shut her eyes tight, a prayer, and switched on her torch again.

164

The beam illuminated the rim of a waste-paper basket, a sliver of green loose-weave curtaining, the leaf of a rubber plant, telephone wire, the side of a steel cabinet. The beam swept wider. Nothing appeared to be in disarray. All seemed as it should be.

A breathy noise. A bubbling.

The smell.

The beam swung wildly across the ceiling.

Someone's vomited, she thought, her nose still wrinkled.

Her heels were sinking back to the floor, the beam of her torch falling down shelves of books and files, coming to rest on a large Victorian partner's desk.

She wanted to speak. 'Hello?' but the word had got jammed. It did not matter how she moved her mouth. No sound came out.

There was another voice. Somewhere here. Very near. 'Ler . . .' it seemed to say. 'Ler . . .' Like wind in grasses.

Mitch, shoulder-blades hunched to protect the nape of her neck, advanced into the room. The beam was making darting forays. But, though it searched, all it found was perfect order.

'Wa-on-on-on . . .' sighed the voice.

The torch touched the wall of files on the desk, the rubber plant, the chair. Nothing. Nothing. Nothing.

'To . . .' the voice said now. 'Hur . . . Le-r-r-r . . .'

Mitch opened her mouth wider. But though the word 'Hello?' formed perfectly in her mind, even rose to turn the word into a question, her working lips could not announce it.

The smell, she realised, was coming from behind the desk. She had to rise almost on tiptoe to move round it. Her heels kept digging in.

Dr Ann Lester had been hit on the back of the head, perhaps as she'd stood up and turned round to reach for one of the files or books ranged on the shelves behind her. She'd not toppled over but had slid down on to her knees and then pitched forward. By the time her knees had hit the floor she had been unconscious, for she'd not put out her hands to protect her head. They'd fallen wide. She lay between the desk and the row of cupboards. There was a gluey patch of blood not far from her left ear. The blood

165

had soaked the tie on her georgette blouse and stained the top of the collar of her taupe suit but most of the mess around the head, Mitch realised, was vomit.

If it weren't for the angle of the head, the staining, the figure could have been that of a Moslim at prayer. Then Mitch noticed the woman's left leg. Below the knee it lay askew, black cuban-heeled shoe pointing inwards.

The head began to move a little, right cheek against the floor, sliding through the vomit. 'Tom.' The word was very clear.

Mitch carefully got down on her knees, training the beam on the mat of hair, moving some of it gently away from the doctor's left cheek. The blue eye was open but did not see Mitch. It twitched from vision to vision in a semi-conscious brain.

'You're going to be all right.' At last finding her voice, amazed at how calm it sounded. 'I'm going to ring for an ambulance.'

Had she heard?

The eye did not see her.

Dropping her bag and torch on the table, Mitch reached for the telephone. When she started dialling 999 she saw the torch beam was falling across Dr Lester's appointment book. The day's list of names ended at seven o'clock. The last appointment – Tom Lerner – had a long doodle attached to the second 'r'. It looked like a pound note on legs. Legs flying so fast, Mitch thought, would have won a gold medal at the Olympics.

18

Freya Adcock lived in a block of flats ten minutes from Mitch's house. It was a flat-roofed art deco building which crooned thir- ties tunes; do-wah-di-do-wa-a-ah, black patent leather shadows high-stepping across steamship windows.

Freya sang a tune to her own devising. She was presum- ably naked behind a not-quite-closed bathroom door which was wreathed in mists of heavily scented shampoo and bath oils.

'Bugger-roo, bugger-r-r-ooo,
What can a jolly girl do!
One was frightfully naughty-eee
Stuffed out of sight
By a big boy in blue jeans
All through the night . . .'

Much splashing and soaping and the buzz of a razor. Hopefully used under arms, Mitch thought, not on the chin.

'Oh don't deceive me,
Oh never leave me,
How could you yooo-oo-use a poor maiden so!'

The whir of a hairdrier. Some slapping of flesh.

Mitch had been let into the flat by Jilly, Freya's secretary, who was on her way out, two files and three boxes of taped programmes clutched to her chest. 'Long time no see,' she shouted after her as she skimmed down the corridor on purple wedge-heeled shoes. Mitch, entering Freya's lounge, found herself studiously ignored by a magnificent Persian cat, its smell pungently working through all Freya's odours. It was sitting in one of the brown corduroy armchairs languidly licking its clitoris.

Mitch had the slightly crazy idea that the cat was called Mummy, named for the cats either drawn on the walls or entombed in graves by ancient Egyptians. Later she'd thought that she'd been so drunk when Freya had told her this that she'd got it wrong.

She had always believed she had to be at the top of her form to cope with Freya. This morning, after a terrible night playing a game of the cop and the criminal with Superintendent Ball, she felt like the dish-cloth which is so revoltingly grubby and greasy and holey you can't even use it as a floor-cloth.

'Been up since six. We had a live two-way with Birmingham in America. Sorry about this. But I needed a jolly good sluice before getting the train to London.' Freya, pink-chopped, her baby-soft hair gleaming, seemed, a buoyant balloon bundled in candy-striped candlewick dressing-gown, to levitate through the bathroom door. 'My dear, you can't believe how hard I've been fighting on your behalf. Coffee, yes? Half a mo.' She shouted from the kitchen. 'Such terrific talent. One simply said. No way. Absolutely not. I can't lose her.'

Mitch's mind snagged on the words 'terrific talent' and reran them two or three times, letting them feed her flesh. Logic, however, warned her there was something extremely fishy afoot. Mitch was not a modest woman. She knew she was a damn good broadcaster. She also knew that she wasn't Freya's kind of broadcaster, not jolly-jolly enough, not straight-down-the-line enough; half a dozen nots. She got this far before actually realising that Freya wanted her back at the station. No sooner had she quickened with delight than she saw Tommy Hung signing the cheque for the Italian chairs she'd bought for her office. No. She couldn't let him down.

All this before Freya said: 'I'm getting ahead of myself. You don't know what I'm talking about! I've got the organisation to agree to take you back. Isn't that wonderful?' She had reappeared with a tray of coffee.

Mitch found herself smiling and glowing because of course she believed Freya and of course she was the best broadcaster this side of Baghdad. Looking for confirmation, she probed Freya's eyes. They were a picture of play up, play up and play the game house-captain sincerity. It came shining through the truest of blue. Who could disbelieve Radio Brum's station manager?

'I've got the organisation to take you back,' Freya had said. The organisation encompassed television channels, radio stations galore, not forgetting publishing interests. It employed thousands of people, very few of whom, outside Radio Brum, would know of Mitch's existence. Those who did had probably sacked her at some time in the past. There was the fact, too, that the radio station managers could hire and fire whoever they liked. All they had to adhere to was a budget. In other words, Freya herself had decided to fire Mitch. And now she'd decided to rehire her. Mitch looked again into all that lying true blue and wondered: Just what the hell is going on?

'Sugar? No? Quite right. If we're not careful we'll get that six months preggers look, won't we? Well, my dear. What do you say? Isn't it great news?'

'I can't work for you, Freya. My partner has ploughed thousands of pounds into our agency. I can't let him down.'

'That's very worthy. And so typical of you, Mitch. You are so loyal, aren't you? But in this day and age one has to think of oneself, doesn't one? I mean, you are a broadcaster, Mitch. Very few have your God-given talents.'

By now Mitch despaired of controlling her ever-rising eyebrows. 'Actually, if I work at it I think I might make a reasonable detective.'

'Don't be ridiculous. What do you know about it? Besides, it's such a sordid keyhole sort of job. You are better than that. And you deserve better than that. I think I can say we can increase your salary by a couple of thousand. But no more than that. These are straitened times.'

'So straitened I hear that there are going to be more cuts at the station. More jobs are going to go.'

'That really need not concern you, Mitch. Weaker brethren will always fall by the wayside. But what one must do, no matter what the cost, is to keep one's top talent.'

'This is all very flattering, Freya. But I've got to say no. As I've told you, Tommy Hung has sunk his all into our venture. I can't let him down. I've no intention of doing it.' Mitch rose.

Freya rose.

The Persian cat rose.

Mitch, alarmed, sniffed battle in the air. But all Freya said was: 'I think you'll find we can come to some arrangement. Even if it means you only working at the station part time. Say two shows a week and a day setting up. Let me think about it and then I'll give you a ring. I really don't want to lose you, Mitch.'

'Could I be tempted?' Mitch wondered aloud, suddenly curious. Just how far would Freya go? 'For the right kind of money.'

'I don't have to remind you, Mitch, that Radio Brum is a local station. We have very little to play with. Less, in fact, this year . . . but, well . . . we'll see. We'll see what we can put together.'

169

Mitch was slowly shaking her head. 'Surely everyone only has one swan-song. If I remember rightly, I've sung mine.'

'Rubbish. We'll get you tuned up in no time. You're a performer. My dear, you'll be broadcasting from your death-bed.'

The Persian cat had leapt from the arm of the chair on to Freya's shoulder. Mitch was perfectly sure that cats couldn't wink. She was also sure this one did.

It wasn't until Freya had shut the door behind her that she realised how unsteady she was. Terrific talent. God-given talent. Can't lose you. No wonder she'd gone weak at the knees. She was in a state of shock.

Of course you're a genius. You know that.

The trouble is, honeypot, nobody else knows it. This is our secret, right?

At last someone else has recognised it. Freya has tumbled.

If you believe *that* you are ready for the funny farm. Three months ago Freya thought so much of your abilities as a broadcaster that she fired you.

By this time the lift she'd got into had brought her down to the ground floor with a jolt. As she got out she saw her ex-assistant Shaun O'Neill hoofing across a white marble expanse of flooring towards her. He'd changed his hair-style. Now it was parted down the middle, cut to fall across his brow. He looked like an escapee from the cast of a *Great Gatsby* remake. He tapped the bag slung over his shoulder: 'In there,' he told her, 'is my first step on the road to fame. *Birmingham Brass*. How about that? A one-hour documentary Freya's taking down to London with her. Possible AMTRAM award contender. Really dramatic stuff.'

'Brass bands?'

'Brass. Tarts. Balsall Heath prossies. Do you know you can have it away for a tenner? Cheaper than a night out ten-pin bowling. All right. All right. Take that concerned mother hen look off your face. I haven't tasted the samples. How are you? You look cream-crackered.'

'Had a hard night.' While Shaun had been talking Mitch had been doing some deciding. She couldn't discuss with Digger Freya's extraordinary offer. His love of tittle-tattling outweighed all ties of friendship. Digger had arrived at Radio

Brum from an acting background where gossip really was meat and drink. Could there be an actor able to think of getting out of bed before reaching for the telephone? She seriously doubted it. Shaun, though, came from journalism. Information was bundled up in pound signs, only worth something as long as no one else knew.

All the same she warned him: 'Keep this under your hat,' before she told him.

'Of course it could be that she does think I've got all this terrific talent.'

Shaun did not waste so much as a second on that line of thought. 'It's a facer,' he said.

'She's gone off her rocker?'

'That presupposes she was sane to start with. Not on,' and he shook his head.

'What could be behind it then? Why is she doing handstands to get me back on her broadcasting team?'

For once, Mitch was sure, he had banished all the multi-track sexual fantasies which usually cluttered his mind. He was bringing his undivided attention to the problem. 'It's extra-ordinary,' he said.

'I know that.' She was starting to get impatient with him.

'On the other hand . . .' and suddenly he'd started smiling.

'You've thought of something?'

'A possibility.'

'What?'

'Calm down. I might be barking up the wrong tree. I probably am. But . . . well, who knows?'

'Shaun!'

'No use wailing. Look, I'll make one or two discreet enquiries. If I'm right I'll give you a ring. Sorry. Got to dash. Wish my tarts luck! Prize-winning material. You'll see. You bet!' He dived through lift doors just as they were about to shut.

What kind of skulduggery would impel Freya to try and rehire her? What connections was Shaun making? She shook her head. She was all out of ideas. Sighing, she made her way back to her car and ten minutes later had run into more trouble.

'I really didn't mean to open it!' A J was wailing. Mitch

had hardly crossed the threshold of her office in the Gas Street Basin.

'Open what?'

'How could I miss it? It's stamped all over it.'

'What?'

'Private. Confidential. In big blue letters. On the front of the envelope. What will Tommy say?'

'A letter to Tommy? You'd better give it me.'

The letter was from Tommy Hung's bank. It confirmed a loan of fifty thousand pounds. The security was his flat. Mitch only just managed to stop herself groaning out loud. Oh Tommy, Tommy, she thought and had to turn her head from A J for fear the girl would see the tears which suddenly swam into her vision. No skulduggery here. Tommy Hung really did have faith in her talents. As a detective. He was putting everything he had on the line for her.

I can't let him do this. I've got to sell my house. I've got to put up some cash myself. My God. Fifty thousand pounds. Oh Lord. I'm going to cry.

The first thing I've got to do is get this agency off the ground. Stop playing nursery games with Radio Brum's Miss Fee Fi Fo Fum. She had straightened her shoulders, blinked away her tears.

'This is what we're going to do.' She put Tommy's letter in her handbag. 'It never came. Right? It simply got mislaid in the post. Tommy is bound to check with his bank when he gets back from Great Yarmouth.' She put her finger to her lips. 'Sealed. OK? And for God's sake be more careful in future. Leave the rest of the post for now. We've got work to do. But first I better bring you up to date on what happened last night.'

When she finished, A J asked: 'Did Superintendent Ball think you were telling the truth?'

'Well, he eventually let me out of his police station. Though not before six this morning.'

'How is Dr Lester?'

'Fractured skull.'

'Who is this Tom Lerner? This seven o'clock appointment of hers?'

172

'I expect Superintendent Ball already knows. But he can take short cuts. Anyway, I want you to track him down for me. I have an appointment at eleven o'clock with Arno Czinner. His secretary rang just before I left home.'

'Where would I begin? I mean with Lerner?'

'There's always the telephone directory. But first you might try Woody. Get him to raid the morgue at the *Birmingham Sentinel*. See if there's anything on the files. He might be a notable. He might even be a notable and a patient.'

'You don't think Daisy could have hit her? I mean, Daisy even told you she'd gone to the clinic. When it comes to opportunity she's in pole position. I mean, I know she said she went in search of Dr Lester but–'

'I have thought about it. But why would she do it? Where's the motive? You told me yourself that they were friends. Mind you, I *am* pretty sure that Daisy is up to something and has been planning it for a long time. There seems to be some tie-up with George Reeves. They were seen in George's pub together. But it can't be a lovers' thing, can it? Not if he was gay.'

'We are sure that George is dead?'

'No. And if both he and Muriel are still alive it would seem likely to me that neither are still in the country. Hopped it with a swag bag would be my guess. Anyway, the police seem unable to trace them.'

'You would have thought the police would have identified that body by now.'

'It can't be that easy. There wouldn't be much more than human porridge.'

A J shuddered. 'Whoever it was must have been dead. I mean, before they were put un – well, you know . . .'

Mitch was silent.

'Of course, Arno Czinner–'

'If George took his money Arno could have killed him. But we can't overlook the timing in this case. The body under the roller came to light just as that little wanker is getting his rights issue off the ground. He needs all the investor confidence he can drum up. What he doesn't need is a bizarrely mashed corpse a few yards from his front door.'

173

'I suppose it was Arno who gave the press the Harry Vine-Muriel lovers-dun-it story. An exercise in damage limitation. Is his whole empire a lot dodgier than the City thinks? Is that why the Glick Hope have been selling his shares? Does Dr Ann Lester know or suspect something and was that why she wished to employ us? Did someone hope to shut her up last night? Perhaps permanently?'

'Hmm. Well, that's certainly a possibility. I must get my skates on. Besides finding Lerner for me I want you to get hold of as much as you can on Harry Vine's health. I want to know if he's been ill recently. Personnel at Aston Clinton should help you there. Right. If you could get on with – Oh hell,' Mitch groaned as the phone rang.

A J lifted the receiver and after listening gave it to Mitch: 'It's a chap called Mr Rooney.' She picked up the pile of post she'd opened before leaving the office.

Mitch glanced across at her handbag. Fifty thousand pounds. Oh Tommy. Oh, what an old fool you are.

19

'I've got to get out of this Mickey Mouse hole! Mitch! You promised me . . .'

What had she promised? 'Ah . . . yes. I . . . right. Oh yes . . . I haven't had time to put out any feelers yet. I–'

'Post-disco bouncy house.'

'What?'

'That's what the arsehole wants me to play on my show.'

'What's that?'

'Politically correct toons for tots. You know. "Rubbers For Lovers". Anti-Aids techno-soul bass lines with funky horn and bumper sticker raga. And a bit of sitar.'

'Yuk.'

'Tweakie and the Trills' "Spray Away The Ozone, Folks". Scalping strings, a lot of Indian percussion. What are my

174

Brummie housewives going to think of that? I daren't even ask for requests because our "Sound Of Music" disc has worn out. This new programme organiser Freya has landed us with is away to lunch, dinner and tea.'

'Look, when I have a moment–'

'Oh, I get it.'

'No. You don't–'

'Too busy playing detective to–'

'Will you shut up, Digger! I'll ring round all my contacts. I promise you. If there's a bloody arts job going in this city you'll hear about it in the next twenty-four hours.'

'Terrific! You'd be going off your rocker too if you had to deal with this front office dick. Jesus. It almost gives one a fellow feeling for Daisy–'

'Daisy?'

'I heard in the bar after you'd trotted. This new producer guy over at *Motel* . . . you know him. He used to do the gardening quiz here before he went across the road . . . the one with the simply astonishing bum. Of course, they say it was his tail-end that got him the job. But they would, wouldn't they? Anyway, he was brought in to jack up the ratings. If he's been jacking up anything else he's been very discreet about it–'

'Daisy's got the chop?'

'Been on the cards for some time, so I hear. Came to a head this week. Lots and lots of nasty-pasties on the *Motel* set yesterday.'

'She never said a word.'

'My dear, I should think not. No doubt her agent is already in negotiations with one of the tabloid Sundays. She and that face-aching kid who is going out with Sharon's brother and having it away with the manager. Both out. That's what a little birdie told me. And the Queen Bee herself might go–'

'Digger, I never watch *Motel*. I've no idea who–'

'Nor do I. Awful load of cobblers. Look, sweetie, when you do your ringing round for me don't let anyone know my real age. I'm twenty-nine. OK?'

'They'll never believe that when they see you.'

'You were letting people think you were forty when you were

celebrating your fiftieth and there was enough flesh dropping off your jaw to start an avalanche.'

'There are times, Digger Rooney, when I don't love you!' She slammed the phone down.

Ten minutes later she was driving north over Spaghetti Junction, noting the HP sauce bottle chimney to her right, the turrets of Aston Hall to her left; taking her bearings. She certainly needed to after what had happened in the past twelve hours.

Threading her way down to the Tyburn Road, filtering right and taking the A38 out towards Derby, TVR sidelights switched on even though it was now almost half-past ten in the morning. Stretching her spine, easing her shoulders back.

The rain began just beyond Minworth junction.

'But it was you? You did it? Didn't you? It was you?' The insistent voice asking, asking, asking; one o'clock drifting into two o'clock and then three o'clock, all this time the doggie eyes got larger. How he pleaded . . . a morsel, a morsel . . . even half a crumb . . . I need . . . I need . . . I need . . . became her need, to feed that terrible hunger which resided in the massive frame of Detective Superintendent Ball. His need was so great she was practically reduced to tears. The poor, poor, creature . . . I must do something for him . . .

And yet not only did she know she'd not hit Dr Ann Lester over the head, she knew he knew.

If she let herself respond to this man's catastrophic need, let pity and charity sway her good sense, she would find herself charged with grievous bodily harm.

He would happily see her standing in dock.

Even though this was a first offence, she might get sent down.

He'd be happy to see her go to prison.

Dizzy with fatigue, she looked over the deal table and up at him.

She didn't say a word. Nothing for the tape to record in that bare interview room. They were so close now, she and Testosterone Tommy, she could tell him anything without even opening her mouth.

You're wasting your time.

He got his sergeant to switch off the tape recorder.

When she got up she could feel the clothes sticking to her back.

'We'll talk again,' he promised her.

But she knew they wouldn't and she smiled at him.

He knew they wouldn't and he smiled back.

At that moment they understood each other better than any pair of lovers could.

He'd almost, Mitch realised now, brought her to the point where she'd have been happy to confess to something she didn't do.

She shook her head, now feeling disbelief at what she knew to be true.

Your jaw-line may be uncertain, Mitch Mitchell, but you did well in that room. You did OK there.

Can I say it?

I'm proud of you.

Do, do say it, she urged herself. I need to feel good. I've got to be good to solve this case. *Tommy Hung is putting everything on the line for me.* She shook her head in bewildered astonishment.

The car-park at Aston Clinton had been closed off with blue and white tape. A heavy-duty polythene tentlike construction shrouded part of it; rain bounced and rolled off the plastic, puddling tarmac. The police had stationed a caravan by the main door; Mitch could see that lights and a temporary telephone line had been installed.

Why hadn't they used a room indoors? Perhaps the police had, on closer acquaintance with Arno Czinner, felt that it wouldn't be safe to set up an information post in his lair.

She followed the arrows and parked her car on turf at the back of the building. She checked her make-up, straightened her short red skirt, smoothed her bow tie and climbed out of the driver's seat. Her heels sank through the soft turf.

She eased up on to her toes until they unplugged with a pop, and tiptoed across the turf to the gravel. On firmer ground, she walked briskly round to the front entrance, passing the suits of articulated plate armour as she climbed the steps to the hall.

The doe-eyed receptionist told her that Mr Czinner was engaged. Would she wait?

Mitch waited. She then asked the receptionist for some paper, pulled her chair nearer the log fire, and made herself at home. Marshalling her thoughts, she started at the beginning of the case, making notes on her interview with Muriel Reeves and then moving on.

An hour later she had reached the events of the previous evening. She was so absorbed in her analysis that she didn't hear anyone approach.

'Miss Mitchell? Mr Czinner can squeeze you in now.' It was Adrian Cain, looking, Mitch thought, surprisingly fetching in his boxy butch suit. 'He's sorry to have kept you waiting.'

Mitch said nothing but did not hurry as she followed the young man to the lift.

'Hi, Miss M.' He was in his private suite, snug in terracotta walls, reclining in one of the kelim-covered armchairs. He didn't get up or offer her a seat. He didn't offer her a drink either, just giving her the ghost of a salute as he drank his.

She saw how it was. She was bought now. His creature.

She went and sat down on the kelim-covered armchair opposite him, saying nothing. What does five thousand pounds buy? It was a question she'd certainly have to answer before she grew any older.

'I want your version of what happened last night. I've heard what the coppers have to say.'

'You have been in touch with Daisy?'

'Nope.' Czinner looked at her. His eyes were like nails, hammered so far back into his head they'd almost disappeared. 'Daisy's fucking me around, Miss M.'

She told him about last night.

'Now stop the frigging BBC news bulletin and give me the juice.'

'The juice is you.'

'What the hell do you mean by that?'

'Glick Hope, so I'm told, have been unloading your shares

by the bucketful. You don't have to understand the finer points of finance to realise that if they continue to do so while you're trying to get away a rights issue your share price might fall below the issue price. And there's the separate question of whether Glick Hope are going to take up their rights. Are they going to buy any of the new shares on offer? Hardly likely, one would suppose, if they have been such heavy sellers.'

'You've told Ball this load of shit?'

'No. But I'm sure he's dug out the information and worked it all out for himself. One would like to think he was stupid, but I don't believe he is.'

'And your theory, I take it, is that I got someone to hit my ex-wife over the head?'

'Did you?'

'Listen, you bitch, I'm paying you and don't you forget it. If you suggest any of this to anyone–'

'Actually, Ball suggested I'd done it. His theory seemed to be I'd been employed by you specifically for that purpose.'

'The man's an arsehole. I mean, the place is a bloody nut-house, for God's sake. It's full of Jesus Christs duffing up Satan. Am I right?'

'I expect the police will take a look at that angle.'

'They'd better. Did Ball tell you the remains in the car-park weren't George Reeves'?'

'Not?'

'That little shit chucked himself out of a two-storey window when he was a kid. Suicide my foot. If you really want to top yourself you go out of a fourth-floor window. Am I right? Anyway, beside breaking a goddamn bundle of bones Reeves chipped the end of the little finger on his right hand. OK.'

Mitch nodded.

'Apparently the blood group was the same as George's. But when they went through Reeves' medical records they came up with this early suicide bid and the chipped finger bone. That out there . . .' he waved his glass in the direction of the window, 'has perfect pinkie bones. Do you know, after they put Reeves back together they decanted the big girl's blouse into a psychiatric hospital?'

179

'So who is under the roller?'

'I don't give a shit. What I want to know is where George Reeves is.'

'Muriel? Was the body male?'

'Male. Dead over a week.'

'But George Reeves is the only one who's been missing over a week.'

'Well, you're supposed to be the detective, Miss M. You work it out. Give me a bell when you've solved it.'

'Not if you're going to keep me waiting over an hour. No way.'

He didn't appear to hear her. 'I got to think,' he said, his eyes so submerged now Mitch thought he'd never be able to dig them back out of his head. 'Piss off.'

Mitch headed straight back for Birmingham. She thought she'd have a light lunch and then get her head down for an hour or two. Later she hoped to corner Tom Lerner, the man listed as Dr Lester's last appointment in her diary. She would have liked to use the drive to mentally review the notes she had made while waiting for Arno Czinner to see her but she was by now stupid with tiredness. But what she would do when she reached home was get in touch with Tommy. He didn't even know she was spending yet more of his money by employing A J Evans. Tommy, the fifty-thousand-pound loan, all this needed thinking about, too. She yawned. Not at the moment.

She tracked Tommy down in the restaurant at the hotel where he was staying. 'Hello, partner,' she said and for the first time meant it. She was still fazed by the fact that he was putting every last red cent into their business venture. Pouring his all into what had seemed to her, until she'd read that letter from his bank, some kind of half-crazy dream.

But losing the roof over your head is real. Oh Tommy. Why did you do it? She was suddenly brought to the verge of panic. What if it doesn't work?

Tommy was asking about her investigation. She swallowed hard, shifted her arm to more easily cradle the telephone and told him. 'The trouble is there are so many lines. So many angles one could follow.'

'The thing to do, my dear, is keep money firmly in mind. Think of that Greek chappie who successfully negotiated the labyrinth with his thread.'

'The thread being the loot? But we must talk about you, Tommy. How's your investigation going?'

He told her and added: 'And the bonus is *my* client is a thoroughly decent kind of chap. With any luck the thing should be wrapped up by tonight.'

She plunged in. 'By the way, did I tell you about A. J?'

There was silence. At some stage, Mitch realised, Tommy must have phoned the office and discovered her.

'It's only temporary.'

The silence grew.

'A week. That's all. You said yourself we needed someone.'

'A secretary. A secretary *without* a Brummie accent. One couldn't have made oneself clearer.'

'No, Tommy,' she said meekly.

'With a good accent one can go a long way. Believe me,' said Tommy. 'One really knows what one's talking about.'

She fulsomely agreed with him.

'Are you all right, Mitch? You're not ill or anything, are you?'

'What makes you say that?'

'My dear, you sound quite unlike yourself.'

My God, she thought as she put the phone down a minute later. Am I never nice to him? Do I never agree with him?

She fell asleep on the sofa half-way through her lunch. She was woken two hours later by A J. She'd found Tom Lerner.

20

'S-sh-shhh.'

'Sorry . . .'

'Shush!'

Mitch cringed as she was forced further down the aisle

181

between the desks. All those at the back of the lecture room had been taken, presumably because of the row of radiators under the windows. There was, however, a gaggle of females gathered in the desks nearest to the lecturer.

Tom Lerner hooked one thumb under the bridge of his red-framed glasses and dropped them out of his curls on to his bony nose. 'Well. Aren't you going to sit?'

Though he topped six feet, Mitch thought that even Shylock would have difficulty in getting a pound of flesh, so little of it did he possess. He was now using this small break in his lecture to rearrange his notes. Most appeared to have been jotted on the back of a neatly deconstructed cardboard box which had once held 250 tea-bags.

Mitch slipped into a seat and looked about her. She found she wasn't out of place in this schoolroom. Some of the students were even older than herself. All had pens poised, pads before them, ready to note the words of this rather fashionable – A J had found out – peripatetic lecturer in financial economics.

'So much for so-called surpluses.' Tom Lerner discarded them with a flick of the wrist. 'Let's move on into even blacker secrets. And let's be blunt. Today's occupational pension schemes are hugely profitable for the bosses and top managers.' He looked round his flock and beamed. 'Why? Well, they pull out a Rolls Royce. They put in a Mini. Yet for the many people who change jobs frequently and for long-serving employees who are declared redundant some years before retirement, they are a swindle . . .'

Mitch, even though she'd slept after lunch, was already beginning to fight drowsiness.

'One of the most insidious effects of the final salary scheme is that it makes it extremely expensive to continue to employ people through their fifties and early sixties. This is what is fuelling the pressures for the early retirement of workers. A survey just published shows a much greater fall in income on retirement in Britain than anywhere else in Europe. Even if a worker stays in the same job the whole of his life – and not many do that – his income after tax will fall by twenty-four per cent against the EC average of fifteen per cent. But it is different for

182

top people. Top people enjoy proportionately higher pensions than elsewhere in Europe.'

Mitch's eyes had closed. Tom Lerner's voice was now a distant drone, the buzz-buzz of a worker bee in sunlike heat. One mustn't slump in one's chair, she found herself thinking. One must sit tidily as one sleeps. Like a politician.

'What if our employer insisted that we deposit all our savings with his company when we went on his payroll?'

Mitch blinked and searched for fingerholes to climb back into full consciousness.

'What if the boss said we could only get these savings back when we left the company? And if we left before we retired we'd get some unspecified sum given back to us? Or if the rate of return for our savings would not be stated? Would not even be related to the return on the savings invested? Or if the company went bust we could lose the lot? Would I – would you – leave our life savings with our boss? Then why leave our pension savings with him?

'Right. Those of us who have managed to remain conscious during this evening's little lesson on one aspect of our household finances might like at a later stage to produce papers for discussion. Time now to refresh the overworked grey cells with coffee, wouldn't you say? Later we shall look at current legislation governing pensions. Right?'

Mitch found she had been much too slow in climbing out of sleep to capture the lecturer. His carcass was already in the hands of five female students, one as fat as he was lean and contemplating him as though he were her favourite dish. If someone didn't come up soon with her cutlery, Mitch had no doubt she'd get stuck in anyway.

Straightening her skirt, Mitch got up and marched down the aisle. She said in her best broadcasting voice, and she had a good one, quite good enough, she told herself, to cut out this babble of witches: 'Mr Lerner . . .'

'Ah. Our sleeping beauty.'

'I'm not one of your students, I'm afraid. And I had a very tough night. I've come to carry you off for a minute or two. If I may. A confidential matter . . .'

183

'Confidential? Very mysterious. One hasn't somehow wandered into a live soap opera? I certainly don't know you? Do I?'

'No, Mr Lerner. You don't.' She wasn't going to say more. Interviewing, she'd early discovered, was as much about not saying as saying.

'Will I learn something to my advantage?'

She was silent.

'Come, come. One can hardly believe that! And wandering in half-way through a lecture too. You'd at least better tell me your name.'

'Mitch Mitchell.'

'Familiar in a way. I do know you?'

'No.'

Tom Lerner was debating with himself; though he was short on flesh, Mitch guessed he was long on ego. Her falling asleep in his lecture was obviously not going to be forgiven. On the other hand . . . 'It concerns Dr Lester,' she told him.

'Are you the police?' He was already tracking his way through to her.

'No.'

'Look, if you are after personal advice on pension provision–'

Mitch found she was too tired to be polite. 'Don't have one. Don't want one.'

'No? What do you intend to do?' He stared at her like a kid looking at a three-legged dog.

'I've always survived on my wits,' she said. 'And when they go I'll be in the happy position of not caring what happens to me.'

'Hardly responsible behaviour–'

'You've just been giving your students a raft of reasons why not to shell out money in pension payments!'

'So you were awake some of the time.'

They were now in the corridor and Tom Lerner was leading the way towards the entrance of the Winterhalt Institute. Mitch was wondering if he intended to show her through the door. She rather belatedly tried charm. 'Unforgivable of me. I really

184

am sorry I fell asleep. I'm afraid I did have a rather terrible night.'

'Ann Lester? You said that was what this is all about? I thought . . . I see I'm wrong there. You were somehow involved in that awful thing–'

'You did hear, then?'

'The police have already been in touch, my dear. I always bring my flask of coffee with me. The stuff in the machines is highly expensive muck, you know. I calculate the profit on each Styrofoam cup at one hundred and forty-six per cent. It's a guesstimate, naturally. Close, though, I wager. Poor little Annie. Oh, I heard all right.'

'I found her at the Glick Hope last night just after ten. You obviously know she's in hospital? That she'd been hit on the head?'

'Fractured skull, they said.' He opened a door with a key and she followed him into a locker room. 'Fine woman, Annie. Most of the garbage on the streets is human, Miss – Mitchell? I can't offer you any coffee. Policy.' He turned the key in a locker. 'Some of the women in my classes are so ferocious they'd tear each other apart to get a drink from my mug. One of the hazards that goes with the territory. Still, you can turn it to your advantage if you can control your fear. It's the telly bits and pieces I do. That's the trouble. Television is a powerful aphrodisiac to the female of the species. But it does bring in extra cash.'

Mitch took a good long second look at Tom Lerner. As a sex object he seemed to her about as desirable as a piece of uncooked spaghetti.

'Ah. I see you haven't caught my little act. When the Chancellor makes a damn fool of himself again or car sales plummet even further I'm the chap they call in to do the quick comment. The resident expert. Quite a profitable sideline if one exploits all its potentialities. I've placed you. You were on television once yourself, weren't you?'

'I did a consumer programme once.'

'Well. You'll know all about it then. Protecting one's dick and all that.'

'I don't have one.'

185

'I was being metaphorical, Miss Mitchell. A figure of speech. Well. What's this all about then?' He measured two-thirds of a cup of coffee in a red give-away mug with a Nescafé logo on it.

'May I ask if you're a friend of Dr Lester's?'

He weighed the matter. 'Certainly I'm more than an acquaintance,' he decided. 'Not a good friend. I couldn't stretch it that far. It's no picnic, you know. A fractured skull. What's all this to do with you? Mmm?'

'I believe you had a seven o'clock appointment with Dr Lester yesterday evening. I'd like to know if you kept it and what it was about. I had an appointment with Dr Lester later that night. That's how I came to find her. She was in need of my services. After what happened to her, you might feel she was right. I'm a private investigator.'

'Good God.'

'I left broadcasting some time ago.'

'Quite a career change. You've put me in somewhat of a quandary, Miss Mitchell. As you must be well aware, I can't consult Annie. Get her permission. She's not regained consciousness yet.' He paused to look her over. He might have been contemplating the teeth in a dubiously aged horse. 'I don't want you to think me an establishment man. No. Not at all. But on the other hand . . . consumer investigator . . . on the box, I mean . . . that's what you used to do. Yes. I remember that. Not quite thorough . . . but all the same . . .' and he nodded. 'What I'm going to tell you, Miss Mitchell, is quite off the record. To be blunt I shall, if necessary, totally forget this little conversation—'

'I wouldn't reveal a source, Mr Lerner.'

'Perhaps not. But whom can one trust, my dear? A devalued currency leads to a slide in all values . . . However, however . . . I mustn't ride my hobby-horse, must I?' He poured the remainder of the coffee into his mug. 'Dr Lester rang me and asked me to confirm for her whether there was a link between Ps and Qs and the Arno Czinner Finance Director Toby Trubberman.'

'What are Ps and Qs?'

'Pargeter Quealey-Smith. Accountants, my dear. They audit

the Czinner Enterprises accounts. Not one of the big five but City blue bloods just the same. Not *quite* what they were. A little caveat here. Six or seven years ago they'd hardly take a chap like Arno Czinner on board. But when needs must . . . It is rumoured that Sir Peter Quealey-Smith – Ps and Qs' senior partner – was caught up in the Lloyd's insurance market scandal. A spiral to disaster, my dear, which has given our auction houses so much work. Cleaned-out Names queuing to sell their mansions and silver to meet their losses. Sir Peter has not been forced into bankruptcy . . . But let's say his firm has taken a . . . a more relaxed view and extended its client base.'

'It is now doing work for companies it wouldn't have touched with a barge pole in the past? To up profits?'

'Rather strongly worded.' He thought about it. 'But I can't fault your assessment.'

'And was there a link? Between Ps and Qs and Toby Trubberman?'

'Czinner's Finance Director used to be a junior member of Ps and Qs. He married Sir Peter's daughter a few years back. I'm told he also left his last job – shall we say, rather quickly.'

'I see. But Czinner still employed him?'

'Quite so.'

'Why would Dr Lester want confirmation of such a link?'

'I really don't know. She didn't want to talk about it on the phone. We made an appointment to meet last night but she cancelled at the last minute and we set up another for today.'

'Did she say why?'

'She was seeing someone else. A matter of urgency. If your appointment was for later, it couldn't have been you. Could it? She phoned me here at the college yesterday afternoon. She sounded . . . well . . .'

'Upset? Frightened even?'

'Good God, no.' He paused and added: 'One doesn't expect people to sound frightened, does one? Even to *be* frightened. I was going to say . . . put out? A little stronger than that, I think. Anyway, not at all her usual self.'

'What is your connection with Dr Lester? I mean–'

'In the first place I was employed by Glick Hope as an adviser.

The Foundation has considerable funds. I never advised on individual bonds or shares, you understand. What they wanted from me every six months was an overall view. Updates if the economic picture was changing rapidly. That's how I came to meet Dr Lester. She has a very shrewd financial brain, you know.'

'I saw her and her ex-husband arguing on the steps of the clinic not long ago,' Mitch remembered.

'I have to say that a lot of people, including the Foundation, have in the past made a lot of money out of Czinner Enterprise shares.'

'But now, Mr Lerner?'

'Oh, I wouldn't care to guess. Any money I have goes into a building society. Not a safe investment, of course. Inflation, my dear, is like a rat. You can't keep it out of the grain store. Nibble, nibble, nibble. And down goes the value of your money. When Harold Wilson devalued in 1967 he promised it wouldn't affect the pound in our pockets. Today Wilson's pound is worth just over two bob. Debasement of the currency shifts wealth into the hands of the debtors. Beggars savers. Thrift is for turnip heads or people like me – the Nervous Norahs of this world. Are you all right, Miss Mitchell? Good heavens. You're dead on your feet.'

'I've had a very trying twenty-four hours, Mr Lerner. I think it's time I packed up and went home to bed. I'm very grateful to you. In the circumstances, many wouldn't have answered my questions.'

'I'm a cautious man. I admit I rarely take chances. But I'm satisfied in my own mind that you're worth it.'

Mitch realised, to her consternation, that she was blushing.

'Well. Yes. I must be getting back to my students, Miss Mitchell.' He, too, had gone a little pink. 'Sorry about the coffee. Frightfully bad manners. It's an odd thing. One always has the best of reasons for shockingly bad behaviour. After you, my dear . . .'

He shook hands with her in the corridor, clicked two fingers back and then bent to relock the door. Mitch, turning to walk to the entrance of the Winterhalt Institute, found that the soles of her feet seemed to have acquired a coating of glue. She leaned almost drunkenly into the swing doors.

Fog was drifting down, just as it had the night before. Now, though, the sight of it brought involuntary tears to her eyes. She felt too tired to brave one more thing that day.

A whisper. 'I don't often take chances. I'm satisfied in my own mind you're worth it.' That, and the pink tinge in the financial economic lecturer's cheeks, brought a glow; just enough light to see you home, she told herself.

She wondered how many times in her life the kindness of total strangers – people she'd never see again – had helped her through.

I bet he's an absolute shit to his nearest and dearest, she thought, as she unlocked the TVR and slid into the driver's seat.

But the light guided her through the fog.

Bed, she thought, when she'd closed her own front door behind her. But how am I to cope with all those stairs? If I'm to yomp through the night again with Testosterone Tommy I'll have to go into training. She was hauling her limbs up to the landing with the aid of the banister.

One shoe was on the bottom step, the other on the half-landing; her jacket swung from the newel post. She was just about to go into the bathroom when the telephone went.

'Oh shit.' She went into her bedroom, flopped on the bed and picked up the extension.

'You have friends in high places,' Shaun O'Neill, her ex-assistant told her.

'Don't talk rubbish.'

'At Cabinet level no less.'

'Pack it in, Shaun. I'm absolutely whacked. I'm going to hit the sack.'

'Just before you do, listen to this bedtime story. Once upon a time there was a very large media organisation which was headed by a Chairperson General. A week after Britain's Chancellor had christened his only son Revell Ullman junior the Chancellor and his wife held a soirée at Number Eleven for some of the great and the good of the land, including one or two arse-lickers from the media. Along went Chairperson General.

'At this little bash our Chancellor got rather tired and emotional and proposed a toast to the Chairperson General's media organisation. A member of CPG's staff, an extremely insignificant provincial cog in a great big international wheel, had saved the Chancellor's life by cool and incredible bravery – i.e. chucking a terrorist's bomb out of the window. Revell Ullman senior would never have laid eyes on Revell Ullman junior if it weren't for this little lady.

'At this moment the Chancellor's wife, radiant with new motherhood, lets the assembled gathering know that she, her husband and the baby are going to their Birmingham East constituency shortly and the family intend to call in at Radio Brum and thank their benefactress, Miss Mitch Mitchell, in person. Hubby, she confides, hopes that he and the wonderful Mitch can carry on with the broadcast which was so rudely interrupted last time by the terrorist's bomb.

'Naturally the CPG sees this as a wonderful opportunity for good publicity for his organisation, which has come in for heavy press criticism lately because of savage cutbacks. All the nation's favourite faces are exiting from screens. He then discovers that among those who have been fired is the woman who saved Britain's Chancellor's life and sees very different stories splashed across the front pages of the tabloids. Headlines like BRITAIN'S BOMB HEROINE GIVEN THE BOOT . . . etc.'

'Oh my God.' Mitch's head was reeling. 'That's what's behind Freya Adcock's sudden desire to rehire me. All that rubbish about fighting to get me my job back, about . . .' She began to taste her rage.

'If you decide to go back, Mitch, you can write your own contract,' Shaun said.

'You've got to be joking!'

'Don't be too hasty. Wrap your mind round all the angles. Apart from the cash, think of this little venture of yours. If you are on the air regularly there will be publicity by association for the Mitchell and Orient Bureau, won't there? That must add up

190

to more clients. People can't ask you to work for them if they don't know you exist.'

'I couldn't . . . That bitch lied through her teeth . . . She . . .' And she heard Freya say again: 'Such terrific talent. One simply said. No way. Absolutely not. I can't lose her.'

'If I were you I'd forget all my injured pride,' he said. 'You listen to your Uncle Shaun. High-mindedness is all very well if you've got the money to pay for it. Or someone else has.'

But Mitch wasn't listening. Her teeth were grinding together.

'Well, that's my advice for what it's worth,' Shaun said. 'At least sleep on it.'

'I'm sorry, Shaun. I'm so busy being outraged – I mean, my God! – but how did you find out all this?'

'Last summer it was me who set up that fateful interview with the Chancellor. Remember? I wangled it through a university chum of mine who works in the Chancellor's office. She put me on to this. Though I must admit it half crossed my mind because I knew the Chancellor was due to come to Birmingham.'

'I really am very grateful for finding this out for me. There had to be something extremely fishy going on. You don't fire someone one month and rehire them the next. If ever I can do anything for you . . .'

'It may have escaped the Chancellor's notice, it may even have escaped your notice, but you have already done something for me. That day you saved my life too. Goddamn it, Mitch. I'll do anything for you. Don't you ever forget it.' He banged the phone down before she could reply.

21

'I'm afraid I've been something of a prize idiot,' Mitch said to Tommy Hung when he rang her at home the next morning to tell her he'd wrapped up his case and would be back in Birmingham by lunchtime.

'What have you done?'

'I think I've made the most elementary mistake imaginable. An absolute purler. I'll have to get hold of Muriel Reeves' sister and have a word with her.'

'Aren't you going to tell me what it's all about?'

'Not on your life. Not until I've confirmed it. I might not be the thick-head I think I am.'

'After what you learned from Tom Lerner you should be thinking of taking a closer look at that Finance Director. What's his name?'

'Our Toby. When I've seen Muriel's sister I'm going to hoof it to Aston Clinton to see what I can dig up about him. Let's meet at the office around two, shall we? I'll be glad when you get back, Tommy. I need another pair of hands.' She was surprised to find she meant it.

By late morning she'd seen Muriel's sister and finished what she could do at Aston Clinton. She decided she'd detour on the way back to Birmingham and take a look at Job's Hall, Toby Trubberman's home.

The first thing to come into view were the roofs, perhaps half an acre of them settling like a fabulous bird on a steep slope to her left, two miles beyond the village of Chorley. She parked her car in the country lane and walked down the track. The west gable of the house and then the front came into view. It was a plain Georgian building, two sets of windows on each side of the door, five windows above and a further five in the mansard roof. A pair of panelled brick chimneys, without pots, rose into a dirty swill of clouds. The hall was substantial; even now, after prices had fallen, she reckoned a buyer wouldn't get much change from five hundred thousand pounds. And that was not including any land there might be.

The grounds were open plan, a large sweep of lawn dipping from the front door to the track. A run of gravel forked to the rear of the house. The main track looped into a huge deserted farmyard a hundred yards beyond the east gable of the house. She took a third branch and arrived at Job's Church. Beyond the bell tower was rolling meadowland, much of it waterlogged. She turned to study the church. It was a curious structure, obviously rebuilt at some time for though the tower and half the nave were constructed in brick, the back of the church was stone.

The small wooden gate was sheened with emerald lichen. The church's stout studded door was set some feet along the wall. To the right was a notice-board with a glass door giving a timetable of services and fund-raising events.

She opened the gate and tried the door of the church. Much to her surprise it opened. An oversight? Even churches as off the beaten track as this weren't safe from thieves and vandals.

And there were plenty of things to steal, she discovered, as she went in. Fine, bell-bottomed candles on an altar covered in a lace-fringed cloth with a purple valance beneath, wrought-iron chandeliers hanging from long chain ropes, even the barley twist rails round the altar itself would make good architectural salvage. An austere place, nevertheless; no stained glass in the graceful stone patterning of the Gothic window behind the altar, no richly carved marble, nothing but jugs of daffodils for decoration. Mitch found she liked its simpleness. But who filled the jugs with flowers? Who worshipped at this place? Apart from the hall itself, she'd not as yet seen any other signs of habitation nearby and yet the hall was not one of those aristocratic palaces which could command a family chapel.

She left the church, shutting the door firmly behind her, and began exploring the graveyard. She realised almost immediately that Job's Hall and the church weren't quite without neighbours. Just above the boundary wall of the graveyard were the outbuildings of a farm which lay higher up a slope, but so well hidden by evergreen shrubs and trees that it was not immediately apparent. Half a mile away, beyond a hedge of rhododendrons on the east side of the church, was a scattering of farms and cottages.

Yet the whole place, free of the usual mooring of clustering houses and shops, tended and cared for by an unseeable congregation, felt eerie. As if, like the *Marie Celeste*, it had been turned over to the elements. But who had just got up and left? Not the nuns in the old religious foundation which had once stood on this site. They had packed their bags hundreds of years ago.

She turned to examine the tombstones. Some had been wrenched to odd angles in long-ago gales; worn-away inscriptions marked the passing of the forgotten dead. But though these gravestones near the bell tower were ancient, at the back of the church there were newly dug ones. A green-painted bench under a yew had been positioned so that relatives who wanted to come and tend the flowers could sit and contemplate their labours when they were complete.

One grave was covered in wreaths and when she bent over it she could see the flowers were as fresh as yesterday. On impulse she bent to read a card.

'Darling Lorraine. Each petal a million tears. Lee.'

The wreath was a heart of lilies on a cross of red roses. She moved back with a guilty start, as though she'd stumbled on an unknown couple embracing.

She carried on searching. She could not find the grave she was looking for.

She retraced her steps and went to look in the large farmyard. There was some stabling which had not been used for some time. The garaging was directly opposite the entrance. Three separate units had been carved out of an old coach house. There were no windows but she noticed that the wooden doors had been salvaged from other farm buildings and there were gaps between the floor and the bottom of the doors. She got down on her knees and peered in. Two were empty. There was a vehicle in the third but the visibility was so poor she had a great deal of difficulty in making it out. She was almost sure it was a saloon car. She could not decipher the number plate but she was pretty certain the vehicle was green. Her heart began to turn, like a rattle at a football match when the game starts to hot up. But no matter how she craned her neck she could not improve her view. She clambered back to her feet, brushing down her coat. She would have to get some tools and come back.

She glanced at her watch. Damn. But she needed to see Tommy and A J. There was much to do and she couldn't manage it all herself. She'd brief them, come back here, force the garage door if necessary and check the car and then have a word with Toby Trubberman.

Don't get your hopes up, she told herself. There are millions of green vehicles in this world.

So many lines of enquiry to follow. She hurried back to the TVR. On her way into Birmingham she picked up some sandwiches.

She could not find any parking spaces around Gas Street Basin. Eventually she corkscrewed up the ramps to the top of a multi-storey car-park and sat there in the dank gloom nibbling an egg and cress sandwich. Tommy Hung had such admiration for her, such faith in her powers. There was A J too, seemingly changing her hair-style every day as she searched for her working-girl image. That kid also had faith in her. And now I've got to face the pair of them and tell them I made the most ridiculously elementary mistake.

It will be good for them, she told herself. Lesson one. Don't rely on Mitch Mitchell. She's a total idiot. She couldn't cross the street without help. She bit her lip. But she couldn't put it off any longer. Got to face the troops. Oh shit.

She shoved the remains of the sandwich in her patent leather handbag. She looked at the bag dispassionately. It was too large, too shiny, and had too much gilt. She always fell for a bit of glitz, a bit of tat, a bit of razzmatazz. A second-class handbag, she thought morosely, a second-class mind. Oh shit. How could I be so dumb? And she hauled herself out of the TVR and slunk across the rain-splattered street. When she slid into the bureau she tried not to see all the money Tommy had lavished on the offices. But she was not going to hang her head in front of her troops. Oh no. Chin up.

'But Muriel Reeves pointed out her husband to you.' Tommy, who had listened patiently to her, now objected. 'On the photograph.'

'Oh, if only I'd been methodical. Done what you always say is a *must*,' Mitch groaned. 'If only I'd written up proper notes as I'd gone along, I'd have tumbled much sooner.'

'What are you trying to say, Mitch?'

'Well, it wasn't until Arno Czinner kept me waiting and I'd time to – as I thought – kill, that I wrote up my notes. I didn't realise at once, not even then . . . I was so tired . . . I'd been up half the night . . . What a fool I've been . . .'

'Mitch!' both Tommy and A J shouted.

'Muriel Reeves did point out her husband to me. Just as I said. She said Georgie's next to Mr Czinner. Mr Czinner's the little chap in the centre. Pink shirt. Georgie's on the left of Mr Czinner. I had the photograph and she was standing in front of me.'

Tommy Hung began studying the photograph very carefully. Since his successes in Great Yarmouth he seemed to have expanded. When he'd first come into her office, Mitch had suspected him of wearing elevated shoes. Later she realised he was swinging further up on his toes as he walked. He might be around seventy years old but this was a man who gave every sign of growing as he pushed himself forward. If he's not careful, she thought, his chest will burst right out of his cashmere jumper. A J Evans, on the other hand, appeared to have shrunk. Today her version of being a working girl – or was she having a shot at being a gel? – seemed to consist of varying shades of beige and grey and a new Princess Diana hair-style, a shape her own soft black hair couldn't hold. It was already slowly deflating like an ill-conceived soufflé. The only thing Mitch recognised from the old A J was the boots she'd bought; they were already scuffed and one appeared to have been submerged in water for a while for a white tide rode up one side. A J had taken up a position behind Mitch's palm and from here, like Jerry peeping through his mousehole at Tom, she viewed Mitchell and Orient's male partner.

'She was standing in front of you so the man on her left was, in fact, the man on your right?'

'That's it, Tommy.'

'And on your right . . . so you actually saw George Reeves and thought it was Harry Vine.'

'What I can't quite understand is why he opened the door to me. He was taking a hell of a risk.'

'Why? Presumably, he'd check through a window to make sure it was no one who knew him. If anyone else called, George

196

needn't identify himself. If the caller knew Harry he'd assume George was a friend and ask if Harry was in.'

'There could just be another explanation,' Mitch said. 'As I drove up, Daisy Sharpe drove away. It could only be her. I found the mauve balaclava and anorak in her wardrobe. When the chap opened the door he'd very obviously just come out of the bathroom. His hair was wet and he was pulling his collar out from under his sweater. He'd dressed in a hurry. Did he expect Daisy to be on his front doorstep? I'd hardly started to pull the bell when the front door opened.'

'Are you suggesting she is in on whatever is happening–'

'Yes. I think she is.'

'George killed Harry Vine and then dressed the corpse in his clothes and drove over it with the motorised roller so it couldn't be recognised except from what it was wearing?'

'No. When I went to the cottage I saw a bottle of an antiarrhythmic heart drug called amiodarone. It sort of rang some bells with me. I'm sure it's used in many conditions but I once did a story about a disease of the heart muscle called hypertrophic cardiomyopathy which carries a significant risk of sudden death. Yesterday, Tommy, A J did some checking into Harry Vine's health–'

'Bingo,' said A J. 'In fact the guy was hospitalised just before Christmas.'

'I don't think the man under the roller was murdered. I think these are the remains of Harry Vine. I think he dropped dead while George was with him or George discovered him dead when he went to visit him at the cottage. George either knew or took the chance that their blood groups were the same . . . Actually, if I've George figured out right, he'd know. He was a man who was used to having to get details right.'

'And as the body was crushed beyond recognition even the old standbys like dental records would be of no use. If it weren't for the chipped finger – a detail George did slip up on? – it could have worked. Probably would have worked,' A J said.

'George set it up, I believe, so his wife Muriel would identify the body. I don't believe the gloved hand survived by accident.'

'It does fit in other ways, too,' said A J. 'When Arno Czinner is away the only people who stay at Aston Clinton overnight are the caretaker and his wife who have rooms at the back of the house. Their son is supposed to act as security man but I was told he's a pretty heavy drinker. I mean, the roller does make a terrific noise. But if the night was stormy – and there were some awful blizzards during that cold snap, if you remember – it is possible no one heard. But, if you think about it, whoever did it must have known the domestic position at the hall – and, of course, must have known the roller was there. An employee is most likely, wouldn't you say?'

'All right. Let us suppose the remains were those of Harry Vine. But why should George Reeves go to such lengths?'

'I think that when I saw George – and I now believe it was George – at the cottage, he told the truth about himself when he said he followed the rule book. I think he was, in fact, a man of probity. But that was before he changed. After all, that's what psychotherapy is all about, isn't it? Change?'

'And you are saying change need not be for the better? But the worse?' In between talking Tommy was humming softly to himself, the noise of a worker bee scenting nectar.

'I think George has stolen some of Arno's millions – or, perhaps more correctly, the banks' millions, as it's they who are funding Arno. I think he planned to disappear when the rights issue was announced because he knew Arno wouldn't go to the police. No one would subscribe to shares in a company whose financial controls were so slack wholesale looting was taking place. Harry's remains, the whole bizarre spectacle in the car-park, was set up in part to make sure Arno was too busy firefighting to do much of anything else.'

'And if the remains *were* identified as those of George Reeves, the man who stole the millions would be believed to be dead,' said A J. 'And that would be of prime importance because when the rights issue was over George couldn't be sure that Arno wouldn't then go to the police.'

'Or even set bloodhounds of his own on to his trail. Arno's roots are in Central Europe and the Middle East. Is he going to sit down and write a protest letter to *The Times*? I'd say he'd be

198

more likely to arrange for George's death. And he wouldn't be squeamish when it came to method.'

'You found Muriel's clothes at Harry Vine's cottage, didn't you? And yet from how you put this together you don't seem to believe she was in on it?'

Mitch shook her head.

'No way? Why?' asked A J.

'In the first place she employed me to find her husband and in the second – according to my group therapy chum – George hated her guts.'

'Could she have somehow found out George was at the cottage and gone there?'

'When I first saw her she told me about George's friendship with Harry Vine. She said Vine could know something. That she should have thought of him . . . meaning, I assume, getting in touch with him. I told her I'd do that. But all the same . . .'

'It is possible that she went out there to see him and found not Vine but her husband George?' Tommy whistled.

'And then they both disappeared.'

'Three possibilities,' said Tommy. 'They somehow patched things up and went off together, George bought Muriel off or . . .'

'Killed her?' asked A J. 'And George, who thought the cottage an ideal hidey-hole, took to his heels.'

'Well, something seems to have upset the apple cart. I think a very nice neat logical plan went horribly wrong somehow and this is why this whole thing is proving . . . so, so messy . . .'

'All this could hold water . . . but it still leaves all kinds of loose ends,' said Tommy. 'I mean, there is the bugging device you found in Daisy Sharpe's wardrobe for a start.'

'Then there's poor Dr Lester. Why was she hit on the head?' asked A J.

'Daisy's bugging activities might have put her in the picture in the first place. On the other hand, she could have always been a player. That might explain why she stayed on long after she'd decided to ditch Arno. I've no idea where Dr Lester comes in,' Mitch admitted. 'But one must, I think, bear in mind that Dr Lester and Daisy are said to be good friends. Could Daisy have alerted the doctor to something and that is why the Glick Hope have been heavy sellers of Czinner shares? If Daisy and George are in cahoots is it something George told her? Oh God. If I've not got a headache I'm shortly going to get one.'

'We did pin down Daisy as the woman George was in the pub with. Remember?' said Tommy. 'What if George and Daisy are lovers?'

'The thing that is bothering me is this,' said A J. 'If Muriel threw in her lot with her husband surely this would include her identifying the remains in the car-park as those of George. I mean, why has she vanished?'

All three were silent.

Tommy said eventually: 'There are the clothes. We know those are at the cottage. And don't forget the cakes. Mitch ate one of those!'

'Then there is the Finance Director. Toby Trubberman. Why did Ann Lester get her friend Tom Lerner to find out if there was a connection between him and Czinner's accountants, Ps and Qs?' asked Mitch. 'I've found out a bit more about Trubberman though I don't know how it fits in. Last autumn the Trubbermans' mongol child died. Since then his wife has hardly been at Job's Hall. In fact, one rumour is that she's left him. There is a church very near the Trubbermans' house. You would think, wouldn't you, that their child would be buried there if they intended to go on living at Job's Hall. Or would you?'

'Could Toby Trubberman and Daisy Sharpe possibly be lovers?' asked A J.

'I suppose you've seen the morning papers? They're full of Daisy leaving the cast of *Motel*,' Tommy said.

'No one got a quote from her. They said she'd gone to ground,' said A J.

'Far too many people in this case disappear,' Mitch said.

'You are not suggesting–'

'Christ, no,' said Mitch. 'But I could kick myself for not pressing Daisy further. She must have had an inkling about why Ann Lester wanted to employ us. According to Daisy, Dr Lester didn't get in touch until after the story of the remains under the roller came out.'

'You can't help feeling that Daisy must be playing a very devious game. A question of two sides against the middle? The whole case seems to have more twists than a corkscrew,' said Tommy.

'That could be put down to the latent influences of Arno Czinner,' said Mitch.

'Dominant people setting the role model, you mean? However much it's not your bag, be with someone like that long enough and something rubs off?' asked A J.

They both turned to look at the kid, suddenly each of them wondering how much of them might rub off on her. Seeing the beiges and greys, Mitch had to admit that Tommy was already influencing her. But that's all right, Mitch told herself; it was influencing the kid in ways neither they nor she realised that could be potentially damaging. Oh God, stop worrying, will you? People are subverting and being subverted all the time.

Tommy had been considering Mitch's theories in more detail. 'But didn't Harry Vine – or the supposed Harry – ring Muriel while you were with him?'

'Not in my presence. He said he was going to ring her and then went out of the room. And then he came back and said he couldn't reach her.'

'My God, if that was George Reeves he's a cool customer. When he realised who you were, he surely must have known Muriel would have shown you a photograph of him.'

'By the time that was on the table it'd be quite obvious that I didn't recognise him. But, thinking back, he did carry it all off wonderfully well.'

'Look here, everything we've learned about George says this is a timid little clerk who was bullied by his wife–' said Tommy.

'On the surface, yes. But when you really think about it we're talking about a complicated fucked-up personality who apparently could make figures do anything. For whatever reason, he was fished out of a boring job by Vine and made a part of Czinner's Development team. New horizons opened up. And he loved his work. He brought home every one of Czinner's past annual reports and read them, according to Muriel, "as though they were bestsellers". He certainly

201

has the expertise, wouldn't you say, to make off with a few million?'

'Though we don't actually know if any money is missing from Czinner's,' Tommy pointed out.

Mitch was silent, thinking again of the events of the morning.

'There's something you've not told us,' Tommy said.

'After making such a fool of myself over the photograph I'm a bit more cautious,' Mitch admitted. She told them about the garages. '. . . but even if this vehicle is green it is a very long shot that it is George's. I mean, it would make more sense to dump the thing in a reservoir or something. But I'm going to have to go back and check. I was thinking I'd have to break in but actually all I'll need is a good torch and the hand mirror from my dressing-table. I should be able to pick up enough of the number plate to ring the police if necessary.'

'I'm going to get back to Willie French, the stockbroker. See if he knows anyone who can help us with Toby Trubberman's past history. We need to know a lot more about that young man,' Tommy said. 'By the way, Willie rang just before you came in, Mitch. Something very odd is going on in Czinner shares. They are rising strongly. Willie reckons that some of the big boys are filling their boots with them.'

'What can that mean?'

'Willie hasn't a clue. But he told me he was still backing you, Mitch. He's still selling heavily.'

'I wish people would stop backing me,' Mitch said, more sharply than she intended. She didn't add what she was thinking: This is terrifying. All this money riding on me. What if I'm all wrong?

'What do you want me to do?' A J asked. 'Go after Daisy?'

'All the newspapers in the land will be hot on her trail. If she's to be found, they'll do it. No. I'd like you to get down to the hospital and see if you can wangle your way in to see Dr Lester. Just grab some flowers or something. If she has regained consciousness she could really tell us something useful.'

A J was the first to leave Mitch's office; Tommy lingered to watch the kid go. Mitch, seeing her through his eyes, for the

202

first time questioned her judgement. She's just the millionth product from the poly sausage machine, Mitch thought, gauche, ill-educated, a closet *Daily Mail* reader. What can I have been thinking of? I won't like firing her.

'By the way . . .' He turned back by the door. 'Freya Adcock was on the phone again.'

Mitch heard Freya saying: 'Such terrific talent. One simply said. No way. Absolutely not. I can't lose her.' Bitch, Mitch thought. She said: 'Freya can go and boil her head in oil.'

She turned to look out of her window. Gas Street Basin oozed with dismal February; even the yellow butt ends of the canal boats looked gloomy, tarts without a trade.

22

She had changed into jersey, jeans and duffle coat, her hair bound up in a russet silk handkerchief which had once belonged to her father. Her tools – consisting of a torch and her hand mirror, so sadly amateurish, she thought – were in her duffle coat pocket. On her feet were navy blue canvas deck shoes, left over from a disastrous boating holiday. She parked her car a little higher up the lane. Phone calls had delayed her both at the office and at home. By the time she reached Job's Hall the light was fading rapidly.

She got out of the car into a roil of wind and spattering rain. It was going to be a noisy night. She skipped frilling puddles as she approached the hall; to her left a bank of rhododendrons swayed oilily.

She heard the engine before she saw the car. She made a dive for the bushes. As they closed around her, headlights raked across the scene and then, as the car turned down the track towards the house, illuminated the puddled gravel.

A black Jaguar. Toby Trubberman's car. It halted in front of the house and two men got out. One opened up a yellow and black golfing umbrella, perhaps in the hope of protecting his business suit. The umbrella slewed sideways in the wind. He fought to close it again. Toby Trubberman. His companion was taller, the hood of his anorak shielding his face. His jeans were stuffed into waders, the tops of which were turned back.

Trubberman propped up the umbrella against the wall and opened the front door. The other man did not take off his waders. He quickly followed him in. Her drumming heart fractured with an arrhythmic flutter. Is that the man I thought was Harry Vine?

Is that George Reeves?

She couldn't be sure. She rose from her squatting position, muscles protesting, bones so stiff she had to shake out her legs. You're too old for this lark, she grumbled to herself. Trying to move through the shrubbery, she found herself caught in a net of twigs. She unpicked herself patiently.

The rain was easing off a little as she tracked round the house.

The light was on in the study. She circled to the rear wall.

Is it really George Reeves? A hand was holding her chest, trying to stop her heart from jumping about so erratically.

She was moving on to gravel now, lifting each foot with infinite care as she passed a downspout, eyes screwing up when each tiptoe touched the shale. Reaching the window, she flattened herself against the wall.

If she looked in and saw them, they could look out and see her.

Suddenly she heard a hoot of laughter. Caution gone, she wheeled towards the window. The man in the anorak was three-quarters turned from her, drinking a glass of whisky. He was looking at Toby Trubberman, laughing. Fair curls falling into his eyes, Trubberman was prancing into the room. Naked? No, he was wearing a pair of aquamarine and lemon bathing trunks. He, too, started to laugh. And then his shoulders flexed, his arms planed out to steady himself as he climbed on to his toes. Suddenly an arm broke free and a clenched fist powered towards the ceiling.

The man in the anorak was laughing so much he was slowly brought to his knees. She found herself looking down on a distorted face, half of it open-mouthed, eyes tight, weeping laughter.

George Reeves.

She wheeled back against the wall.

More than well oiled, she thought. The pair of them. What the hell are they up to? Suddenly George Reeves flung a shooting jacket at the other man. He caught it and as he danced out of the room rotated his bum, gave a little hop and waved his heel.

She stole away from the window and repositioned herself in long grass and trees which lay between the west gable of the house and the entrance to the hall. Under yew branches which swept to within three feet of the ground, leaning against the trunk, she was debating hotly with herself. Why not dash back to her car, drive to the public phone box in Chorley and ring the police? One thing stopped her. Though Toby Trubberman had been in bathing trunks, his companion had kept on his anorak. Surely that meant he wasn't planning to stay long? By the time she eventually got the police to sit up and take notice, he could be gone.

Just why was Toby Trubberman in bathing trunks? And what was so funny about it?

Drunken horse play?

Connected to pre-holiday prankishness?

Were the pair of them about to fly the coop?

She almost jumped forward as she saw the door to Job's Hall open. Light sprang across the lawn. Toby Trubberman came out, well wrapped up. Wool checked ratting cap, scarf tucked into his shooting jacket. Cords stuffed into track shoes. He was carrying waders. The light snapped out and the other man emerged. He toted a long canvas bag, unzipped at one end and something wrapped in dark plastic sticking out in front. The pair moved towards the car, jaunty Jack-the-Lads, one of them whistling up mischief. Both up to no good. She heard a car engine start.

Mitch ducked from under the cover of the yew and raced over bumpy grass to the lane. Her left leg, the one she had broken a few months before, gave way. 'Oh shit . . .' she muttered, forcing herself upright again. She moved more cautiously, tooling along splashing asphalt. She clambered into the TVR. She'd only just banged the door shut when she saw a Jaguar nose out of the entrance to Job's Hall. The car halted at a T-junction of narrow lanes and forked left, towards the city of Lichfield. Mitch disciplined herself to wait thirty seconds before switching on the engine and edging her car off the grass verge. In that time she'd found herself looking round the car for that which was not there, a portable telephone.

She barrelled down the corkscrewing lane, not afraid of catching up with Toby Trubberman. Afraid of losing him. She was remembering the man who had overtaken her at the entrance to Aston Clinton and – without reducing speed – driven in through gates marked OUT.

The lane, she knew from studying the map before she'd left the office, came out on the A5, a north-bound route linking Lichfield to Stafford. She negotiated the final steep descent just in time to see Toby Trubberman turning left towards the coal-mining town of Rugeley. She was four cars behind the Jaguar as it cruised to a halt at traffic lights on the fringe of Lichfield. Toby stayed on the inside lane, moving through filter lights as he continued along the A5. Mitch was now two cars away.

He came off the Rugeley road at a roundabout just below the brim of a rainswept hill and took the road to Kings Bromley. Mitch was recalling more details from the office map. This way you could get to Aston Clinton; it also led to Harry Vine's cottage. Now she was right behind the Jaguar. She dropped back. Dripping hedgerows and belts of trees flared in her vision. The Jaguar slowed a little when it reached Kings Bromley, more a hamlet than a village, the squat bell tower of the church pitch against the less dense blackness of the sky.

The land flattened; the inky sheen of water meadows shelved gently to river banks. Yoxall was beyond a bend in the river. The traffic lights at the single-lane bridge spanning the water were against the Jaguar and Mitch was able to make up some lost ground. The lights changed. She saw the car in front of her pull on to the bridge. When it reached the other side it forked left, away from the village.

'Harry Vine's cottage,' she breathed aloud as she slowed. The lane out to the cottage was little used and she didn't want to be spotted.

What's your strategy?

Well, they're certainly up to something, she thought. For a start weren't the pair of them supposed to be at daggers drawn?

But what has that to do with the death of Muriel Reeves?

She was appalled at the sudden, inexplicable leap her mind had made.

Hold it there.

But her mind was racing on.

'For the last month or two George's been quite aggressive in the group,' Colin Bell had told her. 'He's also declared war on Muriel. So he said.'

Just slow it all down, she told herself firmly. Stop this crazy speculation. You're going to have to be careful and concentrate on being very quiet and watchful if you're to have a hope of finding out what the pair of them are really up to.

Just before she reached the cottage, she ran the car off the road into a nest of trees. All she took with her was the torch.

The plunk, plunk of water funnelling along and off branches and twigs superimposed itself on the soft spraying hiss of rain. Water thickly beaded the top of the Jaguar, parked by the cottage; flanks of metal sweated. The gate was open.

Mitch stood by it, panting a little but not from exertion. Her fingers steepled over her mouth. There was still time to go back, to telephone.

Her anxiety became less acute when she moved. She quietly slipped through the gate. Slowly, taking infinite care to make as little noise as possible, she negotiated the steep, twisting path. It was only when she paused, now near the bottom of the last flight of steps and taking her bearings, that she saw light shivering through the foliage and then she noticed the smoke mushrooming from the lounge chimney, heavy acrid puffs. Noises were coming from the cottage's back garden. She couldn't identify them all but she recognised the slush, slush of disturbed water.

She crept down the last few brick steps, skirted the dripping porch and made her way to the lounge window. She put out her hand, steadying herself on the end of a window-sill. Muscles behind her ears began to tingle as her shoulders bent forward and her neck elongated.

The room was lit by two lamps, a peachy glow beneath pleated lampshades. There was no one there, though the door was ajar. Neatly arranged over the green couch with paw feet was the violet three-quarter length jacket she'd last seen hanging from the coat stand in the hallway of Muriel Reeves' house. On the floor near it were a pair of women's boots. They were unzipped, tongues pulled forward, ready for someone to step into.

A fire was smoking in the inglenook. Slowly she made out a pile of underclothes charring between two logs. A flame was licking its way through the gusset of a pair of knickers. To one side of the firebasket more clothing was piled on the terracotta tiles, ready to be fed to the flames. Cut up pieces of navy blue and orange wool jersey. She recognised the top of a sleeve. The dress she'd seen in the bedroom of the cottage?

The boots appeared to be waiting for feet, not disposal. Was the coat, too, not for burning? She glanced back at them, then at the pile of navy and orange jersey, and at the smoking fire. This time she noticed that there was something stretched round the front railings of the wrought-iron firebasket.

She blinked and looked again.

Smoke cleared and eddied.

A bra? God. Enormous. A size forty, she reckoned.

It toasted slowly.

Suddenly she heard a voice. Beyond the cottage, from the back garden. A tenor as sweet as the night jay.

'Deck thyself, my soul, in gladness,
Leave the gloomy haunts of sadness,
Come into the daylight's splendour,
There with joy thy praises render . . .'

Another voice, deeper, unmusical.

'Roll out M-i-i-zzz Barrel
Let's have a barrel of fun . . .'

Thrump. Thrump. Thrump. A heavy yawing yank, profundo, a descant of splashes and a skiddling pash-pash-pashing.

Then, rising through the night in triumph, notes of pure joy.

> 'Be thy love with love requited,
> From this banquet let me measure,
> Lord, how vast and deep its treasure . . .'

The last note vibrated so sweetly Mitch parted her lips so she could suck it in. She covered her mouth.

I must not panic, she thought.

Oh God.

Thrump. Thrump. Thrump.

Steadying her breathing down, she padded past the lounge window and rounded the gable end of the cottage, moving between the Calor gas storage tank and the wall. She came to the spoon of land at the back and sidled through the bare stems of elderberry. Slithering off a chunk of mossy granite, she clutched at rhododendron leaves to balance herself. She peered through.

They were in the middle of the pond, the water lapping high up on their waders. Like fishermen pulling in a full net, they braced, heaved and backed, braced, heaved and backed. The water streamed off their catch. While one of them hung on to it, the other climbed on to the bank, knelt and firmly grasped it. His friend joined him. Together they heaved.

It was up and on the grass. Something long, palish, shark-shaped.

One said something to the other and a figure detached itself and went into the kitchen. The other dug something out of his pocket. He sank back on his haunches. A light flared. Is that a bit of reedy grass caught in plastic? Mitch wondered. The flare died. The tip of a cigarette glowed.

An upstairs light showed in the cottage. Someone going to the bathroom? Another light snapped on, its beam bouncing over the fishy catch.

Flesh, but firm still, rounded and plump; not dead long enough to lose its shape and bloat on bone.

'My Georgie boy is all the world to me,' Muriel's voice whispered through the days, feathering Mitch's ear.

'We've always been all in all to each other,' Muriel whispered on. 'All in all. All in all.'

Such a fishy shape, Mitch thought, and all those hairdresser's waves now wet wild stalks.

It's not Muriel Reeves, of course. It's not just the hair. This thing has lost for ever its human-like qualities.

She couldn't believe it had ever worn a violet three-quarter length jacket, that it had recommended to Mitch that she should wear boots with zips in them, indeed that it should have zipped boots, tongues pulled out, waiting to receive its feet.

All this and more Mitch thought. Shocked out of her flesh, its emotions, she felt nothing.

She saw it was Toby Trubberman squatting on the grass; in the light she could discern the angle of his cap, the collar of his shooting jacket. He was examining the thing spread out no more than a yard from him. The fingers of his free hand were groping about in the grass. He came up with a twig. He leaned back up off his haunches and, like a child poking a slug, he prodded the corpse. He withdrew the twig quickly. He got up and moved further away.

Did Mitch at this point hear something? She'd no recollection of that. Indeed, she could have stood there much longer, seen much more, but the very last thing she remembered was Toby Trubberman backing from the corpse. She'd no memory of light, striking like an axe; of exploding pain, of dissolution.

Nothing until she became aware of terracotta tiles and something telling her that the remnants of jersey wool had gone. That what was piled there now were pieces of her jeans and her father's russet silk handkerchief. This was important. But the scene faded.

And then she was seeing fuzzy edges of Mrs Reeves. She was sitting in a gaily striped lawn chair with aluminium arms. The stripes and aluminium and violet jacket swam towards her and away and towards her again. Broad orange stripes, thinner green and white stripes, foggy patches of violet. Mrs Reeves' hair, and this seemed very telling, though she couldn't say why, was dry. There was also something very peculiar about her eyes. It was then she realised Mrs Reeves had been turned to stone. This stone stank. 'Like billy-o,' her father said to her. 'By Jove. Talk about bad eggs . . .' But it wasn't her father who now lifted Muriel in her chair. It was two other chaps, hoisting up aluminium arms, carrying her high. She rocked between them, a queen in her carriage, a babe in its cradle. Rocking 'like billy-o,' said her father and she agreed with him because she could talk to him even though he was dead. She only usually did this in dreams.

She was now looking towards a light. Firelight. She saw her sweater being engulfed. There was a tart singeing, a slow shrivelling as it turned browner and browner. This did not surprise her. The same things that were happening to Muriel were happening to her. Yes. That was it. That was the answer.

She wouldn't have to talk to her father in dreams any more. Now she was stone she could talk to him all the time.

Her sweater was almost gone. Muriel had already gone. She, too, would soon be going for a ride in the orange and green striped chair.

There it was. At last.

Such cheery colours. Mummy always used to say she liked a splash of colour.

Orange, green and white.

The smell snapped her back again. She could hear a car engine.

'OK there?' George Reeves-Harry Vine was saying.

'Just watch me . . .' The voice of Toby Trubberman. Breaking into a whistle, rolling out the barrel. Barrelling through.

I've no clothes on under my duffle coat. No socks on under my deck shoes. No knickers. All this was suddenly crystal clear to Mitch, barrelling along in the dark, one of the two tarts out for a lark with a pair of Jack-the-Lads.

But I'm not one of them at all, she realised. It's some ghastly mistake. In the dark she saw the blackness of the stinking lump lolling beside her, hands loose between spreading thighs, tongue protruding out of its mouth.

'You're sure two will fit in?' Toby Trubberman was asking.

211

'We'll stuff the pair of them down somehow. All girls together, eh? How much longer have we got?'

'Six hours. Georgie . . .'

'Yes?'

'Oh. Nothing.'

'It's all right, pal. I'm with you. All the way. Eh?'

'Didn't Sinatra sing that? Fuck me! Watch the road.'

'All righty-tighty, lover lamb!'

Mitch hearing them and not hearing them, seeing the darkness of Muriel Reeves' tongue and not seeing it. Trying to grasp and not grasping at all.

Her head suddenly dizzyingly full of the night jay.

'Deck thyself, my soul, with gladness,
Leave the gloomy haunts of sadness . . .'

A piercing sweetness shrouding her skin, shrouding consciousness.

Muriel was sitting in her camping chair with nothing on. Her coat was folded on the ground next to her, boots on top. The chair had been placed near a bower. 'Darling Lorraine,' Mitch remembered and realised she herself had been dumped on the wooden bench in the graveyard. Job's Church hovered in the background, lit by a watery moon which rode the tip of rain clouds.

Polythene had been stretched and anchored to the lips of Lorraine's grave. The two men were working swiftly. On the far lip they were placing Lorraine's wreaths. On the other polythene sheet were two spades and a pickaxe with a shortened blade.

In George Reeves' hands was a white heart on a cross of roses.

'Each petal a million tears.'

Muriel, softly lustrous and properly prim in her birthday suit, looked almost as if she could have knitting in her hands. Her elbows were perched above the arms of the camping chair, her ankles crossed. Head inclined forward.

Mitch paralysed in the bouncing moonlight. Each bone locked, each root of hair stiff.

212

But something was stirring.

Fed by all this seeing.

Oh, what big eyes she'd got. And they were getting bigger. Bigger and bigger. And bigger.

Pop, pop, popping into rage.

Those shits, she thought, intend to bury me. Her astonishment thrown up out of the volcano of fury.

She was up on her feet. Almost knocked off them by nausea. She stayed up. Me! She moved.

Legs dancing in fury. Astonishment still widening her wide open eyes.

Do they really think I'm going to let them do it?

Bury me?

Put me down with Muriel?

Both enraged feet clean off the ground.

Stuff that.

She took to her heels.

She found herself looking up to the bell tower. It swayed in the pump of blood and fury.

By the time she reached the church door she could hear them behind her. Pounding feet not as loud as the pounding in her veins.

She flung herself through the door, slammed it shut, clawing fingers searching for bolts. She shot two. Feeling for light switches, scratching along walls.

One. Two. Three. Flashing up through darkness the long altar stone. Diamond-edged lace. Candlesticks. Daffodils exploding out of their jars, a fury behind the Cross.

Swinging away from the banks of pews to the back of the church.

It was then she heard them at the door.

Rattle, rattle, rattle.

The rats.

See what kind of a corpse I am!

Drunken farts.

Feet sailing over the tiles. Hands outstretched.

She reached for rope.

The bell began to toll.

213

It tolled for her. God Almighty. You bet.

Clashing discords.

Ringing out across night-soaked water meadows.

Splitting ears, splitting heads.

Down on her knees.

Arm sockets squealing as the bell rebounded in all its fury.

Howling out.

Jesus Almighty.

Me!

23

Willie French looked like a cat who had whacked down a whole fresh salmon. Was his tail up. He'd turned up on Mitch's doorstep with a dozen bottles of champagne. 'Time to glug Krug,' he'd told them. Very smart with a mustard cashmere polo-neck under his worsted suit jacket. Jaunty two-tone loafers on his feet.

A J had shown him into the conservatory where Mitch lay propped up on cushions in the Lloyd Loom chair, her feet on a padded stool.

'You made a million,' said Mitch.

'Not I,' said Willie. 'Just a little something on account. Does one run to champagne flutes?'

'One does,' said Mitch.

'I'll get them,' said A J. She'd given up trying to be a gel. She was now into her third hair-style in a week. She'd had what used to be called, when Mitch was young, a crew-cut. With this she wore a pair of ear-rings large enough for a hamster to do handstands in. Over her Lycra leggings she wore a scarlet sweater which almost came to her knees. A large yellow plastic badge said GENIUS FOR HIRE. She flashed it under Tommy's nose at every opportunity. It made him uncomfortable. He was wearing what Mitch thought of as his granny-is-sitting-on-frog-spawn look. Whoever thought that Chinamen were inscrutable?

If Mitch had been on form she'd have enjoyed the situation. She wasn't. It felt as if someone had untied a bag of marbles in her head and they were bouncing off the bone of her skull. If these children were going to squabble she was going to burst into tears and then be sick.

They simply had to talk quietly and make no sudden moves. Didn't they realise that someone had tried to *bury* her?

A wash of self-pity filmed a pair of eyes that looked like great big bruises.

Bury *me*, she thought, as A J came from the kitchen with a tray of champagne flutes. Why, even Testosterone Tommy had shown a little sympathy. Then he'd said: 'Don't say I didn't warn you, my dear. Didn't I say it was a nasty old world and you were liable to get your head stoved in? Was I right, eh? Or was I right?'

'You were right.'

'Scum. And all of it twice your size.'

'They were going to put me down that hole with Muriel Reeves. Jesus.' She had still been unable to believe the brass neck of the pair of them. 'I hope you hang 'em.'

'Can't be done, girlie. That's against the law. But maybe this'll teach you. You should go back into broadcasting. Can't think why you gave up such a cushy number. Better than pissing about with villains. Am I right?'

'Can't you manage a sip or two?' A J was standing over her anxiously.

'Krug is the best medicine in the world,' said Willie. 'A Lazarus-raiser if ever there was one.'

Mitch, thinking of all her marbles rolling to a drunken standstill, managed a sip or two.

'The thing that amazes me in all this is Daisy Thingummybob. I mean to say. She doesn't strike one as the Mother Teresa type,' said Tommy.

'There's good in everyone.' A J turned her small breasts and their message in his direction.

'Good! She's done a bunk with twenty million!' Indignation momentarily lifted Mitch out of her sick self. She immediately tumbled back in, hands lolling over the chair arms.

'Rather romantic really,' said A J. 'Like Robin Hood.'

'I don't think I caught up with that bit. Missed half the six o'clock news,' said Willie French.

'Well, it hasn't been verified yet,' said Tommy. 'It seems, according to Trubberman – Reeves isn't talking yet – that Daisy had chosen her forty-first year as the one in which she would save lives. Have a go at being a saint. What she plans to do is build an orphanage to house some of the child targets of the Squadra dei Morti in Brazil . . . give them a tip-top education. They are to be her children. She planned to call it Matthew's House – after the child she'd had who died.'

'That's why she didn't renew her *Motel* contract,' said Mitch. 'Though, as it happens, she won't complete the present one. The producer of the show kicked her off the set. Oh . . .'

'Glug the Krug, my dear,' urged Willie. 'Do.'

'I feel like shit.'

'Is she supposed to drink?' Tommy asked A J.

'Probably not,' Mitch answered for herself, dropping her head back down on the cushion. She was wearing an old sweater and a pair of wool tights under her dressing-gown and was aware she must look like a sack of practically dead ferrets. And that didn't help.

'When Daisy saw the writing on the wall – Arno was already pissing about with other arm pieces – she knew the time was ripe. She told Trubberman she'd been thinking about it for a long time. She knew Arno wouldn't part with the money to fund her scheme so she decided to blackmail him into giving it her. You see, Dr Lester had told Daisy that she suspected Czinner of what I think is called teeming and lading–'

'What's that?' asked A J.

'A variant of robbing Peter to pay Paul. Arno needed a huge cash injection – the rights issue – and until he got it he had to disguise the holes in his balance sheet. Daisy wanted evidence of this so she could blackmail Arno. She found out there was going to be a council of war at Trubberman's place and broke in and bugged the place.

'What she actually learned from her bugging operations – and at one stage she later confessed to them she was putting bugs everywhere she could think of – was that Toby Trubberman and George Reeves had already hatched a plot to siphon off millions into a company they'd set up in Switzerland called Ganymede Sons.'

'So she blackmailed them?'

'It turned out there was no need. The pair of them were more than willing to fund Daisy's scheme. Trubberman had a mongol child called Sophia who died last year. Their only stipulation was that the name of the orphanage should be Sophia and Matthew House. In fact, George did a lot of the financial leg work for Daisy.'

'My God,' said Willie French. 'Did everyone have their hands in the till? Trubberman, Reeves, Daisy . . .'

'Chickenfeed,' said Tommy. 'By this time Czinner had already stolen two hundred million and they're still counting. Which was what started Reeves off in the first place. He added up the cash he reckoned Czinner had already stolen and, instead of turning the crook in, decided to siphon off a few million of his own.'

'Pension fund money?' asked Willie.

'Of course. Most of the two hundred million Czinner half-inched was used to shore up the price of Czinner shares in a market-rigging operation two years ago,' Mitch said. 'It was either that or going bust. When it came to his skin or the pensioners you can guess who won.'

'But surely pension funds have trustees and accountants to protect their assets?' A J was surprised.

'The chief trustee was Czinner. Like putting a burglar in an open vault and getting the security people to help load up his van. The accountants were Ps and Qs. My guess is that however dirty their hands are they'll come out of it all looking squeaky clean. But the fact of the matter is that Sir Peter Quealey, their senior partner, had come to grief in the Lloyd's underwriting scandal and needed to refill his coffers. Tom Lerner told me that. But will it ever get to court? No way. It seems to me all the bright guys are on the wrong side of the fence. The dull guys who try to catch them are out-brained.'

'But there must be some safeguards?'

'Well, I think the Prime Minister himself said in another case

217

that there was no defence against a determined fraudster. And a hundred million or so would make any crook determined, wouldn't you think?' asked Mitch. 'Honeypots attract raiders.'

'Let me get this straight,' said Willie. 'Arno Czinner has siphoned off two hundred million of his pensioners' money to shore up his tottering empire? George Reeves found out and decided to skim a little off for himself. But how did he find out?'

'He read balance sheets as if they were bestsellers,' Mitch said. 'Muriel Reeves told me that. She also said that no one read a balance sheet like him. Something must have alerted him – but as he's still not talking we don't quite know what – but he scented something, followed the trail and found out what was happening. By then half the pension fund had been swiped so we must assume there were some fairly glaring clues. Can I have some more champagne?'

'Are you sure you should, my dear? That was a very nasty crack on the bonce.'

'I'm sure I shouldn't,' said Mitch. 'But when your head's like the inside of mine you've got to try something.'

'Coming up,' said Willie. 'Money from the rights issue was going to be used, in part, to refloat the pensioners' fund? After all, you can't keep on doling out money each month if it's not there, can you?'

'That's right. The result of my interfering is that the rights issue has been pulled. Thousands of old folk are going to be on much reduced pensions.'

'That's rubbish, Mitch,' said Willie. 'When the dust settles I expect it will be found out that Czinner was at it again – share-rigging with pensioners' funds. Don't you remember me ringing the Bureau to say that Czinner's share price – which had been dropping like a stone – had suddenly bounced upwards? Once Czinner had found out how to use the pensioners' money as his own private piggy bank he was never going to stop. Was he?'

'Anyway, it seems that there actually *was* bad blood between Trubberman and Harry Vine but the cause was nothing to do with work,' Mitch said.

'I found out that Trubberman was fired from his last job not because of any financial irregularity but because of an incident in the men's lavatory at a firm's Christmas do,' said Tommy. 'Trubberman had become more than a little too familiar with the chairman's son. Trubberman insisted it was no more than drunken horse play and officially his explanation was accepted. But he went.'

'And his father-in-law Sir Peter got him a job at Czinner's,' said Mitch. 'In the circumstances I think we can infer that both Czinner and Quealey thought they could whip Trubberman back into line if he started asking awkward questions. The trouble was that when George Reeves finally did come out of the closet it was he and Trubberman – not he and Vine – who became an item. Anyway, Vine himself suspected that something was going on between them but didn't actually know until last Christmas – just before he was fired. George and Trubberman kept up the pretence that George was going to be fired too because that is exactly what was going to happen – after George had siphoned off enough cash.'

'But why did they kill Vine?' Willie asked.

'They didn't. He died of natural causes,' said Mitch. 'They just decided to use his body and that was where everything came unglued. George was good at planning. But improvisation . . .' Mitch began to shake her head and very rapidly desisted. She looked up beyond the glow of lamps to the windy night beyond the glass and waited for her vision to steady. 'If George Reeves were thought to be dead his fraudulent activities – which had a good chance of coming to light one day – would be written off. Harry Vine was in the clear. That was the point.'

'He was taking a hell of a risk,' said A J. 'It was always on the cards that Muriel might go to the cottage.'

'Well, it was certainly planned that Muriel would be primed to identify the body. But did George have a hidden agenda? Hidden even from himself? Something like the Freudian slip – but in this case the bottom line was killing off Muriel?' Mitch asked. 'All I can say is that was one sublimely happy man hauling that body out of the pond.'

'I've gone all goosebumpy,' said A J.

'The thought of that certainly makes one really want to get to the bottom of a whole crate of Krug,' said Willie.

As they were talking echoes of joy quivered in Mitch's head.

> 'Deck thyself, my soul, in gladness,
> Leave the gloomy haunts of sadness,
> Come into the daylight's splendour,
> There with joy . . .'

Such joy, Mitch thought, her flesh quivering, snagged in cobwebs of ice.

'One should never come between a man and his mate,' said Tommy. 'That was Mitch's almost fatal error.'

'She was dead, for Christ's sake!' Mitch said.

Tommy tapped his head. 'Not in there. They never die in there. Look what happened to Dr Lester – and Arno divorced her years ago.'

'Now we don't know if that's true,' said Mitch.

'What?' asked Willie.

'Dr Lester broke her appointment with Tom Lerner to see Arno Czinner. According to her, he and she had a fearful row about the Glick Hope's selling of Czinner shares . . . he said that was what had caused them to almost drop right through the rights issue price. But he left the Foundation around about eight–'

'So it wasn't him who almost killed her?'

'I think it was,' Mitch said. 'I think the lady isn't saying. He's going to get charged with fraud anyhow and they should be able to nail him. He's likely to get sent down. I think she doesn't want to drag herself and the Glick Hope through the courts . . .'

'That's only a theory,' Tommy protested. 'The fact is, it could have been a patient.'

'It is a possibility,' admitted Mitch. 'They say that transference can be a very dodgy thing and she does have one or two very iffy patients she's in one-to-one relationships with. But the probability is that Arno bashed her one. I saw them together one night at the Glick Hope. I felt that if Arno had had a tommy gun he'd have plastered her all over the door.'

220

'I wonder if she really planned to engage the Bureau?'

'Oh, I think we can bet on that. We know she already had serious worries about Czinner's finances and then the body of a member of the finance department turns up in the car-park!' Tommy said.

A J had been following her own line of thought. 'It's all so murky,' she said. 'All the newspapers and everyone thought that Daisy had gone to ground but she'd run off to Brazil. I thought that so romantic, running off to help those poor kids. And now it turns out she's doing it with pensioners' money!' She looked round them all, her inspection as wide and grave as a little kid's. 'I want to be on the side of the angels. A proper one. That's what I want to be.'

'It does give one a sleazy feeling. I mean, being employed by such a rat as Czinner,' said Mitch. 'I know what you mean, A J. I'd love to be a knight errant. Just for once.'

'It's not that kind of world any more. We're fifty years too late,' said Tommy.

Willie French was the first to go but not before he'd managed to get through a whole bottle of Krug. 'I feel anaesthetised enough to ask you now, Mitch. How did the unfortunate Muriel Reeves . . . well, you know?'

'When I saw Superintendent Ball the results of the post-mortem hadn't come through. But they think Georgie boy socked her on the jaw so hard she was knocked unconscious. And then he stripped her and drowned her in the pond.'

'I never quite followed why he stripped her – or you, come to that, Mitch.'

'The theory seemed to be that we'd be more difficult to identify without our clothes. He burned most of the stuff but kept the coats and that with the intention of getting rid of them later. I mean, if another motorist on the road saw two naked ladies in the back of the car it is possible he'd have rung 999.'

'I suppose the idea of the graveyard was that it was the last place anyone would look for bodies?' said Willie. 'I mean, being the place where bodies are supposed to be.' One hand moved to touch the reassuringly firm pink flesh of the other. 'There are times when imagination is not all it's cracked up to be.'

221

'I suppose if you feel sorry for anyone it's Mrs Trubberman,' said A J.

'Apparently that marriage finally came apart after the child died. She didn't leave for a holiday. She left for good about a month ago,' said Mitch. 'And if you're going to feel sorry for anyone I think Muriel Reeves is first in line. I'm positive that woman really loved her Georgie boy.'

'But was that Georgie boy ever George Reeves?'

'Don't go philosophical on me, Tommy. I could very easily be sick.'

'You shouldn't have drunk that champers,' said Tommy.

'Christ. Why can't anyone be sorry for me?'

'We daren't, my dear,' Willie was just drunk enough to say. 'Given the least encouragement you'd cry all over us. You know you would. Worsted doesn't do too well in the wet.'

He'd enough sense to make himself scarce after that and A J followed him shortly.

Tommy remained a little longer, keeping an anxious eye on her. 'It's all right, Tommy. A bit of champers really isn't going to kill me. I'll be fine in a day or two. Even the doctor says that. I disappointed him rather, I think. Bone head. That's me. Skull as thick as a kerbstone.' She changed the subject abruptly. 'But I can't fire A J until I feel a bit livelier. Can't be done.'

'Fire her? What are you talking about? She's far from ideal, I grant you that. But we have to employ her. A girl like her.'

'What?'

'In the end, Mitch, one must always bow one's head and accept what the gods send one. Even if it is highly inappropriate.'

Mitch felt too relieved to think about Tommy's inappropriateness. 'I wonder why?' was all she said.

'One must toddle. I don't think you're quite in the state to discuss such things. Do go to bed now, my dear. I'll ring you in the morning.'

But it was half an hour before Mitch could haul herself out of the Lloyd Loom chair and walk through the lounge on legs as spongy as a bendy toy's.

222

She knew, though, that basically she was all right when the phone rang and curiosity drove her to answer it.

'I've got your founder. Cost me fifty quid. Do you want me to drop it in or will it wait until we have dinner?' It was Josh Hadley.

'Founder? Oh, that . . .' Mitch's brain slowly uncoiled into a blurring understanding. She supported her body against the kitchen wall. 'What does he look like?'

'Are you all right? You sound dreadful.'

'I've been drinking champers. I didn't think I could feel worse than I did. But I do. Never get hit on the head. It's not a good idea.'

'You should be in bed.'

'I'm going. I'm going. What's he like?'

'She. For-mi-*dar*-ble. One hell of a lot of for-mi-*dar*-ble for fifty quid. Believe me. Just you wait and see.'

At three in the morning Mitch woke up in a sweat of fear. Never mind the head. Feel the fear. She was wringing.

At nine she rang Mitchell and Orient's bank in Waterloo Street. When she had got through to the right department and had filled the clerk in with a few facts, she found she could hardly drag the question out of her quivering flesh.

'Did the cheque Czinner give me bounce?'

There is a sepulchral tone of voice Mitch never heard with her ears but her stomach. 'We are returning the cheque to you. You could always try and re-present it at a later date.'

'When the shit gets out of gaol, you mean?'

There was silence at the other end.

'I should have had it processed by your express service.'

'It doesn't cost much more. Many people express cheques these days.'

'It really has bounced?' It was not that Mitch disbelieved the clerk. After all, her stomach told her it was true. But there was an insouciant spark of optimism in her which would be heard.

Got to be some other poor guy's, the spark told her.

It wasn't.

Oh shit. In the time it took to put the phone down she had made one of the biggest decisions of her life.

She went into the lounge, seeming to see everything with a preternatural brightness. She was already saying goodbye to the home where she and her husband Max had brought up their daughter, had fought and sneaked off early to bed, had bought the chesterfield together and quarrelled over her buying the grandfather clock.

But a Chinaman called Tommy was her partner now.

She had to help him. They had to pull together.

It's time I came out of cloud cuckoo land, she told herself. I can't let Tommy pay the bank interest on a fifty-thousand-pound loan. And when is the business ever going to make enough money to pay back such a huge sum? If I sell this place and buy something cheaper I can inject the surplus into the Mitchell and Orient Bureau.

The thought of putting such a large chunk of her money into the Bureau made her almost panic.

Tommy's done it, she told herself. If he can have faith in me I'm damn sure I can.

But it could take months to sell this place. Meanwhile we are paying out our start-up costs, three wages, VAT bills and God knows what else.

It was then she thought of Freya Adcock's offer of a job.

I could perhaps do just one show a week. That would take only a few hours of my time. I'd make enough to live on and save the Bureau one wage packet. After all, I have Miss Fee Fi Fo Fun Bum by the short and curlies. I'm in a position to drive a deal even Arno Czinner would be proud of. Let's put up the frame and see the picture. A steal of a wage. Plus a nice wodge of expenses. A fat programme budget, a prime time slot, an assistant . . .

Freya will never fall for that.

But Freya will have to, she reminded herself. I mean, all this great talent I've got . . . talent costs, right? Mitch was already laughing to herself. Stuff Arno Czinner. Stuff them all.

I bet I can put the bite on as well as the next lean and mean bastard. I come from the right stock, don't I? Josh Hadley himself says this ancestor of mine is for-mi-*dar*-ble.

Freya Adcock can sit and chew pet vipers until she is blue in the face. She'll pay up.

224